"Did you know my daddy when he was a hellion?"

"Chipper!"

She looked up at Tommy, wide-eyed. "Well, that's what Aunt Fiona always says."

Julia couldn't hold back the laughter. "No, I guess I missed his hellion days," she said.

"I'm going to be a carrot in the Easter play at school. Are you going to come see it?"

She was six, Julia thought. Six years ago, I'd just graduated from college and was headed for New York City with nothing but my dreams to keep me going. "Are you in danger of being eaten by the Easter Bunny in this show?"

Chipper rolled her eyes. "Oh, please. Are you kidding? Frankie Spelling's the Easter Bunny—he'd never be able to catch me. Besides, his nose always runs."

"Frankie has certain deficiencies," Tommy explained, taking Chipper by the hand.

Julia felt a fullness in her throat. What a good father he was. She hated the envious way her own thoughts were behaving: She couldn't stop herself from wishing that Chipper had been *their* child!

ABOUT THE AUTHOR

Amanda Clark is the pseudonym for the mother-daughter writing team of Janet O'Daniel and Amy Midgley. They began collaborating on romances long-distance, when they lived in different states. Now that they've both moved to South Carolina, working together has become a lot less complicated. Janet and Amy are the authors of five Harlequin Romance novels and are making their Superromance debut with *First Love, Second Chance*.

Books by Amanda Clark

HARLEQUIN ROMANCE

3007—BLUEPRINT FOR LOVE
3104—CITY GIRL, COUNTRY GIRL
3219—A NEIGHBORLY AFFAIR
3321—EARLY HARVEST
3333—SULLIVAN'S LAW

Amanda Clark

First Love, Second Chance

Harlequin Books

TORONTO • NEW YORK • LONDON
AMSTERDAM • PARIS • SYDNEY • HAMBURG
STOCKHOLM • ATHENS • TOKYO • MILAN
MADRID • WARSAW • BUDAPEST • AUCKLAND

ISBN 0-373-70640-5

FIRST LOVE, SECOND CHANCE

First Love,
Second Chance

CHAPTER ONE

A FEELING OF FOREBODING hit Julia as she knocked lightly on the door to Bud Winter's office. Something was wrong. Bud wasn't in the habit of sending the boy from the mail room to fetch her. His normal procedure was to step outside his door and bellow, "Julia! Can I see you a minute?"

All of them knew Bristol Publishing had been taken over by a larger firm, and they'd whistled bravely while they reassured one another that their jobs were safe. But now that the moment was at hand, Julia felt a cold tremor pass through her as she pushed the door open. Bud Winter was at the window, instead of in his usual spot behind his littered desk. Plump, balding and disheveled, his rumpled shirt billowing out over his trousers, he turned to her. The light caught and glittered off his glasses.

"Have a seat, Julia."

Remaining where she stood, Julia swallowed twice and said, "I'm history, right?"

He sighed and passed one hand over his thinning hair. "Damn," he said quietly. "I'm afraid so."

For a moment they simply looked at each other. Then Bud Winter gave a short laugh. "If it makes you feel any better, so am I."

"Bud, no." She crossed to him. "They're letting you go?"

"Bringing in all their own people." He shrugged. "Fifty-five years old and I'm going to be pounding the pavement again. If I had any clout left, I'd do my damnedest to save your job, Julia—and the others', too. But I don't. There'll be a severance package, of course. I'm sure it'll hold you until you can find another job."

"Hey, don't worry about it." She tried to sound spunky, but it didn't quite come out that way. "We'll get something else, both of us."

"You'll make it past the front desk, anyway, with your looks," he said. "I'm no Tom Selleck."

"You don't have to be." She gave him an impulsive hug. "Everyone knows you're the best editor in the business."

Looking over his shoulder, she watched the gray New York rain splatter against the window. The damp early March air chilled her to the bone.

THE RAIN WAS COMING DOWN harder when she left for home at five. Her feet were soaked by the time she caught the bus. She'd have taken a taxi if there'd been one, but it was better this way, she reminded herself. From now on she'd have to be careful how she spent her money.

Wearily she studied her reflection in the water-streaked window of the bus. Did she look like someone who'd just been laid off? She examined her image for signs of change. Her oval face was paler than usual, her violet-blue eyes seemed huge, and her hair the color of dark honey, had tendrils curling damply around her ears. Julia sighed. She'd better check how much was left in her bank account. The severance check wasn't *that* large.

When she arrived at her apartment, she kicked off her shoes, and settled down on the couch to riffle through her bank book. Rent was going to be the biggest problem. She'd lost a roommate when Ceil was transferred to Chicago two months before, and paying the whole rent, instead of dividing it was eating a hole in her balance. But the privacy had been so pleasant, though, that she'd been slow to seek out a replacement. She began to calculate how long she could manage with the small amount she had left, and then, turning to the newspaper she'd brought home, she started looking at the want ads.

When the telephone rang she answered it reluctantly. In her present mood there was no one she wanted to talk to.

"Julia? How's it going, kid?"

"Rick!" Her brother was the exception of course. He was the one person she was never too dispirited to talk to. "Everything okay? How's Suzanne?"

"Great. Everything's fine."

"Suzanne's a sweetheart. I really like her—you know that, don't you?" Julia had met her brother's fiancée for the first time at Christmas and they'd become immediate friends.

"Yeah, I do. I'm kind of fond of her, too." She heard him hesitate. "Listen, Jule, I just had word today that Mother Holtz died."

The cheerful room, with its pillows, books and warm lamplight, seemed to spin around Julia and rearrange itself into a bleak chilly parlor. She shook her head and straightened, then heard herself say, "No kidding. When did that happen?"

"Last night. Apparently she had a heart problem. But here's the thing. We'll have to go there and handle the details—you know, the funeral and all that."

"You and me?"

"There isn't anybody else."

"Oh, but—I mean, can't we do it over the phone? You know, with lawyers?"

She could sense his disapproval in the silence that settled between them. Then with a sigh, he said, "Julia. We can't do that. We owe her something."

We don't, said a small insistent voice in her head. *Not a thing.* "You're a better person than I am, Rick," Julia replied. "You always were. All right, I'll go. But the thing is, I'm really tapped out. I lost my job today."

"Oh, gee, Jule, I'm sorry. I know you thought it might happen, but that doesn't make it any easier. Well, don't worry about it. I've already taken care of your plane ticket. You can pick it up tomorrow at LaGuardia. I won't have any trouble hitching a ride on a plane from here."

Julia felt the swell of pride she always did when she heard him say something like that. She thought about the skinny eighteen-year-old, wearing clothes that didn't fit, who'd left home one day to enlist in the U.S. Air Force. Now, ten years later, he was stationed with the Tactical Air Command at Langley Field, Virginia, and "hitching a ride" was a simple matter because today he was Major Richard Marshall.

"Okay," she said. "How long will it take, do you think? Two or three days?" She was free, certainly. She'd already finished editing the last book she'd ever do for Bristol Publishing. Still, two or three days would be more than enough to spend in a town she'd hoped never to see again.

"Guess we'll know more when we get there," he said. "Something has to be done with the farm— I don't know how things have been left. Look, can I send you some money to tide you over till you find a new job?"

"No, no. I'm okay."

"You know all you have to do is ask."

"I know, Rick. But I'm okay, really. I'll tell you all about it when I see you tomorrow."

"You'll need to switch to a smaller plane when you reach Pittsburgh. I'll meet you there."

"I'll call LaGuardia for the time. Give my love to Suzanne."

When the connection was broken, she stared at the hand that still held the receiver; it was cold and white-knuckled. She'd felt chilled almost the whole day, she realized. She got up and went into the tiny kitchen, hunting for the red wine she'd bought the week before when she'd had someone from the office over for dinner. She was sure there was some left. She found the bottle in the cupboard over the refrigerator and poured herself a glass. After a few sips, she started to feel warmer and she willed the tight muscles at the back of her neck to loosen. It was amazing, though, she reflected, that even now she couldn't pour a small glass of wine without being assaulted by guilt.

No, she wouldn't mourn for Elizabeth Holtz. Julia remembered vividly her adoptive mother's prim tight mouth, her cold gray eyes and her repeated assurances that Julia and Rick were wicked through and through and headed straight for eternal damnation.

Julia carried her glass to the bathroom and then ran water into the tub, recklessly pouring in bath crystals. If she was going to feel guilty, anyway, she might as well do a thorough job of it. She lowered herself into the tub and brought the list of her failures up to date. A broken marriage, no job, and very little money in the bank. And those were only the recent ones. Of course she could admit now that she should never have married Bryce Farnsworth, but still, it counted as a failure. And it surely must count as another when your own mother didn't want you. And then of course there was Tommy Black. No, that was going too far. Julia shut her eyes. She wouldn't think about Tommy. That was the biggest failure of all. But she wouldn't put it on the list, because she couldn't bear to.

An inner voice argued with her. Wasn't that being cowardly? Shouldn't she face the hardest things first? Why not look the Tommy Black episode right in the eye and be honest about it? Julia took a deep breath and closed her eyes. She imagined herself back in western Pennsylvania ten years ago, in a bare little room with one small window and a narrow iron bed, where the thermostat was never turned higher than fifty-five. Gideon Holtz's sole concern was that the pipes not freeze; comfort was no consideration with him. Rick had had it even worse. His room across the hall was windowless. Social services had placed them as foster children with the Holtzes when they were eight and ten, respectively. "You'll love it there," the social worker had assured them. "Out in the country, nice clean air and rooms of your own."

There was no mention of getting up at five to do the chores before catching the school bus. No mention of laundry to be hung outside in freezing weather because Gideon Holtz refused to buy a dryer. "A washing machine, yes," he would say, "for sanitary reasons and general efficiency. But God's own air is there to do the drying." And so Julia went through the winter with chapped red hands and skin that cracked painfully.

When they were ten and twelve the Holtzes adopted them, pointing out what a financial sacrifice was entailed. They would no longer receive the foster-care allotment, and raising two children would be a major burden. But they considered it their Christian duty to do so, and heaven only knew, not many people wanted to adopt two near-grown children. Only later did Rick and Julia realize that once they were legally adopted there would be less worry about supervision from the social worker and the Holtzes would have acquired permanent child labor on the farm.

Julia reached up and turned on the hot-water tap, letting it run for a while. Then she turned it off and settled back again, blissfully warm.

She'd been seventeen when she first met Tommy Black. She'd gone to a barbecue, and she could still recall the evening as if it were yesterday.

"Nice party, isn't it?" he'd said, looking down at her with a wide smile. Dark hair fell across his forehead, and his brown eyes studied her.

"It seems nice to me," she replied, "but I'm no judge. It's the first party I've ever been to."

His eyes lit up with amusement and his smile broadened. "Oh, come on. The first this week, maybe."

"No, I mean it. I've never been to a party before."

"Ever?"

"No, not ever."

He continued to study her, lines of puzzlement etched on his forehead. "How can anyone with eyes like yours not have been invited to a party before?"

"Eyes?" Julia wished frantically she'd learned how to make small talk.

"They're like pansies."

She was sure he was making fun of her, but she didn't know how to get away.

"So how come you're at this party?" he asked.

She took a deep breath and wondered how she was going to explain her life with the Holtzes. "My parents—that is, they're not my real parents, my brother and I are adopted—they don't believe in parties. I never was allowed to go to one. But this time, Mrs. Bauer—she's Gretchen Bauer's mother—do you know Gretchen?"

"I know her brother, Fred."

"Well, Mrs. Bauer spoke to Mother Holtz and said that since I was graduating from high school, I should be allowed to go just this once. Mrs. Bauer fixed the dress for me—it was Gretchen's, but she made it over to fit me."

His eyes, softer now, took in the white ruffle around the neck of the dress, the snug waist, the skirt with its two more tiers of ruffles. "It looks beautiful on you."

She was finding it a little easier to talk to him. "The shoes gave us a bit of trouble because Gretchen wears a size larger." She drew close to him and whispered, "I put Kleenex in the toes."

He let out a laugh. "I'd say the whole outfit was a huge success." He went on gazing at her. "And what's your opinion of parties, I mean, so far?"

Julia looked around. The big Owens' living room was filled with people, as was the patio, where the overflow of guests mingled noisily in the soft June air. She could smell the roses and honeysuckle. The Owens, who owned the grandest house in town, had invited all thirty-six of the Wiltonburg High School graduating class. "I think they're wonderful, and this is the most beautiful place I've ever seen."

He smiled at her response, and they went on talking. She learned that he'd just finished his junior year in college and that he'd come to the party because Sherry Owen had insisted on it.

"Otherwise you wouldn't have bothered with a bunch of high school kids," she teased.

"Maybe, but I'm glad I did."

"Then you really should pay a little more attention to Sherry."

"Oh, she's busy enough. I don't really know her all that well. I'm closer to her older brother, Don."

Julia must have made a face, because he laughed. "There has to be a story behind that look."

She shrugged, not wanting to explain exactly what she thought of Don Owen. When he'd been in high school, he seized every chance he could to make a play for her. She decided to change the subject. "Maybe you know my brother, too. His name's Rick Marshall. Well, Rick Holtz now." Julia still hated the name.

"Sure I know him. Where is he?"

"In the air force. He's in college, too. You know, they're sending him."

"He must be pretty smart."

"He is."

They both glanced across the room, and Julia saw Sherry Owen looking at them with a sour expression on her face. Just as Sherry appeared to be about to move in their direction, Tommy said quickly, "Shall we take a walk outside?"

"Is it all right to do that?"

He grabbed her elbow. "Guarantee it happens at every well-run party."

He propelled her through the crowd out onto the patio where barbecues were being set up. Mr. Owen was presiding over them, wearing a large apron. Tommy took her hand and led her across the lawn toward a tall spreading oak with a redwood bench around it.

"How did you happen to be adopted by the Holtzes?" he asked as they sat down.

"We were placed with them when we were younger. You know, foster care. Then they adopted us." Julia hoped he'd change the subject. She didn't want to talk about the Holtzes.

"I was just wondering because I'm adopted, too. Quite a coincidence, isn't it?"

Julia was astonished. "You are!"

"Well, maybe I shouldn't say 'adopted.' I was taken in by William and Fiona Vernon years ago and I just never left. I still have a mother back in West Virginia. I visit her sometimes."

"But why would you leave your real home?" Someone with a home of his own and he'd turned his back on it?

"So they'd have one less mouth to feed. And so I wouldn't have to go to work in the coal mines. I wanted to go to school, you see, but if I'd stayed there I'd have had to go into the mines. I started out hitchhiking, heading north, and Bill Vernon came along in his pickup and gave me a lift. Then he and Fiona took me in and he put me to work after school. I was even able to send some money home to my family. My sister Louise and my little brother Randy are still there. I tried to help them out."

"How old were you? I mean, when you left home?"

"Thirteen."

She studied him in the shadowy light, seeing him differently now. She'd thought him to be a college boy like Don Owen, driving around in his father's car, wearing expensive clothes. Hearing that he'd worked since he was thirteen made him seem like another person altogether—someone more like her.

"I know Mr. and Mrs. Vernon," she said. "He's got all that earth-moving equipment."

"That's right. That's his business."

"Is that the work you did?"

"Yep. Learned to drive those backhoes and big Cats."

She thought of her job hanging out freezing wet laundry in midwinter. "Did you hate it?"

He grinned at her. "No, not at all. I loved it. It's what I'm going to do when I finish college. I'm going to take over Bill's company."

"You are?" The idea of anyone having a secure future already planned was amazing to Julia. "You're really lucky," she said.

"I know I am." He must have heard the bitterness in her tone, for he added, "Things'll work out for you, too. You'll see."

"I'm going to community college, at least for a year or two," she said. "I'm not sure Father Holtz would have gone along with it if the principal hadn't called him and talked him into it."

"Because you made such good grades, I bet."

Julia blushed. "Well, something like that." She didn't add that she knew Gideon Holtz couldn't face being shamed in front of the whole town if word got around that he'd refused to let her go. "I have to earn the money for my books and stuff, but I have a part-time job at the library and I'm a waitress at the diner on weekends."

"Wow. You're really ambitious."

Julia felt the closeness of his scrutiny and blushed again. "What are you studying?" she asked.

"Engineering. Carnegie Tech."

She nodded. "I'm going to study English literature."

"You want to be a teacher?"

"Maybe. Or a writer, or maybe I'll go into publishing. I don't know, yet."

"Sounds as if you'll be keeping long hours while you're in college."

"I will. I have to look after the sheep, too. Now that Rick's not home I spend a lot of time doing that."

"Sheep?"

"The Holtzes raise them."

"And you know all about that, too? Raising sheep?"

She laughed. "Not all, but some. This time of year I have to check them for parasites, and next month they'll have to be wormed. If they're in the orchard, I have to be sure they're not eating too much fallen fruit—that kind of thing."

"It sounds to me like you know a lot." He was studying her curiously.

"Actually I kind of like looking after the sheep. They're nice to be around, and when I'm out there with them I do a lot of thinking. They don't interrupt. And they don't talk back, either."

He reached for her hand and squeezed it. Julia felt a small tremor course through her. "Hey, you know," he said, "I'm glad I met you at the beginning of the summer. We'll be able to spend some time with each other."

Julia had felt her cheeks grow hot and was grateful for the darkness. She hadn't wanted to spoil the wonder of the evening by explaining that the Holtzes would never allow her to see him....

The water in the tub was cooling, and reluctantly Julia climbed out, toweled herself off and pulled on a warm robe and slippers. She finished the last of the wine and made her way back to the kitchen to see what there was to fix for dinner. But memory was treading on her heels.

She'd seen Tommy Black again that summer, after all. He waited for her at the library every day, and he was outside the diner when her shift there was done. No matter where she turned he seemed to be there. It wasn't long before the Holtzes knew something was going on. Gideon thundered at her about sin and transgression, while Elizabeth berated her for unredeemable wickedness.

More chores were heaped on her. Julia got up an hour earlier and worked them all in. By that time nothing they could devise would keep her from seeing Tommy. She became expert at making excuses. Gretchen's mother was experiencing an arthritic attack, she would explain, and needed Julia to help Gretchen finish some sewing she'd promised. And since Mrs. Bauer went to the same church as the Holtzes, it was difficult for them to say no.

Then, late in the summer as she lay in her narrow iron bed one night, Julia heard the Holtzes talking downstairs. Their voices flooded up through the ventilation grill in the floor. She couldn't make out many words, but the discussion was heated, and this in itself was unusual. Usually only the loud booming voice of the hawk-nosed Gideon was heard, with Elizabeth meekly acquiescing.

"... going to do for help around here?" she heard Gideon demand, and then Elizabeth's voice, surprisingly strong, "... just for once think ... my own sister ... turn my back on her ..."

An argument, Julia thought with wonder. Something to do with family. An unusual turn of events, certainly, but not one she cared about. She turned on her pillow and dreamed about Tommy.

The next day she learned that she herself was involved in her adoptive parents' argument. At the breakfast table, before she could slide out the door to catch the bus into town and her job at the library, Gideon called her back to the table.

"Sit down, Julia. We have something to tell you."

Julia pulled out a chair and sat. They'd found out she was still seeing Tommy, she thought. Well, too bad. It would take more than—

"Your mother has had word from her sister in northern New York State," he announced. "She's had a stroke and is bedridden. She needs someone there with her. We're sending you to help out."

Julia looked from one stern visage to the other. "But... but I'm enrolled in the community college. You said I could go."

"There's a college there," Gideon continued stoically. "You'll be able to go—part-time at least—and still look after your aunt."

She's not my aunt, Julia thought savagely. "But that's a different state," she objected. "The college may not even take me. And even if it does, it's bound to be more expensive. How would I—"

"Your aunt is willing to contribute something in return for your help. We will speak to your principal at the high school. I'm sure he'll forward your records and recommend you." It was the closest either of her parents would ever come, Julia knew, to speaking approvingly of her.

Remembering it all now, Julia broke two eggs into a bowl, mixed them with a whisk, then poured them into a pan. As she stirred them with a wooden spatula, she couldn't help thinking how young she'd been, how long ago it all was.

Her reminiscence quickly moved to the night before she was to leave for New York State. Tommy was heading for Carnegie Tech a few days later.

"Want to go to a movie?" he'd asked when he picked her up outside the diner.

Julia's eyes moved over his face, memorizing it. "Not tonight."

"Me, neither. Shall we drive out to the lake?"

She nodded, not trusting her voice.

He drove with one hand, holding hers on the seat between them with the other. When they parked by the water, he put his arm around her and she slid close to him on the seat of the old Pontiac. It was almost summer's end and the crickets were loud.

"It'll only be another year," he said. She could feel his breath moving her hair.

"I know."

"I'll see you during the holidays."

"Yes."

"And once this year's over, I'll be back for good. Then we'll never have to be apart again."

She turned and pressed her face against his chest. "Oh, Tommy, is that really true?"

"Of course it is." His fingers were stroking her hair. "You can make your own decisions then. You'll be eighteen. You can transfer to a college close by."

"You might meet someone else."

"I haven't yet, have I?" He tipped up her chin. "Will you stop worrying?" He bent to kiss her softly, but what started out as a gentle kiss grew stronger as her lips opened to him and her hand reached up to caress his cheek. "There isn't anybody but you, Julia," he murmured. "I knew it the very first night we met. There aren't very many sure things in life—I've known that much since I was a kid. But I'm sure how I feel about you...."

With short angry strokes, Julia scraped the eggs from the pan onto her plate, sat down at the table and stared at them.

She and Tommy had talked for a long time that night by the lake. The stars came out and the moon rose higher. A trail of silver cut across the water.

"Are you getting used to the idea of going away?" he'd asked.

"Yes. At first it seemed awful, but there's nothing here I'll miss. Well, maybe the sheep."

"Because they don't talk back?"

"How did you remember that?"

"I remember everything about you."

She gave him a soft kiss and pressed her head into the hollow of his shoulder.

"Northern New York State," she said. "It sounds so cold and faraway."

"You might be right about the cold part. But we'll both be away at the same time, so what's the difference? We'll write to each other and the time'll go fast. You'll see. Besides, who knows—Aunt what's-her-name might not be so bad."

"Aunt Delia."

"Well, there. What'd I tell you? Aunt Delia. That's definitely a not-bad name."

She giggled and snuggled closer to him.

"And after this year we'll always be together, won't we?"

"You can count on it."

Later they got out and walked by the water. He wrapped his arm around her waist, holding her against him. She shivered, and he pulled her closer.

His nearness and the knowledge that this would be their last night together was doing strange things to her body. They stopped by a big willow, old and twisted. Julia leaned against it and put her arms around his neck. His hands slid down to pull her closer, then up her sides until they were almost touching her breasts. She gave a little gasp as he cupped them in his hands and his mouth found hers with a kind of desperation. She strained toward him, opening her mouth and feeling the warmth and passion as their tongues touched.

"Oh, Julia..."

"Tommy, hold me. I'm going to miss you so!"

"And I'll miss you. But, Julia, if we go on like this I'm not going to be able to stop."

"I don't want you to stop."

"Have you ever made love with anybody before?"

"No. I want you to be the first. Not just the first. The only one—ever."

He gave a low moan and held her closer. "Julia, I love you so much."

They'd slid to the ground and she could see his outline above her as she'd pulled him close....

How foolish she'd been back then, Julia thought, picking up her fork and poking at the eggs on her plate. Not worrying, not caring, not even thinking about consequences. Trusting to luck and love, not realizing that both could suddenly betray her. She'd left on the bus the next morning, daydreaming a love that would never end because they'd promised, and that made it so.

She never saw him again.

CHAPTER TWO

JULIA LOOKED AROUND the bleak room. The funeral guests were piling potato salad onto paper plates and dipping into a jelly mold someone had brought. She spotted her brother talking to the minister and his wife. His eye caught hers and he gave a slight smile. Even though she'd seen him three months ago at Christmas in Virginia, she was always impressed by how handsome he looked in his uniform, how easily he managed every situation. Where had he learned it? He'd had to go to school in ugly hand-me-downs, just as she had. He'd never been able to play on any of the school teams or join a club, nor had he been allowed to take a girl to the movies. Yet he behaved now as if he'd been born with a silver spoon in his mouth.

"She was a true Christian," Julia heard a woman say beside her.

Julia turned to the speaker with a quick automatic smile. "Yes, she was," she agreed. *It doesn't matter anymore,* she reminded herself. *Just try to be gracious and get the thing over with.*

"Well, you should know better than anybody," the speaker sighed. "The way she and Mr. Holtz took you and your brother in...." The woman stirred her tea and eyed the lemon layer cake on the white-covered table. "I imagine you often think about the fate you might have suffered. I mean, on the *streets*," she added.

Julia hated this. She sought her brother desperately, and he, catching her look, spoke a few words to the minister and joined her.

"Hello, Mrs. Durham, wonderful to see you," he said easily.

Mrs. Durham blushed. "Oh, Major. I was just saying to your sister how grateful you two must be. I mean, thinking of the life this good woman saved you from."

"Yes, indeed we are. And how kind of you to come. Would you like to try some of this cake? It's delicious."

Julia watched with relief as he took the woman's elbow and led her toward the table. For the next few minutes she did her best to play the gracious hostess, but she couldn't keep her eyes from returning repeatedly to her watch. The funeral had been a small affair, with only a few mourners in attendance at the church and cemetery. Not many citizens of Wiltonburg remembered the Holtzes fondly, she knew. A handful of neighbors and church members had brought food to the house and said kind things about Elizabeth Holtz. One or two, like Mrs. Durham, conveyed a touch of sincerity. Yet the day was beginning to seem endless. She'd never have gotten through it without Rick.

Howard Westfall, the attorney, came up to her and said in a low voice, "May I stay after the others have left, Julia? I'd like to talk to you and your brother about the will."

"Yes, of course, Mr. Westfall." She knew him only slightly, but he'd seemed kind, offering to help when they first arrived two days ago. He was short and balding and reminded her of Bud Winter, which was perhaps one reason she liked him.

"These things are always a little hard to get through," he said, and she nodded and smiled, appreciating his understanding.

When the last of the mourners had finally gone, the three of them sat in the room the Holtzes had always called the parlor. The same linoleum Julia remembered was on the floor, the same straight curtains hung at the windows. The brocade-upholstered furniture had never been replaced and still showed no sign of wear, since the parlor was entered primarily for cleaning, seldom for sitting. Julia had cleared away most of the refreshments, but the table with its white tablecloth still stood against one wall, giving the room an oddly festive look.

"I know you and Mrs. Holtz were not particularly close," the lawyer said to both Julia and Rick. "Were you aware that she'd asked me to draw up another will for her?"

"No. Father Holtz often mentioned that he intended everything to go to the church," Rick said. "We'd assumed that's how it would have been left."

Mr. Westfall nodded. "I knew of his intentions. But Mrs. Holtz, as his sole heir, specified that it should be otherwise. And of course it was her right to do so. She wanted it divided between you two."

"She left it to us?" Julia was astonished.

"Of course it's not a large estate, but there's the farm and a sum of money. Thirty thousand dollars."

Julia and Rick looked at each other.

"I can't imagine their saving so much," Rick said.

"Well, in addition to farming, Gideon worked at the box factory for years. I believe they were very thrifty."

"Oh, they were that, certainly," Rick said, and it seemed to Julia that Howard Westfall looked sympathetic. The Holtzes' frugal life-style was well-known in Wiltonburg.

Meanwhile, Julia sat there in shock. Half of thirty thousand was fifteen thousand, and even after taxes it would still be more money than she'd ever seen in one chunk. It could be her salvation in this current job crisis. She felt a curious ambivalence toward the woman responsible for it. Resentment mixed with gratitude.

"Of course it will be a while before the will clears probate," Westfall continued. "And in the meantime, there's the farm to think about—I assume you'll want to sell it."

"Oh, I think so," Rick said, glancing at Julia. "My sister and I aren't really interested in returning to Wiltonburg. Our careers have taken us elsewhere."

The lawyer nodded. "Just as I thought. If you do put it up for sale, my brother, Dan Westfall, could probably help you out. He's in real estate, and he handles a lot of farm properties.''

"That would be wonderful,'' Julia said. "We'll certainly need advice.''

"Well, I can tell you one or two things myself,'' Westfall went on. "I've been there when Dan did a consultation. First of all, you should do a few minor renovations to make the house more salable. A little fresh paint and wallpaper can do a lot to make a place more attractive to prospective buyers. It would give it a more up-to-date look.''

Julia and Rick glanced at each other.

"I suppose we could,'' she said hesitantly. "We hadn't planned to stay that long, but if it's important . . .''

"The point is, it'll sell faster if you do it, and the price will be better.''

"What else?'' Rick asked.

"Now this is a bit trickier. We had a flood a few years back that diverted that stream of Gideon's so that it cut a new bed and flooded all those acres in the low-lying part of the farm. Big drainage problem.''

"I know where you mean,'' Rick said. "Over toward the south edge of the property.''

"Exactly. And now it floods there every spring when the snow melts and the stream rises. And since everybody in Wiltonburg knows everybody else's business, there'd be no secret about it when you put the farm up for sale. It'd be sure to be mentioned to any prospective buyer.''

"I wouldn't want to cheat a buyer, anyway," Rick said. "But are you saying we really have a white elephant on our hands?"

"Not at all. It's basically a good farm, and the sheep could be sold with it—the Holtzes always did well with their sheep. Old Fergus Halley's been helping Mrs. Holtz with them the last few years since Gideon died. You'll be hearing from him, I'm sure."

"I saw him at the church today," Rick said. "We spoke for a minute."

"Well, all you need is to have a little engineering done on those acres. Nothing elaborate, but perhaps the stream could be rerouted and some work done to shore up the banks. I'm sure it wouldn't be a big deal. Gideon never liked to lay out money, as you know, so he never did anything about it. But you'd get a much better price for the farm if it were taken care of."

"Who would we see about that?" Rick asked, his brows drawn together in a frown.

"Best fellow around this part of the state is right here in Wiltonburg—Tommy Black. Maybe you remember him from school?"

Something began to buzz in Julia's ears, shutting out the lawyer's voice so that his words seemed to drift toward her from far away. "He took over Bill Vernon's company when he finished college. Of course he expanded into a good many things Bill never handled, some big engineering projects—flood control, road building..."

"Wouldn't this be too small a job for him?" she heard Rick ask.

"Oh, no, he's not like that. He'd be glad to come and talk to you."

"Well, what do you say, Jule?" Rick asked, turning to her.

Julia swallowed. "Why, I suppose, if that seems the best idea... Whatever you think..." They both stared curiously at her, or perhaps she was only imagining it.

Rick looked at her for a moment longer, then said, "Well, why not? It wouldn't hurt to ask."

"Good," said the lawyer. "Here, I'll write down the information. It's called the Vernon-Black Company now, and it's in the phone book. Now you be sure and call me if you need anything else. Meanwhile, I'll go ahead with what I have to do to speed this probate thing along."

Doing her best to behave normally, Julia walked with Rick and Howard Westfall to the front door, thanked the lawyer and saw him out. Then she turned to her brother. "I'd better get into the kitchen and see how much food's left. It ought to be put away."

Rick gave her a concerned look. "Maybe you should take it easy for a few minutes, Jule. This whole thing's tired you out. You look pale."

"No, no. I'm perfectly all right. I'll just tidy up the kitchen and then think about turning in early. The whole day, and then this news—it's been kind of a shock, that's all."

"That's for sure. Last thing either of us would have expected, certainly. Well, I'd better make some calls. You remember Tommy Black, don't you? He lived with the Vernons. In fact, didn't you go out with him a few times? I think you mentioned it to me."

"Yes. Yes, I did," she said in a small voice. "The summer after I graduated from high school."

"How'd you ever get past old Gideon?" He grinned.

"It wasn't easy." She started for the kitchen, but Rick called after her, "Any sign of a dog coming around?"

She turned back. "A dog?"

"Fergus Halley said the dog hadn't been around for a day or two. The one that looks out for the sheep. Her name's Lizzie."

"I'll watch for her."

Julia went into the kitchen and began scraping and rinsing dishes, putting leftovers in the refrigerator. It was a kitchen that had never been modernized. Narrow vertical wainscoting covered the walls, its gray paint peeling. Cupboards with wooden doors rose unreachably to the ceiling. A table with chrome legs and a flowered plastic tablecloth stood in the middle of the room. The bulbous white gas stove was a relic of the fifties. The refrigerator, not much newer, hummed and rattled noisily. Julia recognized both appliances. Nothing had been replaced since she'd left.

She could hear Rick's voice from the hall telephone, obviously speaking to an answering machine. "This is Richard Marshall at the Holtz farm on Firebush Road." He gave the number. "Could you call me, please, as soon as possible? Howard Westfall suggested you might be able to help with a drainage problem here."

Julia stood still, holding a spoon in one hand, her fingers gripping it tightly. Her breath caught in her throat as old promises, never kept, came flooding back. *We'll write every day... I'll always love you....*

When she heard Rick hang up, she breathed out slowly. What was the matter with her? Why was she so nervous at the thought of seeing Tommy Black again? It had been ten years, after all, and besides, if he did agree to the job, Rick would be the one to talk to him.

A faint whining sound came from outside. Julia hurried to the back door and opened it.

A black-and-white dog with matted fur and doleful eyes sat there, shivering. Larger than a true border collie, Julia thought. Maybe a little Labrador mixed in. The dog shrank back, looking uncertain, and Julia said, "Lizzie?" The draggled tail waved slightly. "Come on in, Lizzie," she went on gently. "Let's find you something to eat."

She heard the telephone ring several times as she fed the dog and made friends with it, then brewed herself a pot of tea. She heard Rick talking and could tell from his end of the conversation who was on the line. The real-estate agent Dan Westfall, Fergus Halley in regard to the sheep, finally Suzanne, her brother's fiancée—at which point his voice grew lower and more intimate. Then another call came and he stuck his head in the kitchen. "This one's for you, Jule."

Her heart leapt and then started hammering in her ears as she went out into the front hall where the old black phone sat as always on its doily on the small table against the wall.

"Julia? It's Gretchen Bauer."

"Gretchen!" She let out her breath on a great sigh of relief.

"Julia, I'm so sorry I didn't make it to the funeral today, but I had to be at a meeting in Harrisburg. I just got home."

"Oh, Gretch, it's sweet of you to call."

"How about lunch tomorrow, if you're not starting back to New York right away?"

"Well, actually, I'm not. And I'd love to see you. Where shall we go?"

"How about our old hangout?"

"The diner, of course. Are you still at the library?"

"Yep, afraid so."

"Why don't I pick you up there. One o'clock okay?"

"Great. See you then."

Rick returned to the kitchen with her after she'd hung up.

"Fergus says he'll stop by late tomorrow to check on the sheep. He said we should put some more grain in the creep feed pen."

Julia nodded. "I'll take care of it first thing in the morning."

"You always were better at that stuff than I was."

"How about a cup of tea? I just made some."

"I could use a snack, too. Reverend Simmons kept me talking so long that I hardly had a chance to get anything earlier."

"Well, there's no chicken casserole left—the dog showed up and I gave it to her. But there's other stuff. How about a ham sandwich?"

"Sounds good."

She sliced ham and made the sandwich. Sliding the plate to him, she said thoughtfully, "Rick, were you as surprised as I was about this inheritance business?"

Rick, who'd unbuttoned his uniform jacket and loosened his tie, took a healthy bite of the sandwich, chewed and swallowed.

"Sure was. But it comes at a good time. I mean, we won't see anything of it till the probate business is over—I guess that takes a while. But whatever you need, you can let me advance it to you without getting your back up the way you usually do."

"I don't get my back up," she said indignantly. After a moment she asked, "Why do you suppose she did it?"

"I don't know. Maybe we only saw one side of her. I know I used to wonder sometimes what she was like before she hooked up with old Gideon."

Julia nodded musingly. She poured tea for both of them. Then she said, "That was Gretchen Bauer who called. We're going to lunch tomorrow. You remember her, don't you?"

"Vaguely. I didn't get to know many girls back in those days, if you recall."

"We were a real pair of misfits, weren't we?"

"Yes, but survivors, luckily."

They both sipped the hot tea.

Rick glanced at her over the rim of his cup. "Jule—what about Tommy Black? You seemed...upset when you heard his name."

"Oh, nothing. I was just remembering, that's all." *Once this year's over I'll be back for good. Then we'll never have to be apart again.*

"First boyfriend? That kind of thing?"

"I guess so."

"Nothing more than that?"

"No." She tried to change the subject. "Want some lemon layer cake?"

He shook his head. "I always felt a little guilty because I'd already escaped into the air force when they sent you off to the wicked witch of the north. That couldn't have been easy."

Julia smiled wryly. "I learned a long time ago never to expect things to be easy. Besides, Aunt Delia wasn't really awful. She was a step up from the Holtzes, anyway. I got enough to eat, and the house was warm. I didn't mind taking care of her. And of course Wolfe College was good. Father Holtz would never have let me get that kind of education if I'd stayed here."

"That's certainly true."

"It was just those long winters that got to me. That, and never being allowed to leave, even for holidays. Not that I missed this place, Lord knows. But still, I'd have liked to see . . ."

Her voice trailed off, and Rick asked gently, "Didn't you ever hear from Tommy?"

"No," she said shortly. For a moment she was back there, her feet crunching and squeaking on new snow, her breath making clouds in the air as she walked out to the mailbox with her heart pounding.

"I never blamed you for marrying Bryce Farnsworth, Jule. I mean, even at the time I was able to guess why you did it. You must have been pretty lonesome."

"Marrying Bryce was a terrible mistake. All my fault, too."

"You were awfully young."

"I'm not sure that's an excuse, but thanks." Julia set down her cup and smiled weakly at her brother. "It wasn't fair to him, either."

"Well, at least he had his daddy's money to console him afterward."

"Yes, he had that. And the whole thing was over pretty fast. I heard he's married again to some society girl, so I guess the wound healed."

There was comfort in talking to Rick about the past. It was seldom nowadays that they were together without other people present. Here in the dingy old kitchen they could relax for a moment and do as they'd done years ago—communicate with few words, slip into each other's feelings without effort. They'd stuck together through so much, Julia thought. She could hardly remember when their mother took off and left them. Afterward there'd been the orphanage, two

foster homes, all those different schools and then the
Holtzes.

"I'm glad you had sense enough to wait," she said,
pouring more tea for both of them. "Suzanne's just
right for you."

"I know she is." His eyes lit up. "Don't worry, I
realize how lucky I am."

She felt a sudden ache that was part joy for him,
part sadness for herself. Somehow she felt sure there
was no such happy future ahead for her.

The phone rang again and Rick went out to answer
it. He spoke briefly and then returned.

"Damn," he said.

"What is it?"

"That was Langley. Do you remember that special
training seminar I told you about? It's been moved up
a week. They need me back tomorrow."

"Oh, Rick, no."

"I hate to leave you with all this on your shoulders,
Jule. Look, why don't you call somebody? Maybe
your friend Gretchen can give you a name. Get a guy
to come in and do what needs to be done in the way of
painting and wallpapering." He looked at her apologetically. "How long would you be willing to stay?"

"Well, nobody's beating my door down with a big
job offer. I guess I can stay awhile."

"Great." He breathed a sigh of relief. "Listen, I'll
leave you a check for a thousand dollars." He took a
checkbook from his inside pocket and began writing.
"Take it to the bank and open an account. You can
use it to cover the repairs here, and I'll add more as we

need it. We'll settle up later. Ask Howard Westfall if you need help—he seems a pretty good sort." Rick hesitated. "I suppose Tommy Black will be returning my call. I'm sorry to dump that on you, too, Jule. Can you handle it all right?"

"Oh, sure," Julia said, a little more loudly than necessary. "I'm a grown-up now, remember?" Inside, emotions she hadn't experienced in years were rolling about like marbles spilled out of a bag, going in every direction, scattered and unchecked. *I want you to be the first. The only one—ever....*

Rick gave her a look of concern. "I'll leave you the car I rented. I can arrange for a ride to the airport."

"Whatever you say."

"And you'll remember about the lambs tomorrow? That stuff you're supposed to give them?"

"I'll remember. Grain for the creep feed pen. I'll get to it first thing."

Being on her own was nothing new, Julia reflected wryly. She'd manage. She had so far, hadn't she?

CHAPTER THREE

THE MAN DRIVING the pickup glanced at the little girl sitting beside him. "Got your lunch?"

She held up a metal lunch box.

He swung the car out of the driveway and onto the county road. "Don't forget to buy milk."

"I won't."

"Is your milk money in your mitten?"

She felt for it and nodded, then looked out the window at the snow that still lingered in patches on the hillsides and in the fields. "When's Easter, Daddy?"

"I'm not sure. Few more weeks, I guess."

"Then it'll be spring, right?" She turned her face up to him, squinting in the morning sunlight. Her upper lip was slightly raised to reveal a gap in her front teeth, and her brown hair, short and straight, was held back on one side by a pink clip.

"More or less."

"We've started on the Easter play at school already. I'm going to be a carrot."

"No kidding. Is that a good part?"

"Well, pretty good. Mary Owen is going to be a negg."

"An egg?"

"That's what I said. I'd just as soon be a carrot. I have to wear a carrot costume.''

"Makes sense."

"Frankie Spelling has the best part. He's the Easter Bunny."

"That sounds like a big part all right."

"I guess." She was silent for a moment, then added with a touch of spite, "Frankie's nose always runs."

"Could be a problem," he agreed.

She pulled blue-jean-clad knees up in front of her on the seat, shifted her lunch box and began to hum "I'm a Little Teapot." After a few moments, she interrupted herself to say, "Will you come when we put the play on?"

"Of course. You know I wouldn't miss that, Chipper."

She paused, giving him a sidelong look that he caught out of the corner of his eye. "You'll want to see your picket fence, anyway."

"My picket fence?"

"We need one for the play. I told Miss Carruthers you'd make it. I said my daddy could make anything," she added, pouring on all her six-year-old charm.

Tommy Black controlled a quick smile and said seriously, "I'll certainly do my best."

She looked relieved, and they rode in companionable silence the rest of the way into town. When they reached Wiltonburg Elementary School, he reached over to open the door, and she turned to give him a quick kiss. "See you later, Daddy."

"Later, sweetheart."

She slid out of the truck and immediately ran to join a group of children.

He pulled away slowly and drove toward the center of town. Arriving at the De-lite Diner, he parked in one of the oblique spaces in front of it and slipped a dime in the parking meter. He admitted to himself that he was stalling, and even felt a little disgusted that he was doing so, but headed into the diner, anyway.

Outside, the wintry March chill lingered, but inside it was comfortingly warm, and the air was fragrant with coffee and frying bacon. He slid onto a stool at the counter next to a man with fair hair pulled back into a ponytail. The man sipped coffee and regarded Tommy through horn-rimmed glasses.

"Hey, Van. You're just the guy I wanted to see," Tommy said.

"Here I am. Fire away."

Tommy greeted the waitress and said, "Just coffee, Lorene." Then he turned back to the man beside him. "I wanted to talk to you about the land near the river over on the west side."

"You know more about that than I do."

"But you researched it when you were looking into the early history of the town. Didn't you tell me that land was once filled in? I'd like to know some of the details."

"Sure, come over to the house sometime and I'll show you the records I have. Why are you so interested?"

"I'd just like to keep track of our mayor. I want to know what he's up to when he awards these flood-control contracts."

The waitress placed a cup of steaming coffee in front of him. Tommy nodded his thanks and sipped it.

"I was going to call you, anyway," Van Lightner said. "That stain we ordered for your floors just came in over at Nolan's. I think you'd better stop by and take a look at it. I want to be sure of the color before we do anything with it."

"Okay. I'll try to get over there later today."

Van stirred his coffee and said, "I was talking to Gretchen. Said she's having lunch with an old friend of yours."

"Oh?" A sudden lump rose in Tommy's throat.

"Somebody you used to know pretty well, she said. Julia something or other."

Tommy took a healthy swig of coffee and burned his tongue. "Yeah, I remember her from years ago. In fact, I'm headed over to her place right now to look over a drainage problem in one of the fields."

"Gretch said her old folks were right out of the Brothers Grimm. Really strict."

"They were, as I recall." He hesitated, then added, "Julia and her brother were adopted."

"That's what Gretchen said. She also mentioned you and the girl were pretty tight at one time."

"That was a long time ago," Tommy said shortly. Then, changing the subject, he said, "Wanted to ask you about that stain, by the way. How many coats of polyurethane will we need over it? I could pick that up at the same time—"

They talked for a while, and presently Tommy got up and left. He made his way out of town, turning just past the city limits and picking up a narrower blacktop road. He'd have stayed at the diner longer, if he could have thought of an excuse. His hands gripped the wheel more tightly. It had been Julia's brother who'd called him. Tommy had guessed—that is, until he talked to Van—that she might already have left for New York. She'd come for the funeral all right—it was in the paper—but that was yesterday. He hadn't thought she'd stay on. He'd probably be meeting her brother today, anyway. Rick Marshall—Tommy remembered him. U.S. Air Force career man. It had been late when he got Rick's telephone message last night, so he hadn't bothered to call back. Figured it was easier to come out in person this morning.

He'd heard she was married, but she'd gone by Marshall in the paper. Still, that meant nothing; lots of women kept their maiden names today. He shook his head in disgust. It had been ten years, for God's sake. Even if she was there when he stopped, what difference would it make? Ten years was a hell of a long time. He could still picture her, those big violet-blue eyes and honey-colored hair. It didn't even make sense to *him* anymore.

He slowed down as he approached the place. Usually he tried to avoid Firebush Road. He hadn't been out this way in years. The house looked much the same, he observed, leaning forward to squint at it.

Peeling paint on the old clapboards, front steps listing slightly to one side. He turned into the long lane, feeling his heart start to race in a way that annoyed him.

JULIA HAD BEEN UP since early morning, locating the lamb's feed in the barn and then carrying it in two buckets out to the creep, a sheltered pen just inside the fence of the near pasture. She'd bedded the creep with clean hay and then spread the feed in the trough. The lambs, or most of them, had been quick to come scampering over and push into the pen. The openings were large enough to admit them but not the ewes, so there was a restless crowd of mothers milling around outside.

Julia was glad she'd had the foresight to pack a pair of jeans, a warm red turtleneck sweater and a parka into her suitcase. And luckily, she'd located a pair of boots this morning near the back door. Lizzie had joined her joyfully when she came out, and now the two of them were trying to corral one stubborn lamb, which was refusing to find its way into the creep. Lizzie, who knew enough not to make a lot of noise and worry the sheep, was nevertheless doing her best to help. Her head down, her tail high, she circled and hopped, and at last Julia succeeded in seizing the lamb.

She paused for a moment to inspect the animal while it was in her arms. Same Columbia breed that Gideon had always favored, she noted. Its eyes looked good, its body was plump and healthy, and it was protesting with loud bleats as she held it. Suddenly, over the racket, she heard a voice. "I thought you always said they didn't talk back."

She held the lamb against her protectively, unable to speak as she looked into the sunlight and made out his tall figure standing there. He was rangier and more rugged than she remembered, but a lock of dark hair still fell across his forehead and the brown eyes that were regarding her intently were the same. His face was a little leaner, perhaps. And there were lines that hadn't been there before.

"Hello, Tommy. I didn't hear you drive up." She hoped her voice sounded normal. Something in her chest was tightening painfully.

"No wonder, with all this going on."

They hesitated, then both spoke at once.

"I got your brother's call. I came to look at the—"

"Rick said you might stop by. I guess you want to see—"

She realized she was still clutching the lamb and leaned over to nudge it into the pen.

"I heard you and your brother were coming for the funeral," he said as he stood there looking at her. He was in jeans and work boots. His weatherproof jacket came down to his hips; its collar was turned up against the wind. Both his hands were in the pockets.

"Yes, well, we got through it." The wind blew her hair in her eyes and she reached up to push it back.

He watched the gesture, but said nothing for a moment. Finally he asked, "Is your brother at the house?"

"I'm sorry, he isn't. Unfortunately he was called back to Langley Field. He left early this morning." She added quickly, "I can show you what the problem is. It's in the south pasture where the creek floods."

"Fine." He hesitated. "Is your husband with you?"

She gave a little start. "My husband? No, we've been divorced for years."

He looked at the ground. "Sorry. I didn't know."

She tried to keep her voice offhand. "No regrets. What about you? You must have a wife and family by now."

He didn't answer, but he raised his eyes and looked at her, a long direct look that brought heat to her cheeks. The wind tugged at her hair and she pushed it back again.

"Julia," he said quietly, "are we going to stand here and make small talk like strangers?"

She swallowed. "It's been ten years, Tommy. That's what we are." And it was the way she wanted to keep it, she thought, remembering all those trips to an empty mailbox, all those nights of tears and longing. She never wanted to go through that kind of pain again. "I'm sure we've both changed," she said. "I'm certainly not that same wide-eyed seventeen-year-old who left Wiltonburg ten years ago."

"It's funny," he said, still in a low voice. "I was just thinking you look exactly the same."

He took a step toward her and instinctively she moved back. "I'd like to think I'm a little wiser. And not so easily fooled anymore."

He winced. "I guess I deserved that. But everything wasn't the way it seemed, Julia. I mean, the way it must have looked to you."

Her eyes grew large in disbelief. "I don't see how it could have been any clearer."

"There were so many times I wanted to get in touch with you."

"But you never did, did you?"

He looked away, his eyes narrowed in the sunlight, and she felt her heart turn over with a longing she remembered well. This was a terrible idea, she thought desperately. She never should have stayed on here. She should have left when Rick did and just put the house in the hands of the real-estate people. She could have been gone before she ever saw him. But she'd been so sure it would be different now.

He brought his gaze back to her and said, "Holding a grudge doesn't help, though. When I get mad at my little girl, she always makes me forgive her before she goes to bed at night."

Julia felt her heart sink, but strangely, her resolve strengthened. The last thing she needed in her life was to become involved with a married man who remembered the good old days.

"You have a daughter." It was a statement, not a question.

"She's six. We call her Chipper. Her mother named her Charlotte, but the name didn't stick." He paused. "Neither did her mother."

"Then you're divorced?" She hadn't meant to ask; the words just slipped out.

He shook his head. "I was never married. It's not something I'm proud of, but I am proud of my daughter. Her mother was a girl I knew at a time when I— Well, that doesn't matter. She dumped the baby on my doorstep as soon as she was born and said, 'Here, she's yours. You take care of her.' She left for Arizona with another guy."

"And you've raised her by yourself?" In spite of the prickly animosity she felt toward him, she was curiously touched.

"Yes, but of course I had Bill and Fiona Vernon there to help. I'm not sure I'd have made it without them. I was taking over the business at the time—remember, I told you I was going to do that?"

She smiled bitterly. "Oh, yes. I remember you telling me a lot of things."

A look of hurt clouded his eyes briefly. The sheep were milling and nudging around them, the ewes bleating at their offspring. High above their heads, crows swarmed into an old pine and perched there, complaining raucously.

"Julia, there are things I'd like you to understand. Maybe we could talk sometime. Maybe I could even bring my little girl over to meet you. She'd love the lambs."

Slowly and carefully Julia said, "I don't think that's a good idea, Tommy. That part of our lives—you and me—is over. We've gone in different directions. There's no point unearthing it all again."

"But I just want you to know—"

"Let me show you the field that needs work," she said briskly.

They kept the rest of their conversation strictly on business, walking together out toward the south acreage, examining the course of the stream. Tommy took a notebook from his pocket and made brief sketches, showing them to her as he worked, pointing with his pencil, explaining to her in a distant professional voice what work had to be done. The look of his long square fingers, weathered and work-toughened, made Julia's heart turn over painfully, but she kept her voice steady, asking questions when she didn't understand, nodding and trying to follow everything he said even though she was remembering the touch of those hands and the feel of that long lean body as it had lain next to hers. The ten years that had passed folded together like an accordion. She kept her back straight and was sure to keep a fair distance between them as they walked along together, taking particular care that they didn't touch, not even accidentally.

When he left with the promise to give her a price the next day, she turned and walked, still straight-backed and purposeful, to the back door and into the kitchen before collapsing into a chair. Then suddenly she began to sob, choking sobs that were wrenched from a place deep inside her, and the tears that coursed down her cheeks were just as scalding as those she'd wept ten years before.

THE WILTONBURG Public Library hadn't changed much since Julia had worked there after school. The front desk, complete with signs reading Return Books Here and Check Books Out Here remained the same. But now, there was a scanner in place of the old stamp machine. And against one wall, a new periodical rack displayed magazines to better advantage than the old one had. But the hushed atmosphere, crowded shelves and smell of books were the same. A neat middle-aged woman was behind the desk where she'd expected to find Gretchen. Julia approached her and asked, "Where can I find Miss Bauer?"

The woman gave her a pleasant smile. "Off the balcony. Right there." She pointed upward. "Is she expecting you?"

"Yes, she is. I'll find my way. Thank you."

Julia loosened her coat and climbed the wrought-iron stairway she remembered so well, making her way past reference books and encyclopedias. Finally she arrived at a large door with a frosted-glass window. Written there were the words Dr. Gretchen Bauer, Director."

She knocked and pushed the door open cautiously. "Gretch?"

The woman behind the desk got up and came flying around to hug her. "Julia! Oh, you look wonderful!" She was shorter than Julia, with blond hair brushed back carelessly, but her softly tailored blue suit fitted her with considerable style, and she had a poised confident look that made Julia a little envious.

"Now what's all this doctor business? And what are you director of?" Julia demanded. "Last time I saw you, you were toting books around to the stacks just like I was.''

"Oh, nothing all that great. I've a doctorate in library science, and I'm the director of the county library system, that's all."

"All! It sounds as if you've been burning up the track. Gretchen, you look wonderful."

"I can't believe we never kept in touch. Oh, Jule, it's so good to see you! You look so stylish, so very New York."

"I do not." But Julia was glad she'd taken the time to put on her dark red suit. It set off her honey-colored hair and complemented her blue-violet eyes.

"You look much too elegant for the De-lite Diner." Gretchen laughed. "But we'll go there, anyway, for old times' sake." She turned back and spoke through an open door to an adjoining office. "I'm going to lunch now, Adele. Make copies of those purchase lists, will you, and if anybody calls say you don't know where I am."

Julia heard a voice answer, "Right, Dr. Bauer."

Gretchen grabbed her coat from a chair and picked up her bag.

"Let's beat it before the phone rings."

Gretchen's eyes sparked with excitement as they sat across from each other in a back booth of the diner. Julia marveled at how effortlessly they'd slid into the same easy sort of conversation they'd shared ten years ago.

"I'm sorry we lost touch," Gretchen said. There was obvious sincerity in her voice, and Julia knew it was not just a token remark.

"I know. So am I. But they were hectic years, weren't they?" Because she knew questions would follow, she added quickly, "Tell me about your mom. How is she?"

"Not great. Her arthritis is pretty severe now. She was bothered by it years ago but it's become worse. Nevertheless, she manages pretty well. And I still live with her."

"I remember how wonderful she was to me when I really needed someone."

"I heard you were married," Gretchen said. The waitress came with the salads they'd ordered, and they waited for her to leave.

"I was, yes, but very briefly," Julia admitted. "I've been divorced for a long time."

"Oh, I'm sorry. And you're using your own name again. I saw it in the paper."

"Yes, I didn't feel I was entitled to be called Mrs. Farnsworth after that fiasco, and you know how much I hated being called Julia Holtz. Rick felt the same way."

"How is he?"

"Just wonderful. Handsomer than ever, and he's getting married in June. Unfortunately he had to go back to Langley this morning." Julia shrugged and speared a slice of tomato with her fork.

"So how long will you be in Wiltonburg? I suppose you have to get back to your job—you said you'd been working in publishing."

"I have been, yes. But unfortunately that's over for the moment." Briefly she related the story of the company takeover and her own situation.

"Oh, Julia, what a disappointment. But all the better for us if you can stay for a while."

"Well, I have to get the house in better shape in order to sell it, Howard Westfall says. Paint and wallpaper, that sort of thing. The Holtzes never spent a penny on stuff like that, as I'm sure you remember. So I'll be looking around for someone to help with what needs to be done."

Gretchen nodded. Then, rather diffidently, she asked, "Have you seen Tommy Black?"

Julia's pulse quickened. She reached for a breadstick and broke it in two. "Just this morning, actually. We need some work done in the pasture where the creek floods. Rick called Tommy about it before he left."

"He looks pretty good, don't you think?"

"Oh, yes. He hasn't changed much." She attacked her salad again, keeping her eyes averted from Gretchen's.

The waitress returned with the coffee they'd ordered. When she was gone, Gretchen said, "He's never married, you know."

"I gathered that. Has a family, though." She could hear the bitterness in her own voice.

"Well, yes, he's got a little girl. She's a dear—you'd love her. Not exactly a ruffles-and-curls type. She's just herself." When Julia didn't answer, Gretchen continued, "Tommy had a few years of being pretty wild. He couldn't seem to settle down, drank too much, had a different woman every weekend. I know Bill and Fiona were worried, but they stuck by him."

"Boys have to sow their wild oats, they say." Julia made no effort to hide the resentment in her voice.

"Maybe," Gretchen said, sipping her coffee thoughtfully. "But, anyway, it all stopped when Chipper was dumped on him. From the moment he found himself a father, he was a different man. No more wild weekends, no more heavy drinking. He stuck strictly to business, built that company into an amazing success, bid on every big job that came along and bought more equipment."

"Good for him." Julia felt a desperate need for a change of subject even though a part of her longed to hear more. "What about some of the others? What happened to Don and Sherry Owen? They were always such big wheels in high school. Remember the graduation party their parents threw? Your mother was the one who talked the Holtzes into letting me go." And that was where she'd met Tommy Black, she thought with a pang.

"Don took over from his father at the bank," Gretchen said. "He married a girl he met in college. They had two kids, but then were divorced. Last year he got himself elected mayor, if you can imagine that. Sherry's married and divorced a couple of times. She lives out west somewhere. Las Vegas, maybe. I forget. Remember how she always had her eye on Tommy?''

His name seemed to come up at every conversational turn. Julia concentrated on her salad for a time, then said briskly, "Well, I'd better start thinking about someone to help me with that old relic of a house. Any ideas?"

To her surprise, Gretchen blushed slightly. "There is someone, a man named Van Lightner, who can do just about anything. He was over at our house once, and when he saw the problems Mom was having—she's in a wheelchair a lot of the time now—he made a few suggestions and then started showing up to do the work himself. He built ramps, adjustments to the kitchen counters and any number of things like that. It's made the biggest difference in Mom's life. She's so much more independent now."

"Sounds wonderful. Where'd you find this paragon?"

Gretchen smiled. "At a town meeting, believe it or not. He's very much into environmental issues. He teaches that sort of thing three days a week at the college. And he locks horns with Don Owen frequently, because they differ on flood-control management ideas."

"He sounds terribly busy. Do you suppose he'd consider—"

She broke off as Gretchen's face lit up. "Oh, you can ask him yourself. He just came in."

Van Lightner was the last man Julia would have expected the neat stylish Gretchen to fall for, but her expression clearly indicated that she had. He had a rough thrown-together look. Chambray work shirt and jeans, heavy boots, glasses and a ponytail. He leaned over casually and kissed Gretchen on the cheek before moving into the seat beside her.

"Hi, Gretch. Lunching in style at Wiltonburg's favorite gourmet spot, I see."

"Quit making fun of our old hangout. Julia, this irreverent person is Van Lightner. And Van, this is my good friend Julia Marshall. She went to school with me."

"I guessed as much. Hi, Julia." His hand reached across the table to take hers in a firm warm grip. Julia liked him at once.

"Van, Julia needs help. She's stuck with the job of fixing up an old farmhouse in order to sell it. Do you suppose you could possibly give her a hand?"

"I'd be very grateful," Julia put in. "It'd be mostly things like painting and wallpapering."

Van Lightner smiled and gave a shrug. "Why not?"

Julia stared at him in surprise. "Just like that? You'll do it?"

"Sure. Spring break's coming up—that'll give me ten days free from teaching. And I can work on Tommy's house evenings."

"Tommy?" Her voice wavered. "I wouldn't want to take you away from another job."

"No, it's okay. He won't mind. After three years he's used to it. That's how long he's been working on

that old barn. You know him, don't you? Tommy
Black?''

Julia's mouth had gone dry. "Yes."

"Well, that's that," Gretchen said cheerfully.
"Could you possibly run up and look over the place
this afternoon, Van? I have to be getting back to the
library."

"You bet. I'll see you at the house later, sweetie. I
promised your ma I'd cook my famous pot roast, and
I think she has a grudge cribbage match in mind."

"Why don't you come and join us, Julia?"
Gretchen said suddenly. "My mother would love to
see you again."

Julia was achingly aware of the warmth of Gretchen
and Van's relationship, the closeness and comfortable
habits they'd obviously established. She was glad for
her. Certainly no one deserved happiness more. But in
the face of it, she felt herself more alone than ever,
adrift, rootless. She smiled and said, "Oh, Gretch,
you're sweet to ask, but I still have a million things to
sort through at the house. I'll make it another time,
promise."

Spending an evening with two people in love would
be more than she could handle right now, she thought.
A feeling of cold desolation closed around her heart.

VAN LIGHTNER went through the sad old house like a
breath of fresh air, pointing and making notes, mea-
suring and suggesting. "Actually the place looks
sound enough. Might straighten up those front steps
a tad. But since you're not contemplating anything

major, we'll see what we can do with color. Lighten the rooms up, bring in some sunlight. And how about deep-sixing that linoleum in the living room?''

"By all means," Julia agreed.

"Okay, here's roughly what we'll need to start," he said, handing her a pencil-written list.

She glanced at it, then asked haltingly, "What kind of house are you helping Tommy Black fix up? I mean, you called it a barn."

Van tucked his stub of a pencil back in his shirt pocket and with one finger pushed his glasses up on his nose.

"That's what it is. A real barn. It's on the Vernons' property. They told him he could have it if he wanted. So he's making it into a house for Chipper and him. Actually they've moved in already. It's pretty well finished except for the dining room." He gave a last look around. "Okay, I guess that does it. I'll be ready to start in a few days."

HE HADN'T REALIZED seeing her again would hit him so hard, Tommy thought as he brushed the stain along the short length of board. After all these years he figured the feelings would be finished, played out. But when he saw her in the field behind the barn this morning with that lamb in her arms, the sun glinting off her hair and the wind blowing a strand of it across her cheek, he felt as if someone had slammed him in the middle with a two-by-four. Life never prepared you for moments like that, he mused wryly.

"What do you think, Tommy?" Ed Nolan asked, eyeing the board.

Tommy gave a start.

"Looks good to me. I hope I've bought enough, though."

"No problem. I ordered some extra for stock."

"Good. What about hardware? I still don't have knobs on the kitchen cabinets."

"Take a look. I've got these—" Ed opened a drawer and pulled out several knobs "—or you can take a look at the display in the back room. I stuck a lot of 'em back there with the wallpaper samples."

"I'll do that." Tommy watched as Ed pounded the lid back on the gallon can of stain. "I'll pick that up on my way out," he said, and started through the open archway into the back room of the hardware store where the paint and wallpaper were kept.

He saw her at once, standing with her back to him at one of the slanting easel-type tables where the wallpaper sample books could be spread out. She had removed her coat and tossed it over a high stool. She was wearing something dark red—a suit, he thought, noticing how its tailoring showed off her trim figure. The overhead lighting caught in her dark blond hair, and he felt the same jolt of pain mixed with pleasure that he'd felt that morning when he'd come upon her in jeans and muddy boots. It didn't matter what she wore—she was beautiful.

Suddenly he wished more than anything that he could compel her to talk to him, to listen to what he had to say. But why should she? And why did he think, after all this time, that she'd even care? She had a career now; she'd made a life for herself. Everything had turned out the way it should have. Still, with this trip of hers to Wiltonburg, didn't it almost seem as if he was being offered a second chance? How could he let her get away from him again? He couldn't, he realized suddenly. And he wouldn't. No matter how many barriers she put up between them, he'd get through to her somehow.

She turned a page, sighed, then went back to the one she'd been looking at.

"Pick the roses," he said. "The blue's too chilly." She whirled around, her face flushing. "Sorry," he said. "I didn't mean to startle you."

"It's all right." He saw the wariness leap into her violet eyes, saw the slight tightening of her mouth. He remembered what it felt like to hold her. He knew the taste of that mouth.

She seemed to be casting about for something to say. "I found someone to help me with the work on the house."

"Oh, really? So quickly."

"Yes. I had lunch with Gretchen Bauer this afternoon, and she introduced me to Van Lightner. I understand he's a friend of yours, too."

"And he's agreed to do it?"

"Yes. I hope it's not— That is, he mentioned he's been working for you, and I'm afraid I'll be taking him away from that."

He shrugged. "It's not important. I'm in no hurry." He hesitated. "Why don't you come over sometime and see what we've done with the place? It was a barn originally.''

"Van mentioned that. I'm sure it's really something."

She was holding him off, keeping her distance. He tried again. "But would you like to come and see it?"

"I told you this morning, I don't think that's a good idea." She turned her back to him as if to flip through some more samples.

"I didn't suggest it this morning."

"You know what I mean. Our getting together is not a good idea. At all."

"What scares you so much, Julia?" he asked frankly. The hectic color rose in her face once more. She shook her head and began to turn the pages of the book. "You said yourself you're a different person from the girl who left here ten years ago," he persisted. "You've lived in New York—presumably you know more about life than you once did. What's to be afraid of?"

"I'm not afraid!" she snapped.

He started to move closer to her but then stopped. Everything in him longed to grab her by the shoulders, spin her around and kiss her, but something held him back. If he was ever going to break down her resistance, it wouldn't be that way. She'd draw away, move back into her shell and never come out.

Instead, he said quietly, "How about if I ask Gretchen and Van to come, too? That wouldn't be so bad, would it? Van and I'll cook dinner, and you girls can sit and relive old times."

"There aren't any old times I want to relive," she said, but her voice had lost its hard edge. It sounded slightly husky now, incredibly sensual to his ears. He could feel himself responding to it just as he had years ago when they were both young and neither of them knew that the world had a way of holding out treasures and then cruelly snatching them back. They'd been so sure then that they could make life come out the way they wanted it to.

"Julia?" His own voice thickened slightly, and he jammed his hands into the pockets of his jacket to keep from reaching out to touch her. He was near enough to smell the faint floral fragrance of her hair. "Will you think about it?"

For several seconds she said nothing. Then she gave a tiny nod and said in a low voice, "All right. Maybe."

CHAPTER FOUR

THE PICKUP TRUCK that pulled into the driveway early the next morning had a familiar look. Seeing it through the kitchen window, Julia frowned. It couldn't possibly be the *same* pickup, could it? Even ten years ago it wasn't new. She put down her coffee, slipped on her jacket and boots and went out, shading her eyes against the sun.

"Mr. Halley?"

Fergus Halley got out of the truck cautiously. He was ten years older, of course, Julia thought. But when he turned to her, his smile was as broad as ever.

"That you, Julia? I saw you at the church the day of the funeral. Talked to your brother."

"Rick told me. I'm so glad to see you again." He was a little more bent than she remembered, but agile enough now that he had both feet on the ground. She had no idea how old he was. He'd helped them with the lambing and shearing for as long as she could remember.

He came over and shook hands. He was wearing a leather cap with ear flaps, even though the weather was milder today. He squinted at her. "Well, now," he said. "You turned into quite a looker, didn't you?"

Julia laughed. "You're looking pretty good your-self, Mr. Halley. And I haven't forgotten all the things you taught me about the sheep. I thought I had, but it all came back to me when I got here. I put feed in the lambs' creep yesterday. They seem good and healthy." She hesitated. "I'm sure you must've been a big help to my—to Mrs. Holtz."

"I did what I could. She wasn't too strong toward the end, as I guess you know." Julia didn't know, so she stayed silent. "I suppose you and your brother plan to sell the place."

"Yes, we do. Of course it'll take a while. And in the meantime we have to be thinking about shearing, don't we?"

"Say, you do remember country ways, don't you?" The old man grinned. "That's what I'm doing here right now. Came to pick up the shears and take 'em for sharpening. If the weather stays mild, we could start the job next week or the week after. You going to help?"

"Why not?" She surprised herself with her quick answer. It seemed natural enough, but the minute she'd committed herself, she was sorry. She had no intention of settling into obligations that would keep her here one day beyond what was absolutely neces-sary. She quickly corrected herself. "That is, I cer-tainly will if I'm still around. We're having some work done on the house. Once that's finished, I'll be leav-ing."

"Well, I've got my nephew who'll come. He's a good man for shearing." Fergus's light blue eyes regarded her from their webs of wrinkles. "Back to the city, eh?" She could tell he thought of it as a foreign place, something like Outer Mongolia.

"Well, yes." She changed the subject. "But meanwhile, I want to keep up with everything and see that the sheep are taken care of. We'll be selling them, too."

Lizzie spotted him from the barn and trotted over, her tail wagging in welcome. Fergus reached down to pat her.

"Me and Lizzie'll take care of feeding the lambs for you this morning, and I'll pick up those shears. Good to have you back, Julia."

He started toward the barn. She called after him, "Is that the same pickup you used to drive, Mr. Halley?"

He turned. "Sure is. Two hundred and thirty thousand miles on 'er, and she hums along like a Singer sewing machine."

Julia waved him off, then went back into the house. Her coffee had grown cold. She poured it out and refilled the cup from the pot. Then she crossed to the table and sat down.

What she was feeling, she realized, was a sense of danger. She repeated the words aloud and decided it sounded too dramatic, but even so, the feeling persisted. It was all too cozy, too familiar, too much like a walk down memory lane. And the longer she stayed here, the more difficult it was going to be to extricate herself. Lunch at the De-lite Diner, picking out wallpaper in Nolan's Hardware, feeding the lambs... She was already settling into a routine the homey familiarity of which alarmed her. She'd determined, when she left Wiltonburg, never to return, and in spite of this situation, which she still refused to think of as a family emergency, nothing had happened to change that resolution. She would have to wait a few days for Van Lightner to be free, of course, but once he'd fixed the place up, she'd be out of there.

She sipped her coffee slowly, set the cup down and began tracing the flowers in the plastic tablecloth with one finger. After a few moments, she admitted to herself what it was she really feared—being around Tommy Black.

It was all very well to say to herself that something was long over. She could even convince herself it was true. She could remind herself that that girl—that other Julia—had been barely more than a child ten years ago, and that the wild emotions she'd felt then had nothing to do with today. But when she came up against the physical evidence, the sudden pounding of her heart, the trembling that couldn't be controlled, she had to face up to the truth. That younger Julia was still very much a part of her, and the adult Julia's reactions to Tommy were exactly the same as they'd been ten years ago.

Did she still love him? No, absolutely not, she answered herself firmly. But she couldn't help reacting to him, which was just as dangerous. The longer she stayed in Wiltonburg the more the danger would increase. And if there was one thing she was determined about, it was that she would never again put herself in the position of trusting a man that much.

Well—she took a swallow of coffee—perhaps some man, someday. But it would never be Tommy Black.

She got up, rinsed her cup in the sink and unplugged the coffeemaker, wondering in passing what could have induced Gideon to permit the purchase of anything so up-to-date. Perhaps the old percolator had finally given up the ghost, or maybe Elizabeth Holtz had waited until Gideon had passed on before buying it herself.

Julia sighed. The attic. It was time to face it.

If she wanted to put the house on the market, the attic would have to be cleaned out. A good many things could be given to the Salvation Army or some church mission, but she suspected the attic held the stored possessions of decades. She would have to deal with them—there was no point putting off the job. The sooner these things were taken care of, the sooner she could leave with a clear conscience, knowing she'd done what she had to do.

She left the kitchen and started upstairs. She was sleeping in the same tiny room that had been hers ten years ago. It was exactly as she'd left it—the iron bed, the bare floor, the chest of drawers, the one straight chair. Not a book or a toy to remind anyone of the girl who'd once lived there. She could have slept downstairs in the room that had been Elizabeth and Gideon's, but she had no desire to do that. And in some way, she felt it was good to return to her own room, if only to remind herself of how unhappy she'd been here and what a contrast it was to the life she'd led in New York the last few years.

At the end of the hall she opened the door that led to the narrow attic stairway. A breath of cold stale air greeted her, and she left the door open behind her as she climbed, hoping some of the heat from downstairs would rise. At the top she pulled a string and an overhead light bulb came on.

Julia looked around. The place was crammed with trunks, wooden boxes, cardboard cartons, broken lamps, chairs with ragged cane seats and an ancient hat rack. Plastic-shrouded garments hung from heavy hooks against the wall. Julia began making mental notes of what could be given away at once. Anything wearable, certainly, and furniture that could be restored. Didn't most charitable institutions have workshops for that sort of thing?

One thing was apparent. The Holtzes had saved every scrap, rag and remnant of their lives. Looking around, she didn't know where to begin. With those stacks of cartons, she decided finally. She'd work through them and dispose of the contents and then get in touch with someone about donating the rest of the stuff. She set her jaw firmly and approached the first stack.

By eleven o'clock she was chilled to the bone and absolutely filthy. In spite of the mild day, heat was slow to penetrate the attic, and the trickle of warmth that came from downstairs wasn't enough. She'd sifted through utility bills, feed-store bills, insurance-payment receipts, all dating back forty years. There were yellowing newspapers that disintegrated as she handled them. She tried to discover what had made them worth saving, but never succeeded. She found no reminders that she and Rick had ever existed except in an account book where she found notations in Gideon Holtz's small cramped handwriting. "Winter jacket, Richard: $10." "Sweater, Julia: $2." Rummage-sale prices. She remembered those rummage sales well.

The distant ringing of the telephone floated upstairs. Julia put the book back and hurried down to the front hall.

"Jule! How's it going?" Her brother's voice, so cheerful and normal, brought her back to the present.

"Rick, you have no idea how much stuff they left behind. Records and receipts accounting for every penny. I'm going through the attic right now. You had a winter jacket in 1979 that cost ten dollars. Do you remember it?"

"Oh, Lord, do I. How I hated that thing. Imitation leather and so stiff I couldn't bend my arms." His laughter made her laugh, too. He'd always been able to do that even in the worst times. "Is it too much for you? Getting you down?"

"No, of course not."

"Because I'm sitting here feeling guilty I put too much on you."

"Don't be silly. I'm doing fine."

"Well, what about the other stuff? Did you find someone to fix up the house?"

Julia carried the telephone with her and sat on the bottom step. "Gretchen Bauer helped me with that.

She has a talented boyfriend who's agreed to come and take care of it.''

"Wonderful. And did Tommy Black show up?''

Julia kept her voice under careful control. "He did. He hasn't given me a quote yet, but he's agreed to do it.''

"And was everything...okay?'' She could hear the concern in his voice.

"Absolutely fine.''

"Well, it sounds as if you have things in hand all right. Be sure to let me know if you need more money. Suzanne and I are talking about coming up there for a visit soon. She wants to help. In fact, she made me feel like a heartless clod for dumping it all in your lap.''

"Now that's one smart girl. But don't worry about me, Rick. And you and Suzanne come whenever you can. I don't need advance notice.''

She felt better after his call. She went into the kitchen and made fresh coffee, then returned to the attic to bring down a box. There was no reason for her to stay up there freezing. She could just as easily examine the stuff down here.

The hot coffee warmed her, and she made several more trips, bringing down more boxes. The work began to go faster. Most of the papers she could go through quickly and put aside for discarding. One box contained photographs, and these she looked over more carefully. None of her or Rick, of course. Julia couldn't remember family snapshots ever being taken. Some of them seemed to be of aged relatives, not identified by name, and one was of two young girls who might have been Elizabeth Holtz and her sister, the aunt Delia Julia had stayed with. There were other photos of what looked like church outings, of a stern man holding a Bible—Julia guessed it might be a new minister—and pictures of the church itself undergoing renovations. Several were of the sheep, including a big Columbia ram Julia remembered. Gideon had been proud of that ram. Someone else must have taken the pictures, for Julia couldn't recall ever seeing a camera in the house.

At the bottom of the box was a stack of yellowed newspapers, old issues of the *Wiltonburg Courier*. Julia was about to add them to the trash pile when a front-page picture caught her eye. The headline read *Colin Doyle Named* Courier *Editor*. Julia studied the picture. He was much younger, but Julia recognized him. Colin Doyle had been one of her favorite customers when she worked in the diner. He'd come in for coffee every day, and he always talked to her, asking her what her plans were for the future. He never failed to leave a generous tip. Now *he* was someone in Wiltonburg she'd like to see again. She put the issue aside. She'd take it in to show him.

"GINA BLAKELY," the tall young woman said, extending her hand. "I'm the editor now."

"Oh." Julia tried not to let her disappointment show. "I didn't realize Mr. Doyle wasn't here anymore. It's been a few years since I've been in Wiltonburg."

Gina Blakely smiled. She had short dark hair and eyes that sparkled with warmth. "Maybe I could help?"

Julia wasn't sure how to begin. "Well, thank you, but it was really just a personal visit. I used to know Mr. Doyle. He always encouraged me a lot. I thought of him as a special friend."

"Lots of people did," the young woman said. "Including me. I'm his granddaughter."

"Really? And Mr. Doyle...?"

"He died three years ago."

"Oh." Julia was surprised at the sharp sense of loss she felt.

"He left me the paper, so I moved here and took over."

It sounded to Julia like a shortened version of a much longer story. In spite of herself, she was curious.

"Moved here?"

"From California. That's where I was living at the time. When my grandfather got sick I came back to help out. I was trying for a career in screenwriting, but I wasn't exactly setting Hollywood on fire, so..." She lifted her hands, palms up.

Julia realized they'd launched into a conversation without completing the introductions. "I'm sorry," she said. "I'm Julia Marshall. I'm back here for a short time to settle an estate."

"Marshall? Oh, yes. Elizabeth Holtz's funeral. Well, this is a newspaper, after all," she added apologetically when she saw Julia's look of surprise.

"Of course," Julia said, thinking Gina Blakely was as easy to talk to as her grandfather had been. "I've been cleaning out the attic at the farmhouse and I came across some old issues of the *Courier*." She pulled the newspaper from the protective envelope she'd put it in.

Gina took the paper and looked at it. At once her eyes misted with tears. "Oh, my gosh, this is the day he became the editor. It was before my time, but I recognize it. My mother had the original picture. Several years later he bought the paper himself."

"He was one of my few happy memories of the town."

"Really?" Gina tilted her head to one side. "What a nice tribute."

Julia studied her. "You look—I hope you don't think I'm being too personal—but you look about my age. You didn't live in Wiltonburg when you were little, did you? I mean, I'm sure you weren't in my school."

"No, I lived in King's Crossing—you know, two towns away. So I was in a different school district. But I visited my grandfather quite often. Where do you live now?"

"New York City. I'm unemployed at the moment, but I was in publishing. When I get back I have to start some serious job hunting."

Gina nodded. "Sorry you won't be staying."

Julia had an idea. "Maybe before I leave we could have dinner together."

"I'd like that. We could even settle a few of the world's problems while we're at it."

"Beats trying to solve our own, right?"

Gina's laugh was quick. "Right. Give me a call whenever you're ready."

After leaving Gina Blakely, Julia walked down the main street of Wiltonburg, her spirits considerably lighter. It was the same way she remembered feeling after chatting with Colin Doyle in the diner years ago. He'd always been interested in where she might go to college and what she planned to major in, and he never failed to assure her she could be whatever she wanted to be. "Or you can stick around Wiltonburg," he'd said to her one day. "I'll give you a job." They laughed together over his offer, but Julia always felt he'd been sincere. He didn't say things he didn't mean. She sensed some of the same up-front quality in his granddaughter, and made a mental note to call her soon about dinner.

Not much had changed in Wiltonburg in the last ten years, she observed, looking at the storefronts. The Army Surplus was still on the corner of Main and Oak. Julia had already stopped in there to pick up some much-needed work clothes. Woolworth's was gone, replaced by an unfamiliar menswear store. But Delbert's Shoes was still next door to it, as was Groscher's newspaper-and-tobacco store on the corner. The Federal Bank of Wiltonburg was on the opposite corner, just as it had been since 1927, according to the brass plate in front.

Her eyes skimmed over the other businesses along the street, stopping when she noticed an unfamiliar one. It was a dress shop with a mock-Victorian sign— Rose Boutique, with curlicues and a picture of an old-fashioned lady in a bustle. Julia crossed the street for a better look. It was tastefully done. Soft gray paint with dark red trim, and in the window the nostalgic theme was carried through—a rocking chair, a small marble-topped table and chest of drawers were taste-fully arranged. Only the dresses displayed—one tossed over the chair, one on a hanger hooked over a brass gaslight fixture—were of today's styles. And the chest stood with drawers pulled open, spilling out displays of sportswear—T-shirts, pants, sweaters. All the things had a look of quality. Quite a departure for Wilton-burg, Julia decided, wondering how they were sell-ing.

Staring in the window, she only had an instant to register another reflection before the person who made it spoke.

"Remember when it was Olson's Stationery Store?"

She turned and looked at Tommy directly, wonder-ing if she was blushing again. Why was that one re-action impossible to control?

"I certainly do. Old Mrs. Olson wore an apron." She gave him what she hoped was an impersonal smile.

He stood there in much the same outfit as yester-day—jeans, weatherproof jacket, heavy work shoes. His smile was decidedly personal, she thought.

"There was a cat who always slept on the counter," he said.

"Right near the gum machine."

A small voice piped up. "Is it there now?" Julia looked down to see a little girl clutching his hand.

"No, sweetheart, I'm afraid it isn't. Chipper, this lady is Miss Marshall. We used to be good friends a long time ago."

Julia looked down into brown eyes that were exactly like Tommy's, hair that threatened to come loose from its barrette and fall forward just as his did. Tommy's child. The impact was greater than she'd anticipated. It took her a moment to find her voice.

"I'm very happy to meet you."

"My real name's Charlotte Black, but it's okay if you call me Chipper."

"Thank you. Will you call me Julia?"

"Is that your name?"

"Yes."

"Well, then, I will." The little girl was looking at her with frank curiosity. "Did you know my daddy when he was a hellion?"

"Chipper!"

She looked up at him, wide-eyed. "Well, that's what Aunt Fiona always tells Uncle Bill. She says, 'That boy was a regular hellion.'"

Julia couldn't hold back the laughter. "I guess I missed that," she said.

"I'm going to be a carrot in the Easter play at school. Are you going to come see it?"

She was six, Julia thought. Six years ago I was just graduating from college. Heading for New York City with a check from Rick in my pocket to keep me going. She smiled at Chipper. "Are you in any danger of being eaten by the Easter Bunny in this show?"

Chipper rolled her eyes and said, "Oh, please. Are you kidding? Frankie Spelling's the Easter Bunny—he'd never be able to catch me. And his nose always runs."

"Frankie has certain deficiencies," Tommy explained. "But you'd be most welcome. It's going to be a good show. I'm making the picket fence."

"I see. In the production end, are you?"

"No real talent, I'm afraid."

"Still, I'm sure the fence is important. And not everyone can make one." *Keep it light,* she told herself. *And make no binding commitments.* "If I'm still around, I'll certainly try to make it."

"There's Melissa!" Chipper shouted, pulling away from her father and dashing to meet another little girl who was coming out of a store up the street. The two children immediately started chattering.

Tommy turned back to Julia. "Just left each other an hour ago, I'm sure."

"Lots can happen in an hour—you have to keep up."

His eyes searched her face. "Well? Will you come?"

"Honestly, I'm not sure how long I'll be here."

"Have to admit, it's a pretty attractive invitation." His smile teased her.

"She's a nice little girl," Julia said, evading the issue.

"She seems so to me, but then I'm partial."

Chipper bounded back to them. Her mouth was distorted by something large and purple, which she was chewing on with determination.

"Bubble gum?" he inquired.

She nodded her head, then managed to stow the gum in one cheek. "Melissa's got new sneakers," she said thickly.

"Oh? Didn't you just get new sneakers last week?"

Chipper nodded. "Hers have red laces, though."

"What color are your laces?"

She stuck one small foot out. "Pink."

"Is red better than pink?"

She thought about it. "I guess not."

Julia felt a fullness in her throat. What a good father he was. She hated the envious way her own thoughts were behaving, seeing him in the little girl's face and wondering what happened all those years ago, who Chipper's mother was.

"We'd better be going," he said. "I have those figures almost ready for you. If you like, I can drop them off later."

"You don't have to bother," she said quickly. "You could just put them in the mail." She felt a sudden panic at the thought of seeing him alone again.

"It's no bother." He grinned, then took Chipper's hand and continued down the street.

Julia stopped at the supermarket on the way home, buying a few things she needed for herself along with dog food for Lizzie. The days were growing longer now. After she'd unloaded her purchases, fed the dog and made herself something to eat, there was still daylight left, so she pulled on her jacket and boots and walked back to the barn and the lamb creep.

The sheep were quiet—some of them remained near the pen, and some were out in the field, their lambs close. She leaned over and felt one ewe's coat. Heavy and full, just as it should be. It might be fun to help with the shearing. It would be interesting to see how much she remembered. Without Gideon's sour authoritative presence to dampen things, it could be a good experience. And she'd be the boss this time, she reminded herself. It was her farm now, hers and Rick's. She thought of tight-lipped Elizabeth Holtz with her gray hair yanked back severely, and once again she reflected on the strangeness of the whole business. She'd never expected to walk along this lane again.

She slowly made her way back toward the house in the growing chill of the March twilight. Patches of snow lingered on the higher slopes, but around the house and the farm buildings it was gone, and most of the mud had dried up, too. Even in the south acres, where the drainage problem was, it must be less soggy by now. If so, Tommy or whoever he had working for him would soon be able to start their job. She hadn't given a thought to the estimate he said he had ready for her. She hadn't even considered consulting anyone else or comparing prices, which was probably the right way to do it. Yet she knew she wouldn't. Whatever Tommy said the job was worth, she knew it would be fair.

What made her think that? she asked herself indignantly. Had he been fair with her? She opened the back door, slipped out of her boots and jacket and turned on the kitchen light. She'd left one carton on the floor when she'd taken a break from her sorting and discarding earlier. She lifted it to the table and began going through it, forming a quick mental estimate of how many remained up in the attic. Too many, she thought with a sigh, and gave her attention to the job at hand. One way or another, she'd get through it all.

This box contained the usual mix of tax receipts and fuel bills, but in among the papers was a book. She picked it up and gave a little cry of recognition. It was a paperback, well-worn and barely holding together at its spine. *Modern Methods of Sheep Raising*. The pages were curled at the corners as if it had been left somewhere damp. And so it had been, in a way. She remembered reading it in the barn and sometimes leaving it there. It was the only book she'd ever owned in those days. She'd borrowed library books—although they were frowned upon by the Holtzes—but this one she'd bought with her own money. Leafing through it, she saw all the underlined phrases.

"Plan your breeding program so that lambs are five to six weeks old by the time spring pasture growth starts... Give some thought to raising your own ram, which has many advantages... If artificial feeding of a lamb is needed, be sure to include cod-liver oil, glucose and a beaten egg yolk...."

Julia passed her hand over the ragged page and felt herself slip back into the mind of that young girl, sitting by herself in the barn, poring over the words. Of course she'd never dared mention to Gideon anything of what she'd read. And in fairness, she had to admit he was an efficient and capable farmer. But she could still remember the thrill of learning and understanding. And Fergus Halley, whenever Gideon was not present, would talk to her about it. Adamantly opposed to anything he classified as newfangled, Fergus nevertheless had plenty of wisdom to impart, and he was a good listener. Once when she caught him slipping cod-liver oil into the formula he was giving an orphan lamb, he became flustered. But in the end he conceded defeat and gave her a conspiratorial wink.

She sank into a chair at the table and turned the pages. "The type of wool a sheep produces is a matter of heredity, but its quality is largely due to good health and proper nutrition—"

There was a knock at the kitchen door. Julia gave a start and looked up. It was almost dark now. She walked to the door and opened it cautiously.

"Hi. Have I come at a bad time?"

She stepped back and opened the door wider. "No, not at all. Come on in." Every time she saw Tommy she made an effort to be offhand, yet she felt she'd never quite managed to pull it off convincingly. Or perhaps it was simply that what was going on inside was always so totally at odds with the casual exterior she was presenting. She could feel a slow heat travel through her body, making her face flush and her throat go dry.

"I brought this for you to look at," Tommy said, waving the envelope in his hand. "I didn't know if you might want to think about it or perhaps call your brother and talk it over with him."

"Thank you." She took the envelope and cleared her throat. "Is the weather suitable for starting the job soon?"

"I'd say any day now, if there's no serious rain." His brown eyes seemed to study her features.

"Well, that's good news. The sooner the better."

He hesitated. "Don't you want to look at the figures?"

"Oh. Yes, of course." She opened the envelope and unfolded the sheet of paper. She saw the Vernon-Black logo at the top, and underneath, his handwriting, large and scrawling but legible. "...coarse gravel...six loads of fill...estimated labor..." The words ran together as she tried to concentrate on them. "It seems all right to me," she said, trying to sound businesslike.

"If you're satisfied, I'll let you know when we'll be ready to start. Perhaps as early as Monday. You'll probably be seeing Van then, too. I think spring break's starting."

"That's good."

"The sooner the better?" His eyes crinkled at the corners as he repeated her words. He didn't wait for her answer, but glanced behind her at the carton on the table. "Doing some cleaning out, I see."

"Yes. I've been at it most of the day."

"Could you take a break tomorrow night?"

The air between them hummed like beating wings. "What for?"

"Well, I spoke to Gretchen and Van. They both said okay."

"Okay for what?"

"Dinner. At my house. Remember I suggested it?"

"Yes, but I didn't realize—"

"Gretchen says she'll pick you up. You can check with her about the time."

"Oh, but..." He started to leave, then turned back and gave her a quick smile. "See you tomorrow."

When the door closed behind him she stood for a moment, still holding the paper. She should feel resentful. Everything had been taken out of her hands. Yet all she could feel was a flutter of anticipation—a pleasant youthful feeling, more seventeen than twenty-seven. But twenty-seven was the reality, she reminded herself as she turned back to the table. And what happened after tomorrow night?

CHAPTER FIVE

"WHY'S THAT STUFF tied up with string?" Chipper asked. She was kneeling on a high stool at the kitchen counter, watching her father do the cooking.

Tommy físhed the lamb and salt pork out of the big pot and put it aside. "So I can lift it out easier. It's going back in shortly."

"The string, too?"

"No, I'm getting rid of that. Chipper, we've had this before. You liked it."

"I guess I remember it, only I didn't know about the string. Will you save me some?"

"Sure." He snipped off the string and began cutting the meat into small pieces.

The kitchen was at one end of the big open first floor, separated from the living room by a high counter. The little girl was on one side of the counter, Tommy on the other.

"How'd you learn to cook?" she asked.

"Bought a cookbook."

"How come?"

He gave her a grin. They'd had this discussion before, but Chipper liked to hear it repeated.

"Because there was somebody I had to cook for."

She giggled, supplying the next line. "A lady. Miss Charlotte Black."

"Yes. Miss Black eats like a horse."

The giggle increased in volume. "How come you're having a party tonight?"

"Well, it's not much of a party. Just dinner."

"Who's coming?" She watched as he browned onions and garlic, added tomato puree and then dumped in the meat.

"Gretchen—you know her. And Van."

"Van lets me pound nails sometimes. Is that other lady coming?"

"Miss Marshall? Yes."

"She said I could call her Julia. Did she used to be your girlfriend?"

He got out a heavy cast-iron pot and began creating layers of beans, chicken pieces, Polish sausage, spareribs and tomato sauce. "Sort of, a long time ago."

Chipper grew serious. "I think she should be your girlfriend now."

"Oh? Why is that?"

"Because you should have a girlfriend. You spend too much time alone."

He stopped what he was doing and stared at her. She was kneeling on the stool, looking like a small wise owl. "Where'd you hear that?" he asked suspiciously.

"On Oprah. It was a show about the single parent. Aunt Fiona and I were watching."

"I believe I'll have to speak to Aunt Fiona about your TV viewing." He tried to change the subject. "Where are you three going tonight?"

"McDonald's. Then we're going to watch a movie. Uncle Bill rented *Free Willy.*"

"Didn't you already see that?"

"Yes, but I love it. I want to see it again."

"Sounds good." He finished the layers and shoved the heavy pot into the oven.

"So—" Chipper was relentless "—*is* she going to be your girlfriend?"

"It's not just up to me, you know."

"But do you want her to be?"

He rolled his eyes upward. "I see you've adopted Oprah's interviewing techniques, too."

The front door opened and then was blown shut by a gust of March wind. "Hi, anybody home?"

Chipper scrambled down from the stool and skipped over to him. "Hi, Van. What's all that?"

"Oh, just party stuff." Van Lightner was carrying two bulging shopping bags. He placed them on the counter and then reached into a deep jacket pocket and brought out a bottle of champagne. Tommy raised his eyebrows. "Pretty fancy. What's that for?"

"Never can tell. Somebody might want to drink a toast." He went around the counter to the refrigerator, opened the door and slid the bottle in. "I got the other stuff you said we needed. And a few extras. Come on, Chipper, why don't you help me unload it? Then I want to take a look at that door—the one that was sticking. I brought sandpaper." He reached into the opposite pocket and pulled it out.

"I could help you," Chipper offered. She was back on her stool, already starting to unpack the bags, pulling out the contents and lining them up on the counter.

Tommy surveyed the purchases in disbelief. "All I said we needed was a bunch of grapes and a hunk of cheese." Van had brought red wine, six kinds of cheeses, three packages of crackers of varying sizes and shapes, green, black and red grapes, as well as pears, apples, ripe olives, walnuts and pecans in their shells, and two long loaves of French bread.

"Oh well, everything looked so good," Van said with an offhand wave. "Okay, you deal with that. I'm going to smooth down that door. I don't want to plane it, because that might make it too loose. We'll try sanding first."

Chipper slid off the stool and followed him to the dining room area. It was the one part of the converted barn that still wasn't finished. There was heavy plastic sheeting on the floor to protect it, and the table and chairs had been set up temporarily in front of the big stone fireplace.

"Can I have my own sandpaper?" Chipper asked.

"All right, here. You work down low. I'll start higher."

Meanwhile, Tommy began sorting out the cheeses and rinsing the grapes. In the background he could hear scraps of the conversation from the dining room. But he was more aware of a growing uneasiness that felt a lot like stage fright. Would she like his house? Would she resent it that he'd been so insistent about having her come here? He'd promised himself he wouldn't push too hard, but wasn't he really doing just that? He was worried about scaring her away—she was so determined not to get involved. And he was equally determined to change her mind. As busy as he'd been building up his business and redoing the house, as much joy as he'd had from Chipper, he knew the minute he saw Julia that something was still missing from his life. The whole center of it, the warm core of love that was life itself.

It was obvious she'd had an unhappy marriage, but beyond that he knew nothing about what her life had been for the past ten years. So she'd made a bad choice. Everybody made those at some time or other, didn't they? There'd been hardly a day during those ten years when he hadn't regretted the choices he'd made.

He started preparing a tray of cheese, crackers and olives. Then, finding a corkscrew, he removed the cork from the red wine and set it on the counter. Van reappeared with Chipper trailing after him. She already had a light sprinkling of sawdust in her hair.

"I forgot," Van said. "I've got a pie, too. In the car."

Tommy stared at him.

"*You* made a pie?"

"No. A couple of my students gave it to me." He shoved his glasses up with one index finger. "They raised the berries themselves in organic soil, then froze them. It was sort of an ongoing project.''

Tommy shook his head in disbelief. ''Well, why not? Bring it in.'' He watched as Van went out, with Chipper hopping along at his heels. Then he turned and looked around at the house—at the kitchen where moisture-beaded fruit was piled in a bowl on the counter beside the wooden tray. The cassoulet in the oven was giving off a hearty country aroma. He went over to the fireplace and put a match to the kindling, watching as the flames leapt up around the logs. He tried to see the place through her eyes. What would she think of it? He hardly dared phrase the other question that was gnawing at him. What did she think of him?

''THERE'S NOT a decent mirror in this house!'' Julia exclaimed in frustration as she pulled on the violet-colored sweater and then flipped out her hair.

''Wait, what about this?'' Gretchen got off the edge of the bed where she'd been sitting back, observing. She took the tiny mirror off the wall and held it back at a better angle. Since it couldn't have measured more than eight by ten inches, the field of vision was distinctly limited. ''Any better?''

''Oh, Gretch, it's hopeless. What do I need? A scarf, maybe? How about a belt?''

''Not a thing, Jule. That sweater matches your eyes. You couldn't add anything that would top it. You look gorgeous.'' She hung the mirror on the wall again. ''There. Brush your hair and put on some lipstick.

That's all you need. I could work for an hour and not look so good." Her own blond hair was pulled back in a French braid. "I should've made it to the beauty shop today, but I was at a meeting till an hour ago." She restored the mirror to its hook and plopped onto the bed again.

Julia smiled at her friend. "Gretch, it's so wonderful to be with you again. And, hey, forget about the beauty shop. Every time Van looks at you he turns to putty."

Gretchen grew pink and smiled back at her, but Julia thought she seemed not quite herself—as if she was nervous or perhaps overexcited.

"What was the meeting about? Something important?"

"Well, yes, in a way. Important to me, because I've been pushing for it for a long time. We're going to inaugurate a program of lectures at the library. Visiting authors—whomever we can find in this part of the state—can peddle their books and autograph them too. Some of the old die-hard trustees didn't approve because it smacked of commercialism, but I insisted it would get more people interested in the library."

"Good for you." But not that exciting, Julia thought. Could that really be what had Gretchen acting so hyper? She leaned toward the tiny mirror and applied lipstick. "I went into town yesterday. Met the editor of the *Courier*."

"Gina Blakely? Oh, I like her a lot."

"I did, too."

"She has some good ideas for the paper. She wants to publish it more often than twice a week, for one thing. But I suppose all that takes money."

"I suppose. Is she married?"

Gretchen bounced on the edge of the narrow iron bed. "I'm not sure. I think maybe she was once, back in California, but not anymore."

Julia looked at her and gave a little laugh. "You know, this is like prom night. I feel as nervous as a teenager. Not that I ever went to a prom, of course. But remember that time there was a party at the Owens' house and the Holtzes let me go? I wore one of your dresses, a white one."

"Oh, gosh, I remember that dress. And the shoes— we put Kleenex in the toes."

Both of them laughed. Then Gretchen got up from the bed and paced across the room to the little window.

"Julia, I can't stand it. I have to tell somebody. Can you keep a secret?"

JULIA STOOD just inside the doorway and looked around. *It's beautiful,* she thought. *It's the most beautiful house I've ever seen.* And then Tommy was holding out his hand to help her off with her coat.

"I love your place," she said, trying to sound casual. But her voice came out soft and quavery.

"I hoped you'd like it."

"Oh, I do."

Gretchen only had eyes for Van, who was standing at the other side of the big main room where the unfinished dining section was. "Excuse me, you two," she said, and went to join him. He slipped an arm around her waist and bent to kiss her.

Chipper hurried to Tommy's side, obviously anxious not to miss anything.

"Hi, Julia," she said, smiling a gap-toothed welcome.

"Hello, Chipper. I was just telling your daddy what a pretty house you live in."

"It used to be a barn."

"Well, it's a mighty nice barn now. Will you show me around?"

"Okay."

"Hey, anybody mind if I come too?" Tommy asked.

He and Chipper steered her around the first floor, showing her the big windows and indicating where support columns had been installed. The floors were a burnished wide-plank oak, with rugs arranged here and there in handsome geometrical patterns to divide the different areas, all of which flowed seamlessly into each other—living room, library, kitchen. She could picture how the dining room would fit into the scheme once it was done. The furniture was comfortable-looking, durable enough, she could see, for a growing child and pets, as well. A yellow Labrador was sleeping on the couch. Firelight flickered off the floors and walls. On the coffee table was an array of crayons and a half-finished picture.

"What's your dog's name, Chipper?" Julia asked.

"Nugget," the girl replied. "Daddy said he's pure gold."

"I believe I also said he was eighteen-carat lazy," Tommy put in.

Julia looked at him and voiced what she'd thought earlier. "It's the most beautiful house I've ever seen."

She was surprised at the flush of pleasure in his cheeks.

"There's more," Chipper said. "Upstairs. We go this way."

The bedrooms were located off a balcony that overhung the dining room and library on one side and the kitchen at the far end. Julia followed Chipper up the steps, conscious of Tommy just behind her.

"I have a dog, too," she told Chipper. She was determined to keep the conversation on a cheerful impersonal level. "Her name's Lizzie. She helps with the sheep."

Chipper whirled around at the top of the stairs. "What sheep?"

"The sheep that live on my farm." How odd the phrase sounded, Julia thought.

"Are there babies, too? Lambs?"

"Yes, quite a lot of them." Julia hesitated, then said exactly what she'd been determined not to say. "If you'd like to see them, perhaps your daddy will bring you over one day."

"Hey, could we do that, Daddy?"

"Don't see why not."

Julia purposely avoided looking at him. "Which room's yours?" she asked Chipper.

"Right down here." As the little girl led the way, Tommy leaned down and whispered, "Seems to me I made that suggestion and you vetoed it."

"I know I did. But she's irresistible." Julia still refused to look at him, but she could feel the warmth of his smile. Chipper flung open a door. The room was a mix of feminine softness and tomboy. On the bed was a patchwork quilt with a black-and-white cat sleeping on it. The cat regarded them through slitted eyes and then, ignoring them, started to knead the quilt with his paws. Games and picture books were jammed, none too tidily, into low shelves. Dolls and a teddy bear sat on the windowsill. Soccer shoes peeked out from under the bed. On a dressing table was a jewelry box that Julia suspected played music when the lid was lifted, along with a tangle of ribbons and barrettes, as well as a baseball cap inscribed with the Pirates logo. A book bag hung over the chair back.

"What a nice room."

"My cat's name is Bullet."

"And he sleeps with you?"

"Most nights he does. Come on. I'll show you the rest." She trotted ahead of them and opened another door. "This room's where we keep junk," she said, gesturing toward stacked cartons.

Tommy remonstrated mildly, "I don't think Julia's interested in our junk."

"Well, anyway. And over here, this room is Daddy's." She led the way, opening the door and switching on a light. Julia's breath caught as an unexpected pang that was almost physical pain struck somewhere around her heart. It was a simple room, modestly furnished. There was a king-size bed with a rough tweedy spread in a blue-and-beige plaid, a desk with scattered papers, a bookcase filled with paperbacks, a bureau and a chair with slightly worn leather upholstery. Altogether unremarkable, and yet the image of Tommy coming to this room at the end of the day and sleeping in this bed started a gnawing uncertain feeling in her stomach. Meanwhile, Chipper was explaining, "Daddy has his own bathroom. I have the one down the hall. My shower curtain has Ninja Turtles on it."

"This is a lovely place," Julia said, making an effort to sound pleasant, as if she was simply an ordinary guest expressing polite admiration. *I never should have come here,* she thought with desperation. *I should never have let myself see where he lives.*

Chipper ran to the balcony railing and looked over. "Hey, here they are," she called out, and made a dash for the stairs.

Tommy and Julia followed in time to see the front door open and an older man and woman come in. Van and Gretchen joined the pair. Chipper bounded into the group and the man swung her up in his arms.

"Bill and Fiona," Tommy explained as they crossed toward the entryway. "You remember them, don't you? They're taking Chipper out on the town tonight. Well, McDonald's and a rental film, actually."

"I see." She recognized the Vernons, although Fiona was a little skinnier and Bill a little stouter than ten years ago. She'd known them only slightly, in the way that inhabitants of a small town knew almost everyone. Suddenly the warm firelit house was full of people and ringing with laughter as Van and Gretchen greeted the older couple.

"Come on. Let's go say hello," Tommy said.

Fiona Vernon, a lively little woman with curly gray hair, was not one to cultivate awkward moments. She gave Julia a warm hug and said, "Of course I remember you. Julia. How wonderful to have you back. I'm so sorry about your mother, but it's lovely to see you again, and for goodness' sake don't go running away now that you're here."

"Thank you." Julia accepted Bill Vernon's bear-like handshake, and conversation picked up around her with complete ease. No one seemed to mind whether she said anything or not, for which she was grateful. Her heart was so full tonight, she was hardly able to manage her own thoughts, much less express them.

In all her years in Wiltonburg she'd never known what it was like to hear a door open that way and bring laughter and warmth with it. In the cold barrenness of the Holtz household there'd been only frowns and critical looks, stony silences or else complaints of faults and shortcomings. And yet a homeless boy hitchhiking along the road from West Virginia had been taken in by this loving couple—and now, obviously, so had his child. She watched lovingly as Bill Vernon ruffled the little girl's hair and said, "Go on now. Get your jacket. Let's get this show on the road." It wasn't self-pity she was feeling, she insisted to herself. It was simply disbelief—a sense of wonder that such goodness really existed.

"And go to the bathroom," Fiona called out as Chipper dashed for the stairs.

"I've just been given the grand tour," Julia said, finding her voice at last. "It's quite a house."

"Well, much as I hate to say it in front of him, the best ideas were all Van's," Tommy said. "He's put a lot of thought into the project. And a lot of work."

Van looked embarrassed and poked his glasses up.

"Well, he certainly brought this old barn back to life," Bill Vernon said, looking around. "We always knew Tommy had his eye on it."

"We hated to lose the two of them from our house," Fiona said, her eyes resting fondly on Tommy. "But families like their own place."

"Sometimes we do manage to communicate over that vast hundred yards that separates us," Tommy said jokingly.

Fiona poked his arm. "Just cut the wise remarks, Buster."

Julia smiled as the two of them bantered, but it was that word, "families," that stuck in her mind. A lone man and a little girl hardly seemed like a family, but the Vernons obviously saw it as such and recognized its importance.

"What about that brother of yours?" Bill Vernon asked her. "He's in the military, right?"

"The air force, yes. He wasn't able to stay on after the funeral, but he plans to come back soon to help settle things."

"Hope we get to see him," Fiona said. "I remember he was a handsome fellow."

"Yes, he's still that. He's getting married this year."

The small talk went on until Chipper returned. "Ready!" she announced, tugging at the zipper of her red jacket. Tommy squatted down and helped her with it and then reached up and repinned the red barrette in her hair. It was such a tender gesture that Julia felt her heart turn over. *Chipper could have been ours,* she thought wistfully.

All her worries about the evening dissolved as conversation turned in a dozen different directions. Van announced he would be at her house, ready for work, on Monday morning. He explained to the others how he planned to revive the old place and fully expected *Better Homes and Gardens* to be at his heels, pleading for pictures. Julia mentioned Fergus Halley and his phenomenal pickup truck, and Tommy said Fergus was a legend around Wiltonburg, and so was his truck. As far as anyone knew, he kept the thing running with chewing gum and baling wire.

"I said I'd help him with the shearing if I'm here that long," Julia said.

"Then the rest of us will show up to cheer you on," Gretchen insisted.

"That's if the whole town isn't underwater this spring," Van said sourly.

"Our illustrious mayor, Don Owen, and his management of the town are a pet peeve with these two," Gretchen explained. Van muttered that "illustrious" wasn't the word he'd have picked.

"They're referring to his cut-rate flood-control projects," Gretchen went on. "They feel he's trimmed the budget where it can least be afforded."

"I just can't believe that Don is the mayor of Wiltonburg," Julia said. "Although nothing you say about him surprises me."

Tommy brought the big cassoulet to the table that had been set up in front of the fire. "There. Not fancy, but filling," he announced.

"It smells sensational," Julia said.

The talk went on as they ate, sampled the wine, took second helpings of food and then lingered at the table, eating fruit and nuts and the different cheeses Van had selected.

"Save room for the pie," Tommy warned.

There were protests and groans, followed by an explanation of Van's students' berry-raising project.

"But before that, the champagne," Van said. He got up and went to the kitchen, returning with the bottle and glasses.

"Is this a special occasion?" Tommy gave a puzzled frown as Van popped the cork.

"In a way," Van said, pouring the wine into the tulip-shaped glasses. Julia glanced at Gretchen, who looked back at her with a tiny wink. "An announcement." Van reached out for Gretchen's hand. "We're going to be married."

Julia made sure she acted surprised. Tommy's surprise was genuine. "No! When? That's wonderful!"

"We're not exactly sure," Gretchen explained. "But soon. Maybe in a couple of weeks. And we have a favor to ask."

"Ask away."

Gretchen glanced at Van and he nodded. "We want you two to stand up with us. It'll be just a tiny affair at my house. Will you?"

Now Julia's surprise was real. Gretchen hadn't mentioned this part earlier. For a moment she hardly knew what to say, but suddenly, without looking at him, she could feel Tommy's eyes on her. She remembered how little those eyes had changed in ten years, how they could still kindle a fire in her with their dark intensity.

Van said, "Well, what about it?"

"Fine with me," Tommy said, and Julia knew he was still watching her. "How about it, Julia?" His voice was low and husky.

Julia didn't look at him. Instead, she smiled at Gretchen. "You bet I will," she said. "And if I've returned to New York by that time, I'll come back specially for the occasion."

"Wonderful," Gretchen said. "But please don't go. We love having you here."

Tommy lifted his glass. "To the bride and groom," he said. "They deserve each other—in the very best sense of that overworked phrase."

Julia lifted her glass and took a small sip, finally letting her eyes meet Tommy's, which were still watching her with a dark glow.

At last Tommy got up to make coffee, and Julia helped clear the table and fill the dishwasher. In the kitchen, as he measured out water for coffee, he said, "Would you stay for a few minutes after Van and Gretchen leave, Julia? I'll drive you home later."

Her head came up quickly. "I don't think that's a good idea."

"Please? Just so we can talk for a few minutes?"

She bent over the dishwasher again, answering slowly. "All right." But she felt an immediate regret. Wasn't she making the worst possible mistake? Seeing him with others around was one thing, but being alone with him—mightn't that be more than she could handle?

The coffee was served and the pie sampled and pronounced delicious. "I'd say those students aced the course," Tommy said, and everyone agreed.

Then there were motions to leave, and Gretchen suggested they take her car and leave Van's pickup here until tomorrow. "I only tasted the wine," she pointed out. "I should be the driver." But everyone knew it was really because they couldn't bear to leave each other. "You ready, Julia?"

Tommy said, "You two go along. I've offered to drive Julia home in a little while."

Van and Gretchen's looks were startled but brief. They were obviously too absorbed in each other to concentrate on anything else. At last all the goodnights had been said and Tommy and Julia stood in the doorway waving them off and commenting on how chilly the night had turned. Like a couple, Julia thought. Like an old married couple seeing off their guests.

Back inside, she made a move to finish clearing the table, but Tommy caught her hand and said, "I'll do that later. Let's just talk a little, okay?"

He led her to the couch, keeping hold of her hand. When they were both seated he said, "I've wanted for so long to talk to you about what happened ten years ago."

She would have stood up, but his hand holding hers prevented her. "I don't want to hear this," she said.

He put his other hand under her chin so that she had to look at him. "But you haven't forgotten."

She kept her voice steady. "Yes, I have, Tommy."

His kiss came so quickly it surprised her. A soft searching kiss that turned into passion as it lingered. Julia felt a response leap within her. His hand caressed her cheek. His tongue tasted her lips. He murmured in her ear, "You haven't forgotten."

She looked away from him. "I don't want to remember, Tommy."

"You know what I thought when I saw you again, out there with the sheep that first day? I thought I was being given a second chance." His eyes moved over her face as if memorizing every feature.

"There's no such thing as a second chance."

"I can't believe that. Julia, we were just kids. And if we could only talk about it now—"

"No." This time she managed to pull away from him and stand. She moved across the room to the fireplace and stood looking down at the embers, which had burned low. "It's no good to rehash it. What's done is done." She meant it. She'd rather leave it alone than hear flimsy excuses ten years too late. "It's different for you. You've built a life for yourself—a career, your daughter, this house. I've never been able to do that. Maybe you're stronger than I am. All I know is, I can't go through that again. I just won't. I never want to... to be hurt that way again." She stood very still and straight by the fireplace, her back to him. "I'd like you to take me home now, please."

HE'D DONE IT ALL WRONG, Tommy thought as he climbed wearily upstairs later. She'd hardly spoken to him all the way home, and now it seemed as if they were further apart than ever.

He went down the hall and opened the door to Chipper's room, then remembered she wasn't there. She was staying with Fiona and Bill tonight. She stayed there often, but tonight her absence made him feel lonelier than ever. He turned back, hearing sounds from downstairs as the dog drank from his water dish after his late-night run. He went into his own room and turned on the bedside lamp. He'd done everything he shouldn't have, he reflected glumly. He'd rushed her—exactly what he'd sworn he wouldn't do. But that kiss—he knew she'd reacted to that, just as he had.

He sighed and turned toward the bed. A picture done in bright crayon colors was propped against the pillow. Now when had Chipper put that there? When she dashed up to get her jacket? It was labeled Daddy the Cook and showed a stick figure in a ballooning chef's hat, stirring something with an outsized spoon.

Do you want her to be your girlfriend? he could hear the small voice probe relentlessly.

I sure do want it, Chipper, he thought as he undressed and slid into bed. He was just drifting off into a restless sleep when he heard a small sound and then felt the bed give slightly as Bullet, the cat, jumped up and snuggled close.

CHAPTER SIX

THE OLD KITCHEN already looked different. Van was busy painting it a sunny yellow, and as the dingy gray walls disappeared, light seemed to stream in.

"Amazing," Julia said, standing back to admire it.

Van grinned down from the ladder. "Color works miracles. I did a lot of repainting in Gretchen's house, too, when I fixed things up for her mother. You should stop in and see it."

"I plan to. Mrs. Bauer was always good to me, and there were times when I really needed someone, believe me."

"I can see how there might have been, in this house."

"Think you can do this well with the living room?" Julia asked.

"Sure. Might have to paper there, though."

"Nobody wallpapers living rooms anymore, do they?"

"There are a lot of flaws in that old plaster. But grass cloth ought to cover it. I'll take the linoleum up, too, and cart it off. You might want to invest in one of those natural-fiber rugs. They're not expensive."

"I'll look into it. I already have the wallpaper for the downstairs bedroom." She watched him dip his brush and work skillfully along the ceiling line. "That living room furniture's pretty grim," she said. "Maybe I'll try the attic—see if I can find anything to throw over the couch. Oh, and I've located a sewing machine. I'm going to make curtains for the kitchen." She'd already completed a blue homespun tablecloth to replace the flowered plastic one. It would extend to the floor and hide the table's unsightly legs.

"What'd I tell you? *Better Homes and Gardens*. You're going to have to fight 'em off."

She was glad of Van's cheerful upbeat presence. Her own mood had been less than buoyant since the night of the dinner at Tommy's house and the silent ride home afterward. The atmosphere in the car had been so thick with unspoken memories and fresh resentment that neither of them had been able to cut through it.

"I'll be up in the attic if you need me," she said, and Van waved his brush in acknowledgment.

Stopping to pick up a heavy sweater, Julia climbed to the chilly attic and stood for a moment looking around, wondering where to start. She thought she'd made good progress with the stacks of cartons, but today it looked almost as cluttered and hopeless as before. Realizing she was skirting dangerously close to real despair over the project, she decided to leave the cartons for the moment and concentrate on two trunks she hadn't yet touched. She dragged the first one to the center of the floor and opened it.

The smell of mothballs drifted up at once. Julia frowned and began lifting out stored clothing. Obviously the Holtzes had saved clothing the way they saved everything else. *It might be useful sometime in the future,* she could almost hear Gideon Holtz say, reminding them of the need for frugality.

The Holtzes had both been in their late forties when she and Rick had come to live there. Maybe all these things reflected their earlier years. Yet there was no hint of changing fashions or the march of time here. No crinolines from the fifties, no tie-dyed T-shirts or bell-bottoms from the sixties. Only a steady procession of drab serviceable coats and sweaters, most of them well-worn. Dresses without style or shape, graceless and unlovely. Still, in the bottom of the trunk she found one prize—a quilt that was obviously Amish in origin, its once-vivid colors now softly faded. It would do nicely to throw over the ugly couch in the living room, Julia decided. She would hang it outdoors to air when she went down.

She pulled out the second trunk and opened it. More of the same. Julia began debating whether the stuff was even good enough to give away. This trunk held one dress that was slightly different, however. It appeared to be made of silk and was in a pale ecru color. Although no more stylish than all the others, it did have a round lace-trimmed collar. She'd never seen Elizabeth Holtz in it, not even for church. And then it came to Julia. Elizabeth's wedding dress. It had to be. Digging further, she found a hat, slightly crushed but trimmed with a cluster of pink silk roses. The color matched the dress. She was sure her guess was right.

Had Elizabeth been full of hope and excitement that day?

Voices drifted up from downstairs. She lifted her head to listen. She'd telephoned the real-estate agent to ask if he'd care to come one day and give her some advice. Maybe he'd dropped in unannounced. The voices were followed by footsteps climbing the stairs and then a small voice.

"Hi, Julia."

Julia dropped the hat with the silk roses and turned to see Chipper poking her head up over the top of the narrow stairs.

"Well, hello there. I didn't expect company today. Did your... did someone bring you here?"

Chipper climbed the rest of the way. "Daddy brought me. He picked me up after school. See?" She pointed down the stairs.

Julia moved over to look. Tommy was standing at the foot of the steps. He smiled up at her, his hands in the pockets of his jacket, managing to looking both cautious and apologetic. "We were invited, remember?" Before she could answer, he said quickly, "I'm expecting a delivery of gravel out in your field. Thought I'd better be here for it."

"Of course. And I'll bet Chipper wants to see the lambs."

"I do, but I like your attic, too," the little girl said frankly, and Julia laughed.

"Okay, after we've done the attic we'll go outside," she said.

"Behave, Chipper," he called up to her. "Not too many questions, okay?"

Julia watched him go, his broad shoulders disappearing along the hall and down the stairs to the first floor. Her heart was behaving in that odd way it always did when she saw him. She should be annoyed for this transparent ruse to make contact with her again, but it was hard to stay angry, especially in the presence of the hopeful and interested little girl.

"What *is* all that stuff?" Chipper asked.

"Old clothes, mostly."

Chipper approached the open trunk and wrinkled her nose at the smell. "This is a really neat attic. We don't have an attic. We just have a storeroom. Remember I showed it to you? But Aunt Fiona has one. She says all her life's treasures are up there except me. That's what she always says. Are any of yours up here?"

"My what?"

"Your life's treasures."

Julia smiled. "No, I'm afraid not. These things belonged to Elizabeth Holtz and her husband. This was her house."

"Daddy said it's your house now."

"Yes, mine and my brother's."

Chipper picked up the hat and started playing with the roses. "Wasn't that lady your mommy? How come you call her Elizabeth Holtz?"

"She wasn't my real mother," Julia said. "The Holtzes adopted my brother and me when we were young."

"How young?" It was obvious Chipper was paying no attention to her father's warning about asking too many questions.

"I was ten and he was twelve."

"That's pretty old," Chipper said wistfully. "When I'm ten I'll be in fifth grade." Then she asked, "Where did you live before you lived here?"

"Mostly in a foundling home—an orphanage."

Julia saw another question forming, but the little girl was momentarily distracted by the hat. Cautiously she tried it on. "How do I look?"

"Great. Only I think the flowers should go in front." Julia made the adjustment.

Still wearing the hat with her jeans and red jacket, Chipper began poking about in the trunk. "Where's your real mother?" she asked.

Julia swallowed. "She's— I don't know where she is. I don't remember her."

"Oh." Chipper thought about it. "Why didn't your daddy take care of you, then?"

Julia moved to one of the cardboard cartons and opened it. "I didn't have a daddy. At least I never knew him."

She glanced at Chipper. This news was obviously puzzling to her. Finally the girl said, "My real mommy wasn't able to take care of me, so she let my daddy do it. I don't know what she looks like." The small face had drifted into a slightly different expression, not exactly sad, but thoughtful.

Julia moved in quickly, keeping her voice cheerful. "But how lucky you are to have such a wonderful daddy. And a real family, too—your aunt and uncle, I mean."

"Didn't you have a real family?"

"Not like yours. But I had my brother. We helped each other out a lot."

Chipper turned her attention back to the trunk, handling some of the clothes, but it was obvious she was starting to lose interest. "Which room was yours?"

"I'll show you when we go down."

"Did you have a cat?"

"There used to be one out in the barn."

"Do you have pictures of when you were little?"

"No, I guess nobody took my picture."

"Is there anything of yours in here?" Chipper indicated the trunk.

"There doesn't seem to be."

"Hey, I really like this hat."

"You can keep it if you want to."

"Gee, can I? But I'll have to ask Daddy."

It was an hour later when a voice called, "Ready to go, Chipper?"

Julia and Chipper, who'd been sorting clothing into piles, analyzing what was worth giving away and what was hopeless, looked up with a start. Chipper ran to the top of the stairs. "No, Daddy! I haven't seen the lambs, yet."

"You must've been busy up there."

"We're sorting stuff."

"Well, come on. It's getting late. Where'd you get the hat?" Julia could hear the grin in his voice.

"Julia says I can have it. Is it okay?"

"If she says so."

"Oh, good. I'll be right down."

"Well, be careful. Those steps are steep."

Julia moved behind her, watching her hurry down the stairs. Chipper tripped over the second one from the bottom and fell right into her father's arms. He caught her and held her tight, scolding gently. "Pay attention to what your feet are doing, Miss Charlotte Black. Don't I always tell you that?"

She nodded and wiggled so that he put her down. Julia followed her. "I'm afraid we both got pretty grubby up there. I didn't realize it was getting so late. Has Van finished for the day?"

"He's just packing up to leave."

"Well, let's go see if we can locate any lambs."

They went out the kitchen door and waved goodbye to Van, who was stowing cracked and broken linoleum into the back of his pickup. "See you in the morning," he called.

They watched as his truck rumbled down the driveway, then they started in the direction of the barn, with Chipper running ahead. The early-spring sun was low, the shadows long, and the air was cool but tangy and sweet. Lizzie, seeing them approach, came galloping toward them. She stopped to sniff at the little girl's sneakers, then raised her head for a look. Chipper put out a hand to pat her. Lizzie's tail began its back and forth motion at once, and the two proceeded together. Turning around and walking backward, Chipper asked, "Are there any lambs in the barn?"

"No, we'll have to find them in the field," Julia replied.

"But can I see what the barn's like first?"

Julia nodded, and Lizzie and Chipper dashed ahead while Julia and Tommy followed more slowly. For a time neither one spoke.

"I want to apologize for pushing so hard the other night," he said at last. "I was anxious not to make a mistake, and I went and said all the wrong things."

"It isn't a question of saying the wrong things." Julia was concentrating on the rough dirt driveway, keeping her eyes averted, but with every step, she became more aware of his nearness. "And you certainly don't need to apologize. It's just that you don't seem to understand how I feel about . . . all this."

"All what?"

She took a deep breath. "You know. Seeing you again after so long. I'd just like to keep it simple. I mean, we can be friends, but I don't want to go through all that...emotional part again. I said that the other night and I meant it. I'd like to stay away from the past."

He stopped and turned to her. "Julia, you can't go through life that way." His eyes were imploring.

"I'm not sure I know what you mean. If I hadn't come back to Wiltonburg for the funeral, I'd never have seen you again. I would have gone through life that way. And I'd have been fine."

He put his hands on her shoulders. "But you *have* come back. Can't we at least—"

"No, we can't!" she exploded. "And please try to understand that I'm serious about this."

His hands remained on her shoulders, but his face lost its softness and slowly took on a look of bitterness. "Why don't you say what you really mean, Julia? You don't trust me."

She tried to keep her voice from trembling. "What reason have you ever given me to trust you?"

He let his hands drop. "But if the past is really past—I mean, that's the way you said you wanted it—then what about forgiving and forgetting?"

"I have forgotten, Tommy," she said quietly.

"Are you sure?" he asked. She knew he was thinking about the kiss the other night.

"Tommy, I—" she began, but the air was suddenly torn by a scream from the barn. Lizzie began to bark wildly.

"Chipper!" Tommy covered the distance to the barn at a run, with Julia tearing after him.

Chipper was sitting on the ground at the foot of the ladder that led to the loft. It was clear she'd fallen off the ladder. Blood was pouring down her face from a cut on her forehead. Tommy already had his handkerchief out and was mopping away the blood while he picked up the howling little girl. Without a word, Julia ran to the small room where supplies were kept for the sheep and came dashing back with a roll of paper towels. She tore off several pieces and folded them to make a thick pad, which she handed to him.

"I don't think it's serious," he said, but she could tell he was trying hard to keep his voice steady. "Let's get her to the hospital emergency. She may need stitches or a tetanus shot or something.''

"I can drive," Julia said. "You take care of her.''

"Head wounds always bleed like that,'' he said, obviously trying to reassure himself. They hurried down the driveway toward his pickup. Chipper's howls subsided into intermittent sobs.

"Key?'' Julia said.

"In my jacket.'' She reached into his pocket and pulled out the key as he lifted Chipper onto the front seat and then climbed in after her. Julia had the truck running in seconds. Most fathers would be asking questions, she thought as they barreled down the county road toward town. But Tommy merely held the child on his lap, pressing the towel against her head. He was pale, but in total control. He picked up the truck's mobile phone and called ahead.

"Six-year-old with a head injury,'' he said tersely. "We'll be there in five minutes.''

"Turn left here,'' he ordered as they approached the county hospital on the outskirts of Wiltonburg. "New emergency room added last year.''

Julia nodded and swung into a drive that led to a modern-looking addition she'd never seen before. They pulled up at the entrance, and Tommy slid out with Chipper and hurried inside. Julia parked the pickup in the lot, then went in. She found them in a white-curtained cubicle. A young doctor was already bending over the little girl, examining her eyes with a light. A nurse stood by taking down information on a clipboard. Stretched out on the table, Chipper looked tiny and helpless.

The doctor had just asked Tommy something.

"I don't know," he answered, and turned to Chipper. "Now tell us, sweetie, what were you doing and how far did you fall?"

The little girl gulped and said, "I was climbing the ladder."

"She was playing in a barn," he explained. "And how far up did you climb? How many rungs?"

Her small hand lifted, fingers spread.

"That many? Five?" He turned to the doctor, pleading, "Could be worse, couldn't it?"

The doctor was already cleaning the wound. Chipper let out a protesting yelp and Julia saw Tommy grimace in sympathetic pain.

"Doesn't look bad at all," the doctor said. He glanced up at Julia. "One or two stitches maybe. See? It's right there at the hairline. Won't even show. But she should have a tetanus shot, too. You two might as well wait outside."

Tommy nodded, and Julia could see him take a deep breath of relief. They went out into the corridor together.

Julia leaned against the wall. "Tommy, I'm so sorry. This is all my fault. I shouldn't have said it was all right for her to explore the barn without us."

"Hey, it's not your fault." A little color had come back into his face. "It wasn't anybody's fault. And you heard the doctor—the scar won't even show."

"I know, but I didn't even think of that ladder—"

"Julia," he said tenderly, "you can't protect children every minute. All you can do is try your best to teach them to protect themselves." Suddenly he pulled her to him and held her close. She felt tears run down her cheeks and he reached up with his thumb to wipe them away.

Just then, the doctor came out and said encouragingly, "Hey, she's just fine. The nurse is putting a dressing on now." Then, noticing Julia's tears and Tommy's arms around her, he said, "Not a thing to worry about, Mrs. Black. Your little girl's just fine."

Julia felt the slight tremor in Tommy's arms, but he didn't let go. Neither of them corrected the doctor.

BACK HOME, Chipper was quiet and subdued, lying in her room with pillows propped behind her and a bandage encircling her head. A large new teddy bear in a nurse's uniform and cap sat beside her.

"Be right back, Chipper," Tommy said as he went out to see the Vernons off. Fiona's face was still pinched with worry, and Bill was hovering anxiously.

"She's absolutely fine," Tommy assured them. "Go home, relax and have something to eat. And thanks for the bear. I don't know how you managed to get into town and buy that so fast, Bill."

Bill waved the thanks away. "You let us know, anything you need," he said gruffly.

"We'll be okay," Tommy assured him. "And she's just fine. The doctor said so."

When he'd seen them off, he returned to Chipper's room.

"How's it going, sweetie? Anything hurt?"

She shook her head gingerly. "Not exactly. I feel wobbly."

"That'll be gone by tomorrow."

"Do I get to stay home from school?"

"Maybe. We'll see." He sat on the side of the bed. "Now I want to ask you something. How do you think this happened?"

"Well, I was climbing the ladder to see what was up there, and I turned around to look at Lizzie . . ."

"Yes, I understand that. But what do you think you did wrong?"

"I guess I wasn't hanging on very good."

"And what else?"

She lowered her eyes, long lashes brushing her cheeks. "Maybe I wasn't thinking. About being careful."

"You know the rules, Chipper. Especially in strange new places. You look around first. You try to see where there might be danger."

She nodded and raised her eyes to him. "Am I going to have a scar?"

"No. Well, maybe a tiny one, but it'll be under your hair."

She looked faintly disappointed. Then he saw her thoughts sliding off in a different direction. She put a hand out and he took it in his own. It felt small and warm. He waited to hear what was on her mind.

"Daddy, where's my mommy?"

He thought he'd grown used to the question, but it always gave him a tight feeling in his stomach. "I told you, remember? She's in Arizona. We talked about where that is."

"I don't remember her."

"No, you were too little. You were only a tiny baby."

"But she wanted somebody to take good care of me."

"Yes, of course. That was me."

"Julia doesn't remember her mommy, either. She said so. She said I was lucky because I had a wonderful daddy. All she had was her brother."

He nodded, but he was thinking back to that episode in the hospital. He remembered how Julia had felt in his arms, her head against his chest, as he comforted her.

"Will you stay with me a while?" Chipper asked. "Just till I fall asleep?"

He smiled, taking in the stacked pillows, the new teddy bear. Playing the situation up to the hilt, he thought. But remembering the cold terror he'd felt at her first scream that afternoon, he squeezed her hand and said, "Okay. Just for a while."

"I never did get to see the lambs," she said, starting to sound sleepy. "And I lost my hat."

"We'll go see the lambs as soon as you're better. Julia will save the hat for you, I'm sure."

Minutes later he tiptoed out of the room and went downstairs to use the telephone.

"Julia?"

"Tommy? I was so worried. Is Chipper all right?"

"Of course. She's in danger of being badly spoiled, but otherwise she's fine. She's sleeping right now."

"Oh, I'm so relieved." He could hear it in her voice. "I went out to the barn after you dropped me off. I wanted to look the place over—that ladder—and see if there was anything..."

"Julia," he said calmly. "Kids get into scrapes like this. It wasn't your fault. Now stop thinking about it. But I hope you found her hat. She was worried about it."

"I did. I'll keep it for her."

"By the way, Chipper was disappointed about not getting to see any lambs. That and the fact that her scar isn't going to show."

Julia laughed for the first time, and the sound warmed him. "You must be sure she wears a big bandage when she goes back to school."

"I'll see to it." He hesitated, thinking how good it was to hear her voice. "I wanted to let you know how glad I was to have you there this afternoon."

There was a pause. "I didn't do anything to help, I'm afraid."

"Of course you did. Your being there meant a lot to me. And to Chipper," he added quickly.

"You must bring her to see the lambs another time."

"I will." He wondered if she, too, was thinking about the scene in the hospital corridor. He thought her voice had a different sound tonight, a cautious warmth. Was it just because of her concern about Chipper?

"Well . . . thank you for calling," she said.

"I wanted you to know everything was okay."

They said goodbye and he put the receiver down. "Good night, Julia," he said to the empty room. "Good night, darling."

CHAPTER SEVEN

THE OLD FARMHOUSE on Firebush Road was full of activity during the week that followed. Van Lightner hurried to finish the wallpapering and painting, and with the help of a student assistant, he rebuilt the front porch steps. Julia worked at scrubbing down the living-room floor and then covered it with an inexpensive fiber rug she found at a discount home-supply store out on the state highway. She brushed and aired the Amish quilt and threw it over the old couch, then washed the windows. Now when the sun came in it sparkled across the pale green grass-cloth-covered wall and gave the whole room a look of warmth and hominess.

"I wouldn't have believed it," Julia murmured to Van as they stood admiring the final touch, a pair of framed nature prints she'd hung over the couch. Van had found them in a secondhand store.

"I warned you I was a miracle worker," he said. "But I have to admit this really went beyond my expectations. Are you satisfied?"

"More than satisfied. It's a real transformation. By the time I finish what I'm doing upstairs, that'll be it."

While Van had been busy downstairs, Julia had been painting the two small bedrooms a pale soft blue and, at his suggestion, had painted the wide-board floors white. The effect was charming; the rooms had a country-cottage simplicity. Julia herself was surprised at the result.

The only time she took off all week was to visit Gretchen's mother at their small house in the older part of town. She found Mrs. Bauer as bright and cheerful as she remembered, although somewhat less mobile. She spent much of her time in a wheelchair, she explained, but she was sometimes able to manage with a walker, and things were much easier for her now that Van had made the changes in the house. She pointed out how he'd widened doorways, lowered kitchen counters, then painted the whole place in sunny colors. There was talk of the wedding, and Mrs. Bauer fussed about the couple's plan to live with her.

"I said, no way. That's out." Her blue eyes snapped in emphasis. "A young couple should have their own place. But that Van's as stubborn as an ox and I couldn't budge him. I said we wouldn't all fit in this house, so then he said he'd build an addition for the two of them. He's going to do that this summer."

"He's done a wonderful job on our old place," Julia said, and then went on to describe his work and the painting she'd done upstairs, too.

"White floors!" Mrs. Bauer exclaimed. "Oh, I like the sound of that. Now wait a minute, I've got something you ought to have. Right over there, dear, in that big chest. Bottom drawer. That's it. Bring it over."

Julia returned carrying a red-and-white quilt in a star pattern.

"I made that years ago and hardly ever used it. It'll look good with that white floor of yours."

"Oh, Mrs. Bauer, it's too beautiful, I couldn't possibly—"

"Yes, you could. Now take it. I want you to have it."

"That's so kind of you. I love it. And when we sell the house it'll stay with me. I'll take it wherever I go."

"Oh, dear." Mrs. Bauer's face grew sober. "That's right. Gretchen said you weren't planning on staying." She perked up again. "Never mind. We don't know everything ahead of time, do we? Who knows what's going to happen? Now, let's have some tea."

WHILE JULIA WAS WORKING every day at the house, Tommy and his crew were busy on the drainage project at the far end of the property. She saw his truck coming and going, and from the upstairs window she could even see a tractor and backhoe at work, but there was little chance for the two of them to talk.

Julia was glad. The afternoon they'd driven Chipper to the hospital she'd felt herself dangerously close to a softness that frightened her. Tommy's phone call that night had been so welcome, his voice so much like she remembered ten years ago, that she'd been almost willing, in that instant, to let the past roll back and erase itself just for the chance to be held in his arms again, to feel that sense of belonging....

Once or twice when she lay wearily in bed after working all day, she wondered whether she was hanging on to a grudge out of sheer stubbornness. But then she remembered how seldom life had offered her any reason to trust. Nothing had ever turned out the way her young and hopeful spirit had anticipated, and no one but Rick had ever kept his promises to her. It was time to stop counting on other people, Julia told herself sternly. Time to find strength within herself. Once the house was sold, she'd return to New York, find herself another roommate and another job and get on with her life. And whatever mistakes she ended up making, they'd be *her* mistakes. If there were any successes along the way, they'd be hers, too.

It was an easy resolution to make while lying in bed at night. But as the busy days flew by, the thought of leaving Wiltonburg brought a curious pain that lodged in her chest like a silent cry.

"THAT'S IT," Van said at the end of the week. "I think we're all done." Gretchen was standing beside him in Julia's front hall, having stopped by to admire the finished work. "Now I can get back to teaching— classes start Monday. And after that, wasn't there something else?" He squinted, as if trying to remember. Gretchen gave his arm a punch.

"Just the little matter of a wedding." But her eyes were soft as she looked at him. He put his arm around her, pulling her against him.

"Any date set?" Julia asked.

"Not really. It'll be spur-of-the-moment. How much notice do you need?"

"Only enough to change out of these paint-splattered clothes and wash my hair," Julia replied.

"I'll give you that much."

"There's one other thing," Van said. They both looked at him. "Amazing as this transformation's been, the old place still looks like a chicken coop from the outside. It ought to be painted."

"Oh, Van, really?" Julia couldn't keep the dismay out of her voice. "I was hoping this would be it."

"You've done this much, you really ought to add the finishing touch. But look, it's not such a big deal. It's a small house. I can get a couple of students to help. We'll do it on Saturday."

"I'm off on Saturday," Gretchen said. "Julia, you and I aren't too helpless to paint, are we?"

"And besides, Nolan's was having a sale this week," Van admitted with a wry grin. "I already bought the paint."

TOMMY AWOKE to darkness. He rolled over to look at the illuminated numbers of the clock and gave a small groan. Four twenty-five. He'd planned to get an early start this morning—he'd even left Chipper at the Vernons' so he wouldn't have to wake her when he got up. Still, he was certainly entitled to another half hour. He stretched and pulled the covers over him. But thoughts came crowding in from every corner of the darkened room. And voices. Had he only imagined it the other night, or had Julia's voice really sounded different when he phoned her? Softer, less resentful, somehow.

Time was going by fast, though. Before long she'd be on her way back to New York. How would he feel when that happened? If he'd never seen her again, he could have stood it. They'd been managing all right, he and Chipper. But now that he *had* seen her, spent time with her, everything was different. Nothing would be the same without her, knowing he'd lost her, not once, but twice.

If only he could get her to listen to him. If only she'd give him a chance to explain. He thrust one arm across his forehead. But would that really help?

He turned restlessly. So much of what had happened to her was his fault. That hasty marriage she'd made—would it have taken place if he'd just been able to talk to her? He felt a hollowness inside. Time was running out for him. He was no further ahead than he'd been that first day he'd seen her again, holding the lamb. The soft anxious voice he'd heard on the telephone didn't mean a thing. Or at least, it meant no more than she'd been worried about Chipper. But he was determined about one thing. He wouldn't let her leave without hearing the truth, even if it wasn't enough to make her stay.

He thought of how she'd clung to him when he held her in the hospital corridor. How his cheek had rested against her hair and how her tears had dampened his shirt. He shouldn't attach meaning to things like that, he told himself sternly.

Poor little Chipper—he could still see the expression on her face when he reached her in the barn. Scared and hurt, but also a little guilty. She knew she'd disobeyed him and been careless. Damn. How did you achieve any kind of balance with a kid? How did you let her grow up and discover things for herself and at the same time protect her from harm? And because he was a single parent, maybe he was overdoing his concern. Maybe he was too hard on her, expecting too much of her. Damn, it wasn't easy. Little girls needed a mother.

It wasn't right the way he had to constantly shuffle her around—like now, when he had her sleeping at the Vernons' because he knew he'd have to be up early. His thoughts veered off in a new direction. What would he ever have done without Bill and Fiona? And then he thought, as he had countless times before, what an amazing thing it was that this treasure, his daughter, had come to him out of the darkest period of his life.

He looked at the clock again. Four thirty-two. He clicked on the small bedside radio and listened to the weather report. Rain, starting around noon, the announcer said. Probably heavy at times. The forecast hadn't changed since last night. Still, if the crew started early, they could finish the job at the Holtz farm before the rain set in. There were only a few hours' work left. He'd told the men to meet him in the field as soon as it was light.

He was ahead of the crew by only a few minutes, and as the thin gray dawn broke they were ready to start. Heavy clouds were moving in, so it was obvious there'd be no real sunrise. Still, they worked rapidly and the rain held off long enough for them to finish reinforcing the stream's banks and install the last of the drainage tile.

"Okay, guys, that's a wrap," he said late in the morning. "Take the rest of the day off. We'll finish the widening on Grove Road tomorrow, and after that we're clear to go ahead with Braxton." The proposed huge Braxton office complex between Wiltonburg and Johnstown involved preparing the site and laying the foundation. The job would take several weeks.

He waved the men off and then jumped in his pickup, driving down the rutted lane toward the road. As he drove by the farmhouse, his foot found the brake without any planning on his part. He stopped and opened the door, not giving himself a chance to think about what he was doing or why.

She was wearing jeans and a sweatshirt when she answered the door. Her honey-colored hair was slightly mussed. Her violet eyes widened. He felt desire move inside him.

"Hi. Did we wake you this morning?" he asked.

"I didn't mind. I couldn't imagine what you were doing out there so early, though."

"Rain's on the way, and I wanted to finish."

"You mean it's done?"

He nodded. "I was going to take you out to look at it, but I don't think we'd make it without getting soaked. I hear Van's just about done inside, too."

"Yes. He's made some fairly dramatic changes. Want to see?"

"I'd better not. I'm pretty muddy. Maybe later. I stopped by because I thought we should celebrate."

"Oh . . . well . . ."

"How about lunch? I'll pick you up after I've had a chance to change. Maybe around one?"

He saw her hesitate, but then she asked, "The De-lite Diner?"

He smiled at her. "Oh, I think we can do better than that. How about the River House?"

She seemed to think about the idea for a moment. "All right," she said in a low voice.

THE RAIN ARRIVED at midday, and the restaurant's windows were streaming with it as Tommy and Julia entered. The River House was more upscale than the diner—the Rotary Club and the Chamber of Commerce met there regularly—but it was still pleasantly informal.

Julia had changed into a skirt and a pale yellow sweater, and Tommy, following her in and watching her slim figure glide between the tables, thought how little her appearance had changed in ten years. There'd never been a time, he reflected, not since that first night he met her, that she hadn't been able to make the fixed points of his personal compass wobble furiously.

When they were seated he said, "I hope you and your brother are satisfied with what we did. All this rain will give you a chance to see for yourself—not that I expect you to dash out there in a downpour. But I'm confident we've got the stream nicely rerouted."

"I'm sure it is," she said, unfolding her napkin and accepting a menu from the waiter.

"Then you do trust me sometimes." He smiled.

"Of course I do. You have an excellent business reputation." She sounded cool and careful again, holding him at arm's length.

Don't rush things, he warned himself. "Van seems pleased at how his part went."

"So am I. Van's full of good ideas." She glanced at the menu, and when the waiter returned, ordered a chef's salad. He ordered beef ragout. Then she said, "Dan Westfall, the real-estate agent, stopped by yesterday. He said everything we're doing now will pay for itself several times over when it comes to selling. And of course that was the idea behind it all." She took a sip of water. "How's Chipper?"

"Back to normal. Trying hard to hold on to the invalid role, but it's not really working. She's upset that I've been too busy to bring her to see the lambs."

"I've had an idea about that," she said, and he saw her eyes begin to sparkle. "Fergus Halley and his nephew are coming out to shear next week, and I'm going to help. Think Chipper and the rest of her class would like to come and watch?"

"Are you kidding? They'd love it. Chipper'd feel especially important, since she'd be able to show everybody where she fell and hit her head."

"Well, don't say anything until I have a chance to speak to the teacher," she warned.

He gave her a curious look. "Did you say you're going to help with the shearing?"

"Sure. I always told you that looking after the sheep was the one job I liked."

"I remember." They were back on personal ground again, but he thought some of her earlier stiffness was dissolving. They managed to chat comfortably until the waiter returned with their orders. Then as they ate, he asked, "How's the attic coming?"

She rolled her eyes. "Endless. But wait—I want to show you something I came across this morning." She put down her fork, reached into her handbag and drew out a snapshot. "This is the only one of Rick and me that I've ever found. Father Holtz thought all photography was vanity, so I can't imagine who took it. Somebody at church, maybe. I found it in a box of church programs."

He took the old photograph from her and studied it. Julia and Elizabeth Holtz were sitting on a bench, with Rick standing behind them. Julia looked to be ten or eleven, and her brother, stiff and sober in a white shirt and a tie, about twelve. He was looking straight ahead. Julia's hair was hacked off short, and she had on what looked like a cotton dress, white socks and heavy dark oxfords. She, too, was looking straight ahead, squinting into the sunlight. Tommy's heart turned over. The little girl in the snapshot seemed so sad.

"I wasn't allowed to have Mary Janes," Julia said.

"Mary Janes?"

"Those black patent-leather shoes with straps."

"Oh." He looked back at the picture. Elizabeth Holtz, wearing a plain frumpy dress, was sitting close to the young Julia, but instead of gazing into the camera, she was looking at the girl. Her whole body seemed to lean toward Julia, and her face, which he remembered as grim and sharp-featured, was soft and loving.

Julia seemed to read his mind. "Can you believe that expression on Mother Holtz's face?"

He said slowly, "I have no trouble believing it."

She gave him an odd look. "That's because you never lived in the Holtz household. If you had, I'm sure you'd find it hard."

"Well...Gideon, of course. I know how he was. But Mrs. Holtz...I'm not so sure."

Her voice took on an edge of bitterness. "What makes you think you know anything at all about what she was like?"

Tommy swallowed as he handed her back the picture. A voice in his head told him, *It's now or never.* "Julia—" he began.

He was interrupted by a loud hearty voice. "Well, what's this? You two picking up where you left off?"

They both looked up quickly at the man smiling down at them. Tommy said dryly, "Oh, hello, Don. See you haven't lost any of your old gift for tact."

He saw recognition cross Julia's face like a cloud as she surveyed the plump balding newcomer.

"Hello, Don," she said.

The man seemed impervious to the undercurrents. His eyes glittered as they raked over her with approval. "How are you, Julia? I heard you were back. Sorry about your folks." He said it with the quick automatic sympathy of the professional politician. Julia gave an acknowledging nod but didn't answer.

"Thinking of staying on awhile?" Don Owen's eyes darted meaningfully between the two of them.

Julia's voice turned chilly. "No. I just came for the funeral and to settle up the estate. As soon as that's done, I'll be going back to New York."

"I see. Well, we sure hate to lose you now you're here."

"Hey, Don, does a day like this make you nervous?" Tommy grinned as he nodded toward the downpour.

The mayor gave Tommy a playful punch. "This guy never stops needling." He addressed Julia. "Tommy's trouble is he thinks we need big-city planning here in Wiltonburg, and I try to explain to him we don't have the money for it." He put a hand on Julia's shoulder and Tommy could see her shrink away from his touch. "Listen, you watch out for this scoundrel," he went on with forced humor. "All the rest of us are jealous, the way the women go for him. Well, tell me now—what've you been doing, Julia? Heard you had a career for yourself in the Big Apple."

"I've been working in New York, yes," she said. Her voice sounded small and stifled.

"I don't get there often, but next time I do, I'll expect a personal guided tour. How about it?"

She managed a weak smile.

"Good. Anything I can do for you while you're here, you just call on me, little lady. I'm the mayor now, you know."

"I heard."

"Well, gotta run. I'm over here with some people from the chamber."

Julia watched him walk across the room, shaking her head slightly. Finally she said, "Being mayor hasn't changed him much, has it? He's still got that same winning personality he had when he used to try to grab me behind the lockers in high school."

Tommy's eyebrows shot up. "He did? Oh, well, not hard to believe."

"What *is* hard to believe is that he actually got himself elected. I gather he's not your favorite person, either."

Tommy grimaced. "Got that right." He changed the subject. "Do you remember the last time we were here?"

He saw her hesitation. She looked down at her plate. "Yes, of course. It was that last summer. It was my birthday."

"You had shrimp. You said it was the first time you'd ever tasted it."

"And you had beef stroganoff. I'd never had that, either. You let me taste yours." She looked up at him. He could feel a pulse beating in his temple.

"You haven't forgotten."

"No. But it was a long time ago."

"Not for me."

"For both of us, Tommy. It was another life."

They were quiet, and now it was her turn to change the subject. "Van sprang something on me the other day. He said we definitely need to paint the outside of the house. He's bringing a couple of students on Saturday to help him with it. And Gretchen insists she and I can help."

"Hey, great idea. Can I come, too?"

She blushed. "Oh, that wasn't why I mentioned it."

"I know. You were just trying to think of something safe to talk about. But I'd like to come."

"Well—" she moved one hand helplessly "—if you really want to...."

JULIA MADE a phone call as soon as she got home. "How about that dinner?" she asked.

"Wonderful!" Gina Blakely's voice was full of enthusiasm. "When?"

"Tomorrow night?"

"Okay, where?"

"Well, I was wondering if you'd like to come here. We can eat in my redecorated kitchen."

"Sounds great. I know where the house is. Seven okay?"

"Seven's fine."

Gina arrived bearing a bakery box and daffodils in green tissue paper. A tall woman, she seemed to unfold herself from the little compact car she drove. She had a stylish way about her that Julia observed from the kitchen doorway as Gina came up the path. Loose pants in stripes of brown and beige, a long ivory-colored vest and over it an easy-fitting jacket of buttery yellow. She was altogether more striking than anyone else in Wiltonburg, Julia observed.

"I heard you were doing some renovating." Gina handed her the box and the flowers. "Wish I could claim I raised those daffodils, but I seem to have no green thumb at all."

"They're lovely. Come on in." Julia held the door open. All trace of yesterday's rain was gone. The late sun of the spring evening and Van's paint job made the room glow. Julia's blue-and-white-checked curtains at the window provided crisp contrast, as did the new blue tablecloth.

"Looks like a great old place," Gina said, turning in a circle to admire it.

"Hardly that," Julia said, finding a tall tumbler for the daffodils and adding water. "But at least it'll soon be in shape to put on the market. I'm sure you know Van Lightner—he did the work, with one of his students lending a hand—and he says the house is sound enough."

"What's the rest of it like?"

"Come on, I'll show you."

Julia led the way into the living room and tried to gauge Gina's reaction. "Of course, you didn't see it at its worst," she said.

"Don't worry, I've seen enough of these old places to imagine exactly what it must have looked like."

Julia led her through the rest of the house, pleased at Gina's spontaneous appreciation. "I'm sure you'll find a buyer," Gina said. "That Van's a nine-day wonder, isn't he?"

"Just about literally," Julia agreed, heading back toward the kitchen. "He was on spring break, so he didn't have much more time than that."

"And I suppose you're anxious to saddle up and be out of town by sunset." Gina grinned.

"Well, yes, pretty soon." The suggestion of leaving was curiously unsettling. She waved Gina to a chair at the table and moved to the oven to peer in. Somehow she'd known that eating in the kitchen wouldn't bother Gina. "Actually I'll just be going back to job hunting. Not really a prospect to lift the spirits."

Gina crossed her long legs easily as she settled at the table. "Did you leave anybody back in New York?" she asked.

Julia hesitated. Obviously Gina Blakely didn't mind asking straightforward questions. "You mean . . ."

"I mean a man."

"No, there's no one."

"Really? With your looks?"

Julia blushed. "I was married once. Very briefly. But there's been nobody special since."

"Same here," Gina said, "out in California. I thought I had it made, but then when I wanted to come back here to help my grandfather out—when he first got sick—it all fell apart. The guy dumped me."

Julia bit her lower lip. "I'm sorry. But how do you feel about staying on here? About Wiltonburg?"

Gina shrugged. "It's a known quantity, at least. And I've learned not to think too far ahead. One day at a time suits me fine."

It was an honest answer, but Julia thought there might be more to it. "That's sort of the way I'm operating right now," she admitted. "No idea just how long I'm going to be here, but it's amazing how quickly I'm falling back into the country routine."

She took the chicken out of the oven, stirred the rice and added saffron and mushrooms. She brought out a green salad from the refrigerator and poured oil-and-vinegar dressing over it. When the dishes were assembled on the new tablecloth they were surprisingly colorful and tempting.

"Hey, that looks good!" Gina said. "Hate to admit how many TV dinners I eat—or how many fast-food places I frequent."

Conversation flowed easily all through the meal. "I must admit, I wasn't being exactly truthful when I said I took things one day at a time," Gina admitted. "I'm really planning on staying here. And I even have plans for the paper. I mean, about expanding it and adding to the staff. But it takes money, you know?"

"Have you approached the bank? They're in the money business, aren't they?"

Gina reached for the salad. "Oh, sure. But you must know Don Owen. He's the one I'd have to go to, and I can't stand him. Everything he does has strings attached."

"I can believe it." Julia sketched briefly for Gina her own past experience with Don, and Gina laughed uproariously.

Later, over cheesecake and coffee, Julia said casually, "Tommy Black's been doing some work for us—

redirecting a stream out in one of our fields. Yesterday he and I ran into Don Owen, and I had the impression Don and Tommy don't care much for each other. Has there been a quarrel?"

Gina shrugged. "So I hear, but a lot of it happened before I took over the paper. Apparently it involved the flood-control project in the old part of town."

"What happened?"

"Nothing anybody can be sure of. But Tommy seemed to think there was something peculiar about the awarding of the contracts for the work."

"I think he has doubts about the work itself." Tommy had never spelled this out in so many words, but Julia felt intuitively that this was the case.

"He does?" Gina sipped her coffee and put her cup down. "How do you know? Is he an old friend of yours or something?" She studied Julia's face. "Oops. Said the wrong thing."

To her horror, Julia found her eyes filling with tears. She quickly lifted her own cup, but when she tried to swallow, her throat closed painfully. She set the cup down and stared at her plate until the pattern around its rim ran into a blurry circle.

"I'm sorry," she whispered. "I don't know what's the matter with me."

Gina's voice grew softer, more compassionate. "Maybe I can guess. You used to live here. Was he somebody you knew back then?"

Julia nodded, and then, almost without her willing it, she began to tell Gina about those days—the whole story tumbling out in bits and snatches. The cold house where the thermostat was never set above fifty-five, the ugly brown oxfords, being sent away to New York State, marrying Bryce Farnsworth out of desperation and loneliness after Tommy dropped her from his life. Losing her job just when things were looking good. On and on, with pauses only to blow her nose and wipe her eyes. When she paused for breath she was astonished at herself for revealing so much to a near-stranger.

Gina only said quietly, "Boy, you've needed somebody to talk to for a long time, haven't you?"

Julia took a deep breath. "I didn't know it, but I guess maybe I have." She gave a shaky laugh and added, "And just imagine. I spilled it all to a newspaperwoman."

Gina grinned. "Strictly off the record, Julia."

"I guess I knew that." Julia got up and started clearing the table. "The thing is, there are people I could have talked to—my brother, for one. But I don't see him often. And Gretchen Bauer—she's a real friend, but she's to be married soon. She's so full of her own happiness I just couldn't—"

"Put those things down," Gina ordered, and Julia got rid of the two plates she was holding. "Come on back and sit down. Tell me what's next."

Julia sank back into her chair, then absentmindedly reached for the coffeepot and poured more coffee for each of them. "Oh, I'll finish up here and head back to New York. I've got to start job hunting. Once I do that I'll be okay."

"And Tommy Black?"

"That's all over. It would never work. There's just too much..." She paused and started again. "I could never..."

"Come on," Gina said gently. "Anybody can see you're crazy about the guy. And don't they always say you have to make peace with the past before you can move on?"

"I thought I'd done that. I was so sure..."

"Besides, how long do you want to punish him for something that happened ten years ago?"

Julia sipped the coffee, which was lukewarm now. "I'm not punishing him, really I'm not. It's just that I can't go through all that again. The pain..."

Gina hooked an arm over the back of her chair and gave Julia an appraising look. "Haven't you changed in ten years? What makes you think he hasn't?"

A series of scenes rolled through Julia's mind—Tommy showing her around his house, Tommy cooking a dinner for them, the way he'd held Chipper as they sped to the hospital, his arms around her, comforting her, in the hospital corridor.

She said in a low voice, "Once I'm back in New York, it'll all work out. It'll be fine then."

"I'm not sure that it matters where you go," Gina said, and her eyes met and held Julia's in a frank gaze. "It looks to me as if part of you will still be here."

CHAPTER EIGHT

"THE WEDDING'S TWO WEEKS from Saturday," Gretchen said.

"Wonderful."

"And, Julia, could I ask a big favor?"

"Of course." Julia balanced the telephone on one shoulder and put down the box she'd been carrying.

"Go shopping with me?"

"Shopping?"

"For a dress."

"You bet. Sounds like fun."

"Mom's having a fit because I won't let her make it, but sewing's too hard for her these days, and there's a nice shop in town now."

"I know. I saw it."

"How's tomorrow afternoon sound?"

"Great. Maybe I'll buy a dress, too."

Two weeks, Julia thought after she'd hung up. After two more weeks there wouldn't be anything to keep her here. The house would be finished, the attic cleared out. She could hand the key to the real-estate agent and leave. Considering how reluctant she'd been to come to Wiltonburg at all, it was odd that she now felt a nagging reluctance to leave the place. But perhaps that was only because of the uncertainty that loomed ahead of her. Still, she was no longer in trouble financially. There was that strange and still inexplicable inheritance from Elizabeth Holtz, which she'd have as soon as the probate formalities were finished. When the farm was sold, there'd be more money. She'd be negotiating for a job from a position of strength. That ought to lend her some confidence.

She walked slowly back to the kitchen. Would it feel strange, she wondered, with Tommy and her standing up with Gretchen and Van at their wedding? Not at all, her mind said quickly, but her heart was telling her otherwise. However, she wouldn't think about that now. She had other things to worry about. For one, she needed a new dress.

THE ROSE BOUTIQUE was as tasteful and inviting inside as its window display indicated. The rose theme was carried out in the color of the carpet and in the floral-print swags over the doorway to the dressing rooms. The owner, a handsome middle-aged woman, greeted Julia and Gretchen with a friendly hello and an invitation to take their time and look around all they wanted.

Gretchen and Julia began browsing through the racks. The shop was small but well arranged, and all the dresses had a look of quality.

"What about this?" Julia held up an ivory-colored chiffon dress with satin piping around its jewel neckline and tiny faux pearls dotted over the bodice.

"I love it," Gretchen breathed.

"All right, that's a possible," Julia said. "But this is nice, too." She held out a crepe chemise in pale pink with short puffy sleeves.

"Yes...."

"Well, let's start with these two. Come on."

Gretchen gave a delighted chortle, and they went back to the dressing rooms.

A quarter of an hour later they had narrowed down the choices, but were still looking. The shop owner joined them. When Julia uttered the magic words, "a small spring wedding," the woman's eyes lit up and she went to the rear of the store to bring out some new arrivals.

"This one's linen and cotton," she explained, emerging with a buttercup yellow midcalf-length dress. "Doesn't it have a wonderful springtime look?"

"Go ahead and try it," Julia urged, and helped Gretchen slip the dress on. When she stepped out of the dressing room to look at herself in the three-way mirror, Julia could only say, "Oh, Gretch, that's the one."

The dress was lovely. With scooped neckline and delicate embroidery all the way down the front, along with tiny covered buttons, it had a truly bridal look.

Gretchen fumbled for the price tag, but Julia slapped her hand away gently. "Don't you dare. It's for your wedding. Whatever it costs, it's worth it."

"Are you a member of the wedding party?" the proprietor asked Julia. At her nod, the woman held out another dress. "What do you think?"

This one was a floral print with a full skirt and a fluffy white chiffon collar that fell in graceful folds. Its coral, pink and green shades were the essence of the season.

"Oh, Julia, yes. Try it," Gretchen begged.

When Julia stood in front of the mirror wearing the dress, she looked like a different person. This was someone with no connection to the Julia who got up in the morning and pulled on jeans to go out and feed the lambs. This wasn't even the Julia who wore plain sensible clothes for the office. This was a Julia in a dress that floated around her in a soft whisper.

"Wait till Tommy sees you in that," Gretchen murmured.

Julia shot her friend a look, but Gretchen was standing there with stars in her eyes, a picture of total innocence. There was no way Julia could be cross with her for wanting to spread her own happiness to others. Yet inside, an old familiar resentment was welling up. Why did everyone in Wiltonburg assume she was ready to pick up where she left off ten years ago?

Her whole life seemed to be repeating itself. Every new phase since she was a child had been engineered from outside, with someone else placing her in the situation and saying, there now, you'll adapt in no time. The orphanage, the foster homes, life with the Holtzes, then being sent to care for Aunt Delia... Even her college had been selected for her. And of course the only decision she'd ever made for herself—her marriage—had turned into disaster.

"...and maybe Delbert's will have shoes close to this shade, or else what about off-white?" Gretchen was saying. Julia realized she hadn't been listening.

"Let's go there and find out," she said gently, shoving aside all the sharp resentful images that had been crowding her thoughts. As they paid for their dresses, she realized that Gretchen deserved her happiness. So why not relax and enjoy the occasion? Every wedding should be fun.

It was late afternoon by the time she got home. After hanging up the new dress and putting away the matching shoes, she changed into jeans and sweatshirt—what she'd come to think of as her farm clothes—and went out the kitchen door, whistling for Lizzie. The dog came galloping toward the house.

"Let's go for a walk, Lizzie," she said, and Lizzie's tail wagged in excited agreement. Tommy had finished the work in the south pasture earlier in the week, but Julia hadn't had a chance to look at it. She did now, though, and besides, something in the warm spring air was making her restless, reluctant to be indoors.

Lizzie trotted ahead, looking important, showing how well she patrolled the fence lines, how capable she was at her job of keeping strange dogs away from the sheep. All around them the grass was starting to spring up with its new green, and a few meadow flowers were already blooming. The sheep and lambs browsed widely and peacefully in a hilly pasture to their left. Late April, Julia thought. Time to speak to Fergus about culling the ewes—those whose fleece was poor or who hadn't proved to be good mothers. She made a note to remind him, but today she couldn't seem to keep her mind on practical matters. The soft air brushed her hair across her cheek, and the sweet scent of spring was in every breath she drew.

Just how much was she really looking forward to going back to New York? The question made her stop for a minute as she remembered what Gina Blakely had said—that it wouldn't matter where she went, part of her would still be here. And the other thing, too. *Anybody can see you're crazy about the guy.*

She resumed walking slowly. Was that what was making her drag her feet on the issue of leaving? Using Gretchen's wedding as an excuse, of course. But there was the matter of the sheep-shearing, too, and that had been her own idea. She'd spoken to the first-grade teacher, Miss Willett, and received enthusiastic thanks for the invitation. Now she was looking forward to it herself.

Maybe spring was the culprit, she thought as she tossed a stick, sending Lizzie into raptures of chasing and retrieving. Wiltonburg's winter face was nowhere near so beguiling. Perhaps it was just that she was in the best season, and it was working on her senses where they were most vulnerable.

Or maybe Gina was right.

Lizzie returned with the stick and Julia threw it again, quickening her step and hurrying toward the south pasture.

The area that had formerly flooded was now dry. It bore the signs of recent upheaval—new earth and the marks of heavy machinery, but Julia could see that in no time the coarse grass would take over, covering it with green. The stream that had caused the trouble now headed in a new direction, its banks reinforced. Tommy and his crew had done an efficient and thorough job.

It occurred to Julia that it was probably also a very small job for the Vernon-Black Company. Howard Westfall had mentioned that Tommy took on big projects now—flood control, road building. Rerouting a meadow stream had probably been no more than a nuisance. Julia made a mental note to have a check ready for him next time she saw him. The balance in the account at the bank was getting low. That was something else she had to take care of. Yet even this didn't seem to worry her today.

She called to Lizzie and started walking back toward the house. The sun, low in the sky, was casting long shadows, but it was still bright enough to make her shade her eyes. When she saw a tall figure striding toward her, waving, her heart gave one of those ridiculous leaps. She could only stop walking and stand there. He'd said he'd be on hand to help with the painting, but that wasn't until tomorrow.

"Hey, Julia!" He was still waving, and suddenly Julia realized it wasn't Tommy.

"Rick!" She ran toward him and as they met he swung her up in a hug. "Why didn't you let me know you were coming?"

"Last-minute decision. Got up early this morning and drove. Jule, you look terrific." He held her at arm's length. "Hey, is that the same girl I left here last month? I never thought Wiltonburg agreed with you that much." He was out of uniform today, casually dressed in chinos and a blue sweater.

"It's the hard work and fresh air."

"Sure that's all?"

"Of course. I haven't had time for anything else. I just walked out here now to see how the job in the field turned out."

"Oh. I'd like to take a look."

"Isn't Suzanne with you?" Arm in arm, they turned back toward the stream.

"Sorry, she's not. She sends all kinds of apologies, but a big commission came along and she grabbed it."

"Good for her. What kind of job?"

"Wedding, I think she said."

"Well, it's the season for them." Suzanne was a talented designer, as well as seamstress, and she'd recently started her own business. "She must be really busy then—getting ready for her own wedding, too." Julia had a sudden picture of herself, up to her knees in other people's happiness.

"Oh, she hasn't even started that. But I told her she can get married in jeans, as far as I'm concerned. She didn't exactly agree to that, but it doesn't seem to be worrying her. Hey, this looks great." He stood with his hands on his hips, inspecting the reinforced banks.

"The stream drains off in a new direction now, see?" She pointed. "Tommy says he doesn't think we'll have any more trouble from it."

He gave her a quick glance. "Everything go smoothly?"

"Oh, yes. And with the house, too," she said, deliberately steering him away from the subject of Tommy. "Come on, I'll show you. And talk about timing, you couldn't have managed it better. We're going to paint the outside of the place tomorrow. Think you can still handle a paintbrush?"

"Sure. Who's we?"

"I've got quite a crew coming," she said, and as they walked back she filled him in.

Rick was astonished as she led him through the house. "I can't believe it," he kept saying. "The old place is really starting to look sharp. Jule, you've done wonders."

"Actually it got to be fun after a while," she said.

"I'm leaving you my car," he said. "That's why I drove. There's no use your hanging on to that rental— I can use Suzanne's. I'll take your rental back when I go to the airport on Monday. Oh, and we'll need to put more money in the bank for these expenses."

"Yeah. The balance is getting kind of low," she said, then showed him all the bills so far. While she was at it, she pulled out the old photo she'd found.

"Seems light-years ago," he said softly, holding it up for a closer look. "And Mother Holtz looks almost human, doesn't she?"

They ate the simple supper Julia prepared, and Rick said it was the best meal he'd ever eaten in that kitchen. He'd hardly finished before he started yawning, and Julia could tell fatigue was catching up with him. "Up at five this morning," he apologized. "Sorry."

"Go to bed. You'll need to get some rest or you won't be any good to us tomorrow."

He gave her a wry look. "Slave driver. I can see how you worked all these miracles."

The sun was setting as Julia cleaned up the kitchen, and she'd just decided to turn in early, too, when the telephone rang. She hurried into the hall and picked it up.

"Julia?"

"Yes. Who's this?"

"Bud Winter. Lord, I had a time finding you. How's everything going?"

"Great." Now that she recognized his voice, Julia could almost see her former boss on the other end of the line, rumpled and round-faced, his glasses halfway down his nose. "What about you, Bud? Any luck?"

"That's why I'm calling. Amazing thing happened. I landed another job, with C. P. Grayson and Sons."

"That sounds wonderful, and it's not amazing at all. They're lucky to get you. That's an excellent house."

"It is that. And I'm being given pretty broad latitude, which means, among other things, that I'm allowed to bring in somebody to work with me. You're my first choice, Julia. And the money sounds good. What do you say?"

Julia swallowed and tried to catch her breath. "I'm absolutely at a loss for words. Bud, that's wonderful...and you're wonderful, too, for thinking of me."

"Go ahead, keep flattering me. I love it. What about the job?"

Julia hedged. "I've been working like mad here trying to get the old farm in shape to sell. It turned out to be a lot more work than I'd imagined. I'm afraid it'll keep me here another couple of weeks, but after that I should be able to get my thoughts together. Could I possibly let you know then?"

"Sure. I'll give you that much time. Tell you right now, though, Julia, you'd love this company. So give it serious thought."

"I certainly will."

She hung up and walked slowly upstairs. It was the answer to everything—working with someone like Bud, who was talented and easy to get along with, all the agonizing job hunting canceled, and she might even be able to keep her little apartment to herself, instead of sharing. It really solved every one of her problems.

Then why did she feel as if someone had just built a fence around her, instead of setting her free?

THE FIRST TO ARRIVE the next morning were Van Lightner's students, a young man and woman. They started scraping rough spots on the old house with putty knives and wire brushes before Julia had even made coffee. When she called to invite them in for some, they waved her away with thanks and said they'd just keep working—Professor Lightner wanted to be able to start painting early.

Van was the next to appear, and by then Rick was up and dressed. Julia introduced them and gave them coffee, and was pleased to see them hit it off at once. Rick repeated to Van his amazement over the changes in the house.

"All the good ideas were his," Julia said with a grin at Van.

Gretchen arrived soon after, and the kitchen began to fill up with chatter and laughter as Julia went on pouring coffee and making toast. She was glad to be busy. Something inside her had been pounding with anticipation since she first opened her eyes this morning. She deliberately kept from looking out the window, but when the next knock came and she saw the door push open, she felt her pulse race.

"Hey, I didn't think anybody heard me," Tommy called out. His tall frame filled the doorway as he stood there in worn jeans and an old denim shirt. Chipper was holding his hand. She, too, was in jeans and a denim shirt. "I brought a helper," he announced.

"Wonderful," Julia said, trying to keep her voice normal. "Chipper, you and I'll make a good team."

"I'm going to do the low parts," the little girl said.

"That'll save the rest of us a lot of bending," Van said.

"Tommy, you remember my brother, Rick? You were in high school together, weren't you?"

"Were we!" Tommy crossed the room to Rick, who had risen to shake his hand. "We were on the track team together."

"Only for a brief time." Rick grinned. "Then Father Holtz got wind of it and my career as a quarter-miler was cut short."

"But it was long enough for him to break the school record," Tommy said to the others. "We ran against each other that day, remember? I suffered ignominious defeat."

"But for good reason, as I recall. Wasn't there something about eating a whole pizza before the meet?"

The laughter in the old kitchen bounced off the walls, and again Julia was struck with the strangeness of joy in a house that had never witnessed such a thing before.

Then Van pushed up his glasses with his finger and announced that it was time they all got to work. Everyone trooped outside, and supplies of paint and brushes were allotted. Julia watched as Tommy led Chipper to a quiet spot near the back of the house, handed her a brush and a little sand bucket into which he'd poured a small amount of paint.

"Let someone know when you need more," he said. "Don't put too much on your brush at once. Do it like this." He let her hold the brush but covered it with his own hand as he showed her how to stroke it on. Julia felt a tightening around her heart as she saw the long square-tipped fingers guiding the little girl's hand. Standing beside them, watching, she was able to imagine for that moment that they were a family, doing this project together on a Saturday.

She remembered her thought the first time she met Chipper outside the Rose Boutique. *She could have been mine.*

"There. Think you can manage?" Tommy stood up and patted her head, then looked at Julia.

Afraid that everything she'd been thinking must be showing nakedly in her face, she said quickly, "I'm sure we'll both do just fine."

His eyes lingered on her for a moment and then he said, "Well, then, I think I have a date with a ladder. See you two ladies in a while."

For the first five minutes Chipper concentrated hard on painting, while Julia began working near her. Gaining confidence and beginning to use large splashy strokes, the little girl said, "Daddy wouldn't let me wear my new sneakers because he said I'd get paint on them. These are my old ones."

"That's sensible. Painting can be messy." Julia was working on one of the kitchen windows.

"Miss Willett told us about our class coming here to see the sheep. It's going to be on Tuesday."

"Yes, that's the plan. Do you think it'll be fun?"

"Yep." Chipper hesitated, then looked up at Julia with concern in her face. "Does it hurt the sheep?"

"Goodness, no. Sometimes they fuss a little bit because they don't like being held down, but it doesn't hurt at all. And when it's done they're very happy."

"They are?"

"Of course. They like getting rid of those winter coats now that it's spring."

Moments later several splotches of white paint had landed on Chipper's denim shirt. "Aunt Fiona's making my carrot costume for the play. Are you coming to it?"

Julia hesitated, but only briefly. "I'd certainly like to. Yes, I definitely will."

"Good. Because Daddy's going to ask you again. He told me so."

Julia felt her cheeks grow hot, but Chipper went on, "Aunt Fiona says making my costume is a real stretch for her because I'm not shaped like a carrot. She says it's a major challenge."

"I'm sure it'll turn out fine."

The sun was warm, and the project went ahead rapidly. The men worked on ladders, and the two students concentrated on window frames. Gretchen attacked the front door while Julia and Chipper continued working at the back of the house.

At noon Julia offered to make sandwiches, but everyone had brought lunch—orders from Van so that less time would be wasted. She took Chipper inside to clean her up at the kitchen sink, however, and when they returned, Tommy was waiting for them.

"We brought plenty of food," he said. "You can share with us."

"I'm the hostess," she objected. "I should be doing the providing."

He ignored her. "Peanut butter and jelly, or roast beef?"

"Well, roast beef, I guess—if you're sure you have enough."

When everyone sat down on the new porch steps to eat, however, Julia announced that once the job was done, she and Rick would provide hamburgers and hot dogs for everyone.

"Hey, wait, I want to get a picture," Rick said, and hurried inside for his camera. After he'd gotten his shot, one of the students offered to take another so Rick could be included.

This time Tommy lifted Chipper onto his lap and put his free arm around Julia, pulling her close. Julia gave a tiny gasp, but she didn't pull away. What difference did it make? she thought. It wasn't a relationship that was going anywhere, but why not at least enjoy today? She smiled into the camera.

Early in the afternoon the Vernons stopped by to admire the progress of the work and to pick up Chipper, rightly guessing that her interest in painting would have begun to flag by now. They found her off in the meadow pursuing lambs, her hair and face paint-streaked, the denim shirt a mass of dribbles. Julia thanked Chipper for her help and then leaned over to give her a hug.

"See you Tuesday, Chipper," she said.

The only crisis of the day occurred moments later when Van confessed he'd underestimated the amount of paint needed. "That's thirsty old wood," he said, shaking his head. "Going to take a couple more gallons." He was on his knees painting the new porch steps in a heavy gray enamel.

"I'll go pick it up," Tommy said. "My truck's the last one in the driveway. Ride along with me, Julia?"

She hesitated for only a second. "Okay, sure."

Neither one of them spoke for a few minutes as Tommy backed the truck out and swung down the road toward town. Then Julia, slanting a mischievous look at him, said, "A *whole* pizza? Before a track meet?"

He sighed. "The confidence of youth. And the ignorance. It did me in on the last turn."

They both laughed. Then he reached for her hand. "What is it?" he asked. "How come you're different today?"

"I didn't know I was..." She stopped and started over. "Well, maybe I am. It's just that I've been doing a lot of thinking, and I've decided that I shouldn't hold on to the past so tightly. I just want to forget it—at least for the rest of my stay in Wiltonburg."

"Does that mean—" he began. She interrupted him quickly. "It doesn't mean a thing. That is, it doesn't change anything."

His eyebrows shot up. "What I was going to ask was, does that mean you'll go to the Easter program with us?"

She couldn't help laughing. "I've already told Chipper I would."

"Great. And there's a dance the following night in the high-school gym. How about that?"

"Hey, wait a minute. You're rushing me."

"I figure I'd better get in on this good mood."

"It isn't a mood. I just feel a whole lot better about everything all of a sudden. Besides, something nice happened to me last night."

"Oh?" He waited at a stop sign and then turned right onto the main street, headed toward Nolan's Hardware.

"Bud Winter, the man who used to be my boss, has joined a different publishing house. He wants me to work for him again when I get back."

Tommy smiled at her, but some of the light faded from his eyes. "You must be very good at what you do." She gave a little shrug, and he asked, "Are you going to take it?"

"I'm not sure," she said slowly. "It's a great opportunity. But . . . I'm not sure."

"Why not?" He kept his voice calm as he pulled into a parking space in front of the store.

She remembered what she'd been thinking the other day in the dress shop—that other people had made decisions for her all her life. "The next decision I make is going to be all my own. No outside influences. And I want it to be right." She wondered if he'd have any idea what she was talking about.

He turned off the ignition. "I don't blame you for that," he said. "I don't know that anyone can guarantee it'll be right, but it should certainly be your own decision." He seemed about to say more, but then he opened the door and got out. "Be right back."

He returned moments later with two gallons of paint, but then he held up his index finger and hurried into the small grocery next door. This time when he came out, he was carrying two Popsicles.

"Raspberry all right?" he asked as he got in.

"My favorite."

They sat for a time peeling off paper and making inroads on the Popsicles. Then he started the pickup and they drove back onto the main street.

"Wonderful idea," she said, licking luxuriously.

"Don't say I don't know how to treat a lady."

Halfway along the county road his Popsicle fell apart, and he pulled off the road under a big maple while he retrieved it. Julia was already down to the stick on hers.

"Some people know how to manage these things and still stay neat," he grumbled.

"You make that sound like criticism," she said airily.

"I do think it shows a certain rigidity. My approach is looser, more aesthetic."

"And decidedly messier."

She was watching as he licked the last bit of Popsicle from the stick. His mouth was stained and she supposed hers must be, too. She swallowed as she saw the bright pink ice disappear into his mouth. Now he was looking at her, a long slow look that made a blush start somewhere around her neck and work its way upward.

He dropped the stick into the trash bag on the dashboard and started to reach for the ignition key. Then he drew his hand back and turned to her, instead, pulling her against him in a swift movement that surprised her, yet seemed, at the same time, completely right and inevitable.

Her arms came up to circle his neck as he bent to kiss her. She tasted the raspberry ice on his mouth, felt the chill of his tongue as it searched for hers. One of his hands moved to slide up along her side and then close over her breast. She gave a little gasp, and he pulled back to look at her face for an instant. Then he kissed her again, and she felt herself answering the kiss with a passion compounded by ten years of longing.

"Tommy," she murmured against his mouth. "Tommy, I can't fight you any longer. I don't know what's going to happen next, but just for today I don't care, either."

"Would you believe me if I told you there was never anybody but you, Julia?" he whispered.

Her rational self would never have believed such a thing, but sitting here on a sunny April day, his arms around her and his lips like fire against hers, she was ready to believe anything he told her. She didn't answer, but raised her face to him again and parted her own lips to meet his.

THERE WAS no such thing as an outdoor grill at the Holtz farm, but Van had brought his, and he and Rick did the honors, cooking hamburgers and hot dogs after the painting was finally finished.

Everyone sat outside, eating coleslaw and potato chips, admiring the now sparkling house and talking until the sun began to sink in the sky. Then the two students left and Van and Gretchen drifted off. Rick went inside to telephone Suzanne, and Tommy said he'd better go pick up Chipper at the Vernons'.

Julia walked with him to the pickup and lingered next to him. He pulled her close and she could feel the hard length of his body against her as he bent to find her mouth and kiss her again.

She was feeling surprise and wonder. Was it right? Was it sensible? Her mind tried to put up arguments, to be rational. But she felt them melting away like Popsicles.

CHAPTER NINE

TOMMY AND CHIPPER walked along the old farm drive that led from their house to the Vernons'. Trees on either side were leafing out rapidly and birds were racketing about overhead, busy with nest building. Tommy was looking over yesterday's mail, going through circulars and bills.

He paused when he came to an envelope with a West Virginia postmark, addressed in his sister's handwriting. Chipper, skipping at his side, kept up a running commentary that demanded only occasional responses from him. He opened the envelope with one finger and read as they walked along:

Dear Tommy,
We sure do appreciate the check you sent. It was a lot more than you should have sent us, but it sure will come in handy. We plan to use it for some new spring things for the kids, but mostly for Randy, who is growing awful big now and sure does need them. Tommy, if you could find the time to give him a call sometime, it would be real nice. I think hearing from his big brother now and then would do him a lot of good. Not that he's ever got into any real trouble, just kid stuff, but you know how it is...

"Could we, Daddy?"

He glanced down at his daughter. "Could we what?" He knew from past experience that he should pay attention to this question. Saying yes absentmindedly could be disastrous.

"I said, could we have some sheep?"

"Why do you want sheep? You already have Nugget and Bullet."

"Yes, but sheep would be fun. And Julia knows all about them. She'd show me what to do. We could train Nugget to be a sheepdog."

The pleasurable stab that went through him at the sound of Julia's name was new to him. Since Saturday, when they'd stopped along the way home, parking like teenagers at the side of the road, he'd experienced a hundred times in memory the sweet touch of her lips, still faintly tasting of raspberry, and felt her soft yielding body melting against his.

He brought his attention back to the child. "Where would you keep them? You'd need some kind of shed for wintertime, and one of those feed things for the lambs."

"Well . . . I could probably do most of it," she said doubtfully. "Van showed me how to hammer nails. I mean, you might have to help me a little bit."

That afternoon must have meant something to Julia, he tried to convince himself. And she'd even said she wanted to forget about the past. She still refused to commit herself any further than that, but at least she'd lost that chip on her shoulder. Maybe if she was willing to meet him halfway . . .

"Are you, Daddy?"

"Am I what?"

"Are you coming to the sheep-shearing today? At Julia's?"

"I thought you were all going on the bus. Anyway, I have to work."

"I know, but don't you want to watch Julia shear the sheep?"

He turned back to his letter, uncomfortably aware of his face turning warm. "We'll see," he said.

The Vernons' big kitchen was in its usual state of comfortable chaos. The sewing machine was open against one wall. In the center of the room was a round wooden table littered with newspapers, coffee cups, seed catalogs and uncleared plates. Bill Vernon sat there with the Pittsburgh paper while Fiona stood at the window watering potted begonias and geraniums.

"I swear I'd just as soon read the local paper," Bill said, starting the conversation without preamble. "Nothing here but crime and politicians—same old thing," he said, putting the paper down and holding out both arms to Chipper, who ran to give him a hug.

"How's Louise?" asked Fiona, spotting the letter in Tommy's hand.

"Everything seems all right, as far as I can tell."

Fiona finished her watering and turned back. "That Louise is a real good woman, I swear. All those kids of her own to raise and taking in her little brother, too. Hello, sweetie," she said to Chipper, who ran over to throw both arms around her waist. She looked at Tommy. "How old is Randy now?"

"Seventeen."

"Staying out of trouble, is he?" Bill asked.

"Louise says he's getting into kid stuff, whatever that means."

Bill snorted. "What a boy that age needs—"

"What a boy that age needs," Tommy interrupted, "is to start out hitchhiking and have someone like you pick him up."

Bill snorted and Fiona's eyes misted over. "Well, come on now, Miss Charlotte. Try this costume on. You two had breakfast?"

"Yeah, sure," Tommy answered, but Chipper inquired, "What did you have?"

"Some first-rate French toast," Bill said. "Want me to fix you a piece?"

"Chipper..." Tommy said warningly, but she'd already nodded, and Bill went to the stove to prepare it.

"Just slide out of those jeans while you're waiting, Chipper," Fiona ordered. "And it might be a good idea if you stood on a chair so I can see better." Chipper hurried to undress, climbing up and standing on a chair in her underpants and T-shirt. "All right—arms up. Easy, easy." She slid the narrow orange shift over the little girl's head. "Now the hat." The headpiece was a bright green cap that tied under her chin and had leaflike protrusions on top.

"Those leaves were a challenge," Fiona admitted. "I stiffened 'em with buckram. They don't look much like carrot tops, but the general effect is good."

"You're a wonder, Fiona," Tommy said.

"Aunt Fiona, don't you think we should get some sheep?" Chipper asked.

Fiona bent over to examine the hem of the carrot shift. "Whatever for?"

"Because I know a lot about them, and Julia can teach me more."

Fiona turned to look at Tommy, who quickly picked up the newspaper and began scanning it.

"Well, what I'd say is, if you still want sheep by the time get into the 4-H, then your daddy might say it was okay. But right now you'd better let me fix this costume."

"The show isn't till Friday night."

"I know, but I'm not the world's fastest seamstress, either."

"Where'd you get the idea of wanting sheep?" Bill said from the stove, where he was beating an egg with milk and then dipping bread in it.

"Our class is going to Julia's farm to watch the sheep getting sheared today," Chipper explained.

Now all three pairs of eyes turned to Tommy.

"I want Daddy to come, too, only he says he has to work. But you could take time off, couldn't you, Daddy? Aren't you your own man?"

Tommy burst out laughing. "What does *that* mean?"

"That's what Uncle Bill always says. When you have your own business, then you're your own man."

Bill shook his head and dropped the dripping bread in the pan. "Lord, you gotta watch what you say around here."

"Now, how does that feel?" Fiona asked.

Chipper moved her feet slightly. "It's awful skinny. I don't know if I can walk in it."

"Just take little tiny steps. Do you have to walk much?"

"No, not much. Mostly I stand still. But I have a line to say. I say, 'Please don't eat me, Mr. Rabbit. I'm on my way to the Easter-egg hunt.'"

"I had an idea carrots don't do a lot of walking generally. Well, that ought to do it. Here, let me get you out of this getup." As Fiona untied the cap and lifted the costume over Chipper's head, the little girl repeated her line in muffled tones, practicing various interpretations. Tommy swung her off the chair.

"How soon are you starting that Braxton job?" Bill asked, bringing the plate of French toast to the table and sprinkling cinnamon-sugar on it.

"We should be ready in three or four days. I've got the men over on Grove Road now, finishing up the work there."

Chipper scrambled back into her jeans and sat down. Bill tied a kitchen towel around her neck.

"Why don't you come over to the Braxton site and look it over once we start?" Tommy suggested. "There's a couple of things I'd like your input on." Tommy often thought that Bill Vernon must miss work. As much as he enjoyed his retirement, there had to be times when he longed to be out there again with the big machines. And Tommy still respected his knowledge and long experience. "It's got to be planned just right—they want to allow for a reflecting pool, underground parking and a lot of other features."

"Fancy stuff," Bill said gruffly. "Well, I might just drop by sometime."

In the truck later, headed toward Wiltonburg Elementary, Chipper said, "Now that Julia's house is so pretty, maybe she'll decide to live there." Her tongue darted out to capture a morsel of cinnamon sugar on her upper lip.

Tommy felt a muscle in his jaw flex. "Oh, I doubt that."

"Well, I wish she would. I bet she wants to."

"What makes you think so?"

"I just bet she does," Chipper said thoughtfully.

He made a call from the pickup after he'd dropped the little girl at school. "Frank? I'm going to stop by the Highway Department—check on those new specs. Got enough to keep you busy there at Grove Road for a while? Good. I'll get there as soon as I can." He knew he could trust Frank Wooten to keep the men busy and see that no time was wasted.

He spent half the morning at the Highway Department, then got back in the truck and headed for Grove Road. But at the turnoff for Firebush Road he braked sharply and made a left. He shook his head, smiled in a self-mocking way and said aloud, "Damn. I can't believe I'm doing this. Going to a sheep-shearing with a bunch of first-graders. What's the matter with you, anyway, Black?''

He parked behind the yellow school van and walked slowly past the newly painted house and up the drive to the barn. A bunch of children were clustered outside it as Julia talked. Her eyes were on them and she was obviously concentrating on what she was saying. She was in jeans and a gray sweatshirt, and her hair was tied back with a piece of red ribbon. There was color in her cheeks. She held up a pair of clippers as she spoke. Tommy stayed back, his arms folded. She hadn't noticed his arrival.

"These are hand clippers," Julia was saying. "Both Mr. Halley and I prefer them, but later he'll show you how electric clippers work, too."

"Don't you ever cut the sheep?" a small boy asked.

She smiled. "We try very hard not to, but sometimes, of course, a sheep will get a nick. If that happens, we keep this can of antibiotic spray handy so it doesn't get infected. The important thing in shearing is how you hold the sheep. You want to put her in a position where she can't struggle. If you try to use force, she'll just struggle more. All right now, ready to see how it's done?"

There was a chorus of yeahs, and some clapping, and then Fergus Halley, in jeans, boots, flannel shirt and sacroiliac belt, led one of the ewes over to Julia.

"First slip your thumb into the sheep's mouth like this—" she demonstrated "—then bend her head over her left shoulder and swing her toward you. Now you can lower her to the ground and start cutting in this area—it's called the brisket—and on up into the right shoulder area."

Tommy watched, fascinated, as Julia deftly immobilized the animal and began clipping. She seemed completely sure of herself. He thought it must have been years since she'd done this, but obviously she remembered how and hadn't lost her touch.

"From this position, you hold her left front leg up toward her neck and then you can reach her side and belly," Julia explained. As she shifted the animal, it let out a cry. Tommy heard a voice that was unmistakably Chipper's saying, "It doesn't hurt a bit, does it? It's like getting rid of your winter coat, that's all."

"Yes, exactly," Julia said, glancing up long enough to smile at her. In so doing, she spotted Tommy, and she faltered and her face grew pink. The sheep gave a lurch, but Julia quickly regained her hold and went on with the demonstration.

"Now you hold one ear, but gently, so it doesn't hurt, either, and trim down the side of the neck." Quickly and efficiently, she finished shearing the animal and released it. The children clapped as it trotted away and immediately began munching grass in the meadow.

"We roll up the fleece like this, folding the side edges in toward the middle, then the neck end and the tail end. Then we roll it all up and tie it. Since this isn't a large flock, most of the wool will be sold to craft stores and small companies for hand spinning. Now Mr. Halley will show you how the electric clippers work." She helped Fergus bring in another ewe and begin to shear it. Her eyes moved to Tommy and she smiled faintly.

For the next hour the demonstration continued, with Julia and Fergus explaining how the sheep were raised and cared for. Small voices continuously interrupted in an unending volley of questions. The teacher, Miss Willett, finally called a halt and said the driver of the van was waiting and it was time to return to school. The last few minutes were occupied with petting the lambs, a treat Julia had saved for the end, and with Miss Willett taking pictures. Tommy, leaning against a tree with his arms folded, waved to Chipper. Then at last the class was rounded up and herded back into the van.

Fergus Halley drew a deep breath. "Well, now that that's over with we can get down to business here. My nephew oughta be along any minute to help."

"Mr. Halley, you were the hit of the show," Julia said. "The children loved your demonstration."

Fergus made a flapping motion with his hand and said, "Well, I ain't headed for Hollywood anytime soon. I'll take the dog now and start bringin' 'em in."

He whistled for Lizzie, and he and the dog started out for the field.

Tommy crossed to where Julia was standing in front of the open barn door looking at him. Without a word he took her hand and led her inside. In the soft grain-smelling shadows he pulled her to him. As his lips found hers, her hair, blown loose from its ribbon, brushed across his face. He could feel the warmth of the sun on her skin. He held her close, one hand low on her back so that it rested on the gentle swell of her hip.

At last she pulled away slowly and looked up at him. *God, those eyes,* he thought. Deep soft violet-blue— they'd captivated him from the first moment he'd seen her. Her beauty didn't need anything, he marveled. Fashion and cosmetics couldn't add a scrap to it. Jeans and sweatshirt couldn't hide it. He kissed her again, slowly and softly, feeling her response.

When they pulled apart he murmured, "You've caused a major problem at my house, know that?"

"How?" The violet-blue eyes moved over his face lovingly. His heart felt close to bursting.

"Chipper's decided she wants to raise sheep."

"Oh? What's so terrible about that? Sounds like a good idea to me." Her hand rested on his shoulder, one finger tracing the seam of his vest. "I mean, why not?"

He planted light kisses on her forehead. "Because guess who'd wind up locating strays and acting as midwife?"

She chuckled and raised her face for another kiss, opening her mouth to him eagerly. In the distance they could hear Fergus signaling Lizzie with whistles.

"I think that daughter of yours can do anything she sets her mind to," she said when they drew apart again.

"Well, she has it set on something else right now." He moved his hand up and down her spine, feeling the slight responding tremors course through her body.

"What?" she whispered.

"She says that since your house is so pretty now, you should stay in it."

He felt a faint stiffening in her and quickly added, "Okay, okay. It was her idea, not mine. She likes you a lot."

"I like her, too. And I liked doing this—you know, having the kids here."

"That was obvious."

"Was it?"

"Yes, because you looked beautiful doing it. That's a sure sign. Not that you could ever look anything but beautiful."

She let her head drop into the hollow of his shoulder, and he couldn't help thinking how well it fit there.

"Still, you can't blame us for wanting you to stay," he said, his hand still moving over her back.

This time her reaction was more noticeable. Her whole body grew rigid and she pulled back slightly. "You know I can't do that," she said in a low voice.

As mildly as he could he answered, "No, I don't know. I imagine you can do whatever you want to do."

She took a step away. "I mean, it's ridiculous to think a person can change the direction of her whole life just like that."

"Just like what?" He leaned back against the wall of the barn and folded his arms on his chest.

"You know perfectly well what I mean. Just because we've met again and had some nice times together, that doesn't mean I'm suddenly going to throw away a good job offer and a way of life that suits me fine, all because you think it would be a great idea."

He could feel anger welling up and kept it down with an effort. "It isn't only what I think. I had the idea it might be something we were both thinking. Isn't that what's supposed to happen when two people love each other? They start planning on being together, don't they?"

"I did think that once," she flung out bitterly.

"Oh, Julia, come on. Are you still talking about what happened ten years ago? That was another life, for God's sake."

"Well, it might have been another life, but I'm still very aware that it was *my* life. I haven't forgotten it, even if you have."

"I thought you wanted to forget it. I thought you'd decided to put the past behind you and start thinking about the future."

"Maybe I was being too optimistic."

"Are you going to try and tell me you don't love me?" he demanded. "The way you kissed me back just now—"

"I *always* loved you," she blurted angrily. "That was never the question, was it? It was whether you loved me. As soon as I went away and you were back in college, it became too much of a hindrance for you to be tied down to a girl you probably had only a passing interest in, anyway—"

"A passing interest!" His anger rose, bubbling and boiling. "Is that what you think it was?"

"Well, if it wasn't, you certainly found other women to comfort you soon enough. Chipper's evidence of that." She moved to the open doorway and stood with her back to him.

He caught up with her in two strides and grabbed her arm, pulling her around to face him. His voice pulsed with fury.

"You've got some nerve passing judgment on me when you don't know the first thing about what happened ten years ago. And every time I've tried to discuss it with you, you refuse to listen. You're so full of your own grievances and injuries you don't even stop to think that other people might have been hurt, too. Is that the way you want to go through life—feeling sorry for yourself? If so, go ahead, I won't stop you."

She yanked her arm out of his grasp. "How could I possibly believe a word of what you told me now? You'd say anything to make yourself look blameless, wouldn't you? My mistake was trusting you back then, and I certainly don't intend to make it again."

"Then I'll be sure and not make the same mistake, either. Like asking you to marry me."

For a moment her stony look altered slightly, and her lips started to tremble. Then she flung herself away from him and marched off toward the house. He watched her go, seeing the determined set of her shoulders, the firm stride of her blue-jeaned legs, the bobbing of the red ribbon in her hair. When she'd slammed into the house, he walked back down the drive to his truck. Its wheels spat gravel as the pickup roared off.

CHAPTER TEN

JULIA WAS GLAD she had the sheep-shearing to concentrate on for the rest of the day. It left no time for thinking and regrets. Working alongside Fergus and his nephew gave her sore muscles, an aching back and a sunburn on her face and the nape of her neck. The usual sense of accomplishment that came with the job was missing, however. When at last she saw the two men off and went into the house, she was overwhelmed by a weariness that was only partly physical. The job had taken up the hours and kept her concentrating, but now that it was over, the memory of her quarrel with Tommy rushed back over her like a cold wind.

She climbed the stairs to her room, undressed and then ran a hot bath in the old claw-footed tub down the hall, sinking into it with a groan. Almost at once she felt herself bombarded by questions for which she felt compelled to find answers.

Was she afraid to take a chance? To confront her own feelings? No, of course not. She simply didn't want to be rushed. Then what about this business of his betrayal ten years ago? Why did she refuse to talk about it? Because her pride was hurt, of course. A perfectly human reaction. He'd been young and he'd forgotten her and turned to someone else, and it hurt.

Then why had he said, "You don't know the first thing about what happened ten years ago"? Why hadn't she given him a chance to explain? Because hearing it would be like living through it all again. Because hearing it spelled out would be new hurt and humiliation piled on top of the old.

She reached for the soap and washcloth and lathered it furiously, thinking of other things he'd said. "Isn't that what's supposed to happen when two people love each other?" And the most painful one of all, "I'll be sure and not make the same mistake, either. Like asking you to marry me."

Had he really meant to ask her to marry him?

She remembered what she'd told him the day they drove to town for the paint—that now she wanted to make her own decisions. But was going back to New York what she really wanted? Or was it merely easy? Once again, was it just a quick way of making those decisions without answering any of the important questions? She tried to picture her Manhattan apartment, her own small place that had once seemed so snug and so right for her. She found she had trouble recalling what it looked like, what color the couch was, what the view was like from the window. This old farmhouse that she'd spent most of her life hating seemed the only reality now.

She dragged herself reluctantly out of the tub and toweled herself dry, wrapped her terry-cloth robe around her and shoved her feet into slippers. For a moment she recalled the dizzying passion of their kiss, how they'd clung together, bodies fitting each other perfectly. Didn't that mean something?

She hugged herself tightly. Feelings like that could lead you astray, deceive you. How could you know they were real? Hadn't they fooled her before? Yet even as she cautioned herself, some deeper instinct told her the truth. They were real. Feelings didn't get any more real than that.

She was on her way downstairs when the telephone rang. Her heart gave a jump but then quickly subsided. He wouldn't be calling, not after the things she'd said to him.

"Jule? How's it going?" Rick's voice was cheerful, reassuring. It always managed to comfort her.

"Just fine. How was the trip back? Do you miss your car?"

"Trip was fine. And yes, I miss my car, but it's only a loaner, you know. Don't get any ideas."

"Can't promise. It's a whole lot better than that rental I was driving. How's Suzanne?"

"Busy, but fine. We took some time off and went looking at apartments today."

Julia sat down on the bottom stair. "That beats what I was doing—shearing sheep."

"No kidding. But hey, you know something? I've never seen you looking better than you did last weekend."

"Oh, come on."

"No, I mean it. I thought it was all that fresh country air till I saw you with Tommy Black."

"What's that supposed to mean?" Julia straightened.

"Oh, nothing. Just the way you two looked together. And you've blossomed so much in a few short weeks. You going to tell me cleaning up an old farmhouse did that?" She couldn't answer, then she heard his voice again. "Jule? You still there?"

"Yes." She hesitated. "Oh, Rick, I don't know what to do."

"About him?" His tone was gentle.

"Yes. I do have feelings for him, but I'm so afraid of being hurt again."

His voice turned sober, thoughtful. "Well, you're right to think it over carefully. Nothing wrong with that. But don't start closing doors too quickly. I mean, you can't go through life being afraid, getting bitter, keeping people at arm's length. You've seen what that can do—what it did to the Holtzes, for instance."

"I know, but...I do have to choose, Rick. I've had a job offer in New York. It won't wait forever."

He was quiet for a moment, then he said, "Hey, don't agonize over it. I have a lot of confidence in you, and I think you'll make the right decision. One day soon it'll all come together for you, and you know something? When it does you'll know it."

After she'd said goodbye to him she went into the kitchen. Although she hadn't eaten since noon, she didn't feel hungry. Nevertheless, she opened a can of soup, heated it up and ate it. Then she went about making a cup of cocoa, thinking of what Rick had said. Not much, really, and if his words had come from anyone else she'd have dismissed them as mere platitudes. But Rick was different. Rick came from the same place she had, and his life had been just as hard.

He understood her, and more than that, whatever he said she knew he meant.

"Don't go closing doors too quickly," he'd advised. Well, she'd done that already, hadn't she? And now, would she wonder for the rest of her life what might have been? What was she scared of? Why was she turning Tommy away when he was trying to be honest with her? All right, maybe he hadn't been honest ten years ago, but at least now he certainly seemed . . .

She shook her head to clear it and poured the cocoa into her mug. Over in the corner she saw the last two boxes from the attic. She sighed. Facing them now was too much. She couldn't handle one more scrap of memory tonight. She took the cocoa and a book and went upstairs to bed.

She read for a time, then turned the light out and tried to sleep. Despite her exhaustion sleep didn't come, and she turned the light back on and picked up her book. Finally she looked at her bedside clock. Eleven-thirty. She threw back the covers and pulled on her robe. She seemed to have kicked her slippers under the bed, so she walked barefoot downstairs to the front hall. Then she crossed to the old black telephone and dialed Tommy's number. He answered on the first ring.

"I'm sorry—were you asleep?"

"No. I'm in bed, but not asleep. Staring at the ceiling, as a matter of fact." His voice sounded carefully noncommittal.

"I couldn't sleep, either." She hesitated, then said quickly, "Tommy, I'm sorry. I started that argument—it was my fault. Will you forgive me?'' She pictured him in the king-size bed, perhaps propped up on one elbow, his hair falling over his forehead. Her heart contracted.

''I was pushing too hard. I shouldn't have,'' he said.

''It's just that I've only been here a few weeks, and it's all happened so fast. I don't know what's right.''

''I've been trying my best not to rush you, but I'm so afraid of losing you a second time.''

She cradled the telephone against her cheek with both hands as if doing so could bring him closer. ''I was afraid of coming back here. I'm not ready to feel this way all over again. I don't know how to act.''

''I know you don't believe me, but I never stopped loving you, Julia. When I saw you again that first morning—you were standing there with a lamb in your arms—I knew I couldn't let you get away again.'' His voice was full of tenderness. ''And I guess I overdid things. But look, I want you to do what's right for you. If that should include me and Chipper, so much the better. But I'm not going to put any more pressure on you.''

''So I'm forgiven, then?'' she asked. ''Am I still invited to the show Friday night?''

''There's nothing to forgive. And yes, you're still invited.'' She heard his low chuckle. ''Chipper would really take it out on me if you didn't come.''

ON FRIDAY MORNING Julia called Gina Blakely.

''Will you be needing a story on the Easter program at the elementary school this evening?''

"Oh, boy. That's tonight, isn't it? And I'm rushed off my feet today. Electricians working on the wiring here and leaving everything in a mess. And I'm already a day behind schedule. I'll send someone to get a picture, but I'm not sure—"

"Could I write it?"

"Julia, you're really brightening my day. Of course you can. I'd be terribly grateful."

"I don't have a typewriter here, but I could bring my notes around and do it at the office tomorrow."

"Wonderful."

THE SETTING WAS the least romantic imaginable, Julia thought with amusement as they took their seats that evening in the gymnasium of Wiltonburg Elementary. Hard folding chairs were lined up under merciless overhead lights and the whole place smelled vaguely of sneakers. She sat wedged between Tommy and Fiona Vernon, and her toes were stepped on twice by latecomers pushing past.

At last the lights were lowered and the curtains parted on the small stage. Miss Willett, seated at the piano below, began thumping out "Here Comes Peter Cottontail," and Julia felt Tommy's hand move out to grasp hers. She gave him a reassuring smile and squeezed his hand, telling him silently that Chipper would be fine. But in that instant they were in it together, nervous and excited. And again the thought came to her that Chipper could have been hers. Tonight it almost seemed as if she were. There was applause at the sight of the scenery, and she leaned

toward Tommy to whisper, "The picket fence is out-
standing."

She saw his quick grin. He kept holding her hand
tightly as the Easter Bunny came on stage, followed by
several decorated walking eggs and an unmistakable
carrot. Julia heard Fiona's quick intake of breath.

The four of them watched without stirring as the
play moved forward with only minor mishaps. One of
the eggs was badly out of tune in a quartet, and the
Easter Bunny needed to be cued twice, but Chipper
said her line loudly and clearly, and had no trouble
managing her costume. By the final scene a chorus had
been added, and the stage was full. The curtain closed
to loud applause, and Fiona got a handkerchief out of
her bag and wiped her eyes.

"Lord, I hope I don't have to go through this again
anytime soon," she said.

"The costume was wonderful, Mrs. Vernon," Julia said.

"Fiona, please." She reached out to yank on her
husband's arm as Bill continued to clap loudly.

Early the next morning, Julia was at the *Courier*
office transferring her notes to a word processor.
Gina, when she'd read it, laughed delightedly. "Julia, it's perfect. I think you managed to say something nice about every single kid in the show. And it
has such a big-city sound. 'Charlotte Black gave a
sensitive interpretation of the carrot.... Frankie
Spelling showed real flair as the Easter Bunny.' I love
it." She opened a desk drawer and brought something out. "Sorry we aren't in a financial state that
allows payment, but you do get a present."

"Goodness, that's not necessary!"

She held out a print of the old newspaper photograph of Colin Doyle Julia had given her. "I told you my mother had the original. I made a print for you."

"Oh, Gina, you shouldn't have gone to so much trouble. But I'm very happy to have this."

Shortly after she got home Tommy called her. "You haven't forgotten about the dance tonight, I hope."

"No, of course not. Wiltonburg's social scene is keeping me a lot busier than New York's ever did," she said, and they both laughed.

Later, though, when she began to dress for the evening, she felt nervous and full of anxiety. She was experiencing the jitters of a teenager, something she'd missed the first time around. No one had ever called at this house to pick her up for a date. No one had ever taken her to a high school dance. Of course it wasn't that she'd never handled social situations—in New York she'd gone out with plenty of men. It was just that this chunk of her young life had always been missing.

She paused a moment, hairbrush in hand. She remembered telling Tommy the first night she met him that she'd never been to a party, and he hadn't believed her. Now, doing this slightly ridiculous thing—going to a dance in the high school gym—she was feeling giddy and girlish and totally unsophisticated. Would her dress be right? Would everyone be staring at her? How would she look to *him?*

She had pulled out a simple green silk dress, the only one she had with her, except for the flowered one she was saving for Gretchen's wedding next week. It had covered buttons from the round neck to the hem and a wide belt in the same fabric. She wore a heavy gold necklace with it and let her hair hang loose to her shoulders.

As soon as she opened the door to him, his face told her what he thought of her appearance. He gave a low whistle. "You look terrific. You may have to fight off Don Owen all over again."

"Don't tell me he's going to be there."

"I'm sure he will be. The dance is for the scholarship fund, and he never misses a chance for a little back-slapping in a good cause." Tommy was wearing a wide-stripe blue and white shirt, tan trousers and a navy blazer. She was all the more aware of his rugged good looks.

"You never picked me up at this house ten years ago," she said a little shyly.

"I know. You wouldn't let me."

"I didn't dare. Father Holtz was pretty terrifying."

He bent over to give her a light kiss. "Then we have a lot to make up for, don't we?" But his kiss was so quick and offhand it seemed an indication that he intended to keep his promise to not press her.

"What's this?" she asked as they started down the front steps toward a neat little red compact parked in the drive.

"It's Fiona's," he said. His hand on her back guided her lightly. She tried not to notice it. "Fiona says trucks are for guys. She didn't approve of my taking you to a dance in a pickup."

Julia had to laugh. As he opened the car door for her, she turned to him, and this time he hesitated only briefly before pulling her to him and kissing her again. Her arms came up to circle his neck and the kiss lingered briefly, but then he pulled away and waited for her to get in, closing the door behind her.

The Wiltonburg High School gym was larger than the one they'd been in the night before, and the lighting was carefully subdued for the occasion. Ferns, flowers and crepe-paper streamers softened the atmosphere, and music from a rather impressive sound system was already playing when they walked in. Tables were scattered around the rim of the gym, with plenty of space left in the middle for dancing, which several couples were already doing.

Tommy noticed Van and Gretchen waving from one of the tables, and he and Julia threaded their way past the dancers to join them. Van rose as they approached, and so did a tall lanky blond man who was sitting with them.

"Julia, Tommy, sit with us," Gretchen said. "You both remember my brother, Fred, don't you? Fred, you and Tommy were in school together, right?"

Fred Bauer nodded to Julia, and then he and Tommy got talking about old times. At one point, Rick's name was brought up, along with the famous quarter-mile race, another mutual memory.

"This thing tonight is going to be a lot like a class reunion, I suspect," Gretchen said. "I wish Rick could have come, too. Fred is now Dr. Frederick Bauer, by the way."

"Another doctor in the family?" Julia laughed. "You people are overachievers."

"Oh, Fred's a real doctor," Van said with a sidelong look at Gretchen, which prompted her to poke him. "A GP, in fact, with a practice over in King's Crossing."

It was hard to believe Fred and Gretchen were brother and sister, Julia thought, looking at them. Fred was long and spare and rawboned where Gretchen was small and compact. But they had the same quick friendliness, although Fred was a little on the shy side.

"On vacation?" she asked him.

"Came for the wedding, actually, but I decided to take a few days off to visit Mom, too, and start my annual harangue."

"About what?"

"How she needs to move to a more convenient house. Van's done wonders making this one better for her, but if she'd just let me contribute and get her settled in a small modern place, it would help her a lot now that she's getting older."

"I don't need to tell you this perfectly plausible argument is falling on deaf ears," Gretchen said.

Tommy leaned toward Julia, giving a nod across the gym. "What did I tell you? His Honor's already working the room."

Julia followed his gaze and saw Don Owen moving through the crowd, shaking hands. She guessed, by the ruddy look of his face and booming voice, that he might have had a few drinks earlier.

The gym was starting to fill up. Julia saw several faces that looked familiar, and a few people, passing by their table, recognized her and stopped to chat. All of them were cordial, and even those who hadn't been close friends of hers seemed pleased to see her again. One or two glanced curiously from her to Tommy, but no one remarked about their being together.

When the disk jockey put on a slow song, Tommy pushed back his chair and said, "How about it, Julia?" She smiled at him and got up to slide into his arms. Moving across the floor, he held her close, his cheek resting against her hair. She murmured, "We never did this before, either, did we?"

"No. It seems we missed out on a lot." His hand against her back moved in a slight caressing motion, and she let her head rest in the hollow of his neck, the place that was beginning to seem so right to her. With her eyes half-closed, she was content to follow his lead, moving dreamily to the music. When it was over and they returned to the table, Tommy went to the refreshment booth to get them both a cool drink. Fred Bauer had strolled away and found an old acquaintance. The music started again, and Van and Gretchen got up to dance.

Julia's glance moved around the room, picking out familiar faces. Mr. Dorn, the principal, looking much the same as he had when she was in high school; Miss Goodspeed, her old math teacher—

"Well! What's this? All by yourself, pretty lady?"

Julia's heart sank as she looked up to find Don Owen leaning solicitously over her. His face was shiny from the warmth of the room, and she could smell the liquor on his breath.

"Hello, Don." She managed a weak smile and tried not to recoil noticeably. "Isn't this a nice affair?"

"Well, maybe not up to your New York watering holes, but we manage." He gave a loud bark of laughter. "How about a dance, Miss Julia?"

"Oh, thanks, Don, but I just sat down to rest for a minute. Maybe later."

His arm slid around her shoulders. "You know you always were the best-looking girl in high school, even with those clothes the Holtzes made you wear."

She tried to wriggle out of his grasp, but the arm that held her shoulder tightened. "Don, really—"

"Want to know something? I even made sure you got a special invitation to that party at my house. Remember that party? Lot of good it did me, though. You never looked at anybody once you'd met Black." His mouth twisted unpleasantly. "C'mon. Why don't we have a little dance for old times' sake—"

"I don't think the lady wants to dance, Mr. Mayor." Tommy set the drinks on the table and turned to Don. His face was dark with anger, but Julia could see him holding it in, not wanting to make a scene.

Don released her, suddenly affable again, his public image back in place. "Julia and I were just having a little talk about the old times. Say, this is a good crowd here tonight. See you two later. Enjoy the evening now."

Tommy shook his head as he sat down. "Doing the same thing he used to do in high school. He leaves a bottle in the car and runs out every now and then for a nip."

"How'd he ever get elected mayor?"

"Surely you're not naive enough to think that kind of behavior disqualifies a person."

"Guess you're right." Julia took a sip of the ginger ale he'd brought.

"How are you enjoying the dance so far?" He placed his hand over hers on the table.

"It's fun. And I'm amazed at all the familiar faces, all the people I recognize. Hey, look, there's Gina Blakely, over there by the door. You know her, don't you?"

He followed her gaze to where Gina stood, tall and elegant in dark blue silk pants with a long matching tunic. A man, slightly shorter, was with her. He had a camera around his neck. "Sure, I've done some advertising with her. She's doing a good job on the paper."

Julia caught her eye, and Gina said a word to the man with her and then threaded her way through the dancers to their table.

"Hi. I hope we're not too late for the principal's little speech. Hank's going to get some pictures."

"Nobody's made any speeches yet except Don Owen," Tommy said, standing and holding out a chair for her. "He's working the room as usual."

"Oh, well, that's not really news, is it?" Gina sat and then said, "Hey, am I taking somebody's place here?"

Julia assured her she wasn't. As the dance ended, Van and Gretchen returned, and so did Fred Bauer, his hands stuffed in his pockets. He was the only one who didn't know Gina, so introductions were made.

"King's Crossing?" Gina said. "That's where your practice is? But that's where I'm from. My mom still lives there."

"Blakely? Not one of my patients, I'm afraid."

"No, she's Mrs. Doyle."

"Mrs. Doyle? Harriet Doyle?"

"That's her."

"Then I do know her."

"And you're *that* Dr. Bauer? She's mentioned you. She thinks you're great."

Gretchen's gaze swung to meet Julia's, and Julia caught the spark of amusement in it as shy Fred Bauer went on talking to gregarious Gina.

The next time Tommy and Julia got up to dance, he whispered, "That wasn't some deliberate matchmaking, was it? As I recall, Fred Bauer was always a little scared of girls."

"It wasn't deliberate, no." She smiled up at him. "But he doesn't seem scared of this one, does he?" Both of them glanced at Fred and Gina, who were also dancing, the two tallest people in the room.

A few minutes later it was time for the principal's speech. Mr. Dorn stood up and said a few words about the scholarship fund and how rewarding it was to see so many guests attending for a good cause. Hank, the *Courier* photographer, got his picture. Then there was more dancing, and finally Julia said to Tommy, "I think I'm about ready to leave. How about you? I keep farmer's hours these days."

"Anytime you say."

"Just let me stop at the ladies' room first."

"Remember where it is?"

"Good heavens, yes. You don't forget things like that."

She said her goodbyes to the others, then left and went out into the corridor, making a right turn and then another to locate the door with GIRLS written on it. This part of the school was quiet and deserted at the moment, but the sound of the music could be heard distantly. She hummed along with it as she repaired her makeup and hair, thinking of Tommy waiting for her, feeling her pulse throbbing pleasantly. She was still humming as she pushed open the door to the hall.

The second she stepped into the hall a hand shot out and grabbed her. She felt herself shoved against the wall. She let out a cry as the smell of liquor assaulted her, and then Don Owen was pressing himself against her, forcing a loose-lipped kiss on her.

As she struggled to free herself, he rasped, "You never did have time for me, did you? You might have had holes in your socks, but you always had that nose in the air when you were around me. Maybe you could make some time now, eh?"

Julia pushed with all her strength, and Don stumbled backward against the lockers where he slowly sagged to the floor. Julia heard footsteps pounding down the corridor and suddenly Tommy was there, putting his arm around her. "Are you all right? What happened?"

"I'm fine," Julia said, straightening her dress and taking a deep breath. "It's just Don up to his old tricks."

Tommy looked down at the mayor. "Go home and sober up, Don," he said. "Just be glad it was me who saw you like this and not some of your constituents. I never voted for you, anyway." He turned to Julia. "Are you sure you're all right?"

She nodded, but she was trembling all over, and he kept his arm around her as he led her out of the building. "That really came out of left field," she said in a shaky voice.

"You're not hurt?"

"No, of course not. I'm fine."

He helped her into the car. "I'm beginning to understand why Don's always disliked me so much."

"I didn't realize he had."

Tommy shrugged. "There's not much we see eye to eye on, but I always thought there might be a little more to it than that." He went around to the driver's side and got in. "Feeling okay now?"

"Of course."

He pulled her face close and kissed her softly, protectively. "Damn. I never did like these bucket seats." He released her and turned the key in the ignition. "Well, what did you think of your first dance at Wiltonburg High?"

"I can't say it wasn't eventful." She glanced at him, seeing the sharp chiseled line of his jaw lit by the glow from the dashboard. Desire for him was churning up a storm of emotions in her.

"If you'd ever gone to one ten years ago, chances are the same thing would've happened," he said, sounding amused. "I think Don must have always had the hots for you."

"Well, maybe it's a good thing I never did go to a dance back then." She kept her eyes on his hands as they rested lightly on the wheel, watching how effortlessly he drove through the night. Then he was turning in at her lane, parking the little red car near the front steps and walking with her to the door.

"Come in for a cold beer?" she asked.

He hesitated briefly. "Better not. Things have a way of—" He stopped and started again. "It's better if I don't."

She unlocked the door and turned to him. "I'd like you to," she said softly.

He acquiesced and followed her inside. She'd left a low light on in the living room, but the hallway where they stood was dim and shadowed. She turned to him, and his arms came around her in a slow, sensual movement, sliding over the smoothness of silk to rest low on her hips. She put her arms around his neck and raised her face to his. His lips touched hers tentatively, moving across them in a soft caress, then parting to taste them more fully. She felt herself yearning toward the kiss, opening herself to it, and to him. Her fingers moved up to tangle in his hair.

He pulled his mouth away from hers, but still held her close. "Julia. Darling Julia," he whispered.

She hadn't actually believed Rick when he'd said it would all come together for her. But now, suddenly, she knew it had, and the knowledge was a blinding revelation. Nothing else mattered. Nothing else had ever mattered. How many people had a second chance at a love like this?

She murmured his name and sought his mouth again. But slowly and carefully he released her and stepped back. "Let's give it a little time, Julia," he said. "I don't want you to be sorry again."

"You're thinking about those things I said the other day."

"You said them because you felt them. There's nothing wrong with that. But I want you to be sure this time."

"Oh, Tommy..."

But he took another step away from her, stopping only to push a strand of her hair back from her cheek. Then he opened the door and moved out into the soft spring night. She stood there in the darkness long after she heard the car leave.

CHAPTER ELEVEN

CHIPPER BOUNCED on the edge of the bed and regarded her father critically as he worked at tying his tie.

"How come you're wearing that dorky suit?" she asked.

He swiveled around to look at her. "What's the matter with it?"

She gave the dark blue suit another frowning perusal. "It's awful plain."

"It's supposed to be. This is a wedding. Calls for conservative dressing."

"What's that mean?"

He turned back to the mirror. "It means that weddings are serious affairs. You know, solemn. You're supposed to dress accordingly. Nothing flashy."

"I don't like that tie, either." She hopped off the bed and ran to his closet.

He sighed. "Well, I think you might have a point there. I can't seem to get it to look right." He undid the knot and tossed the tie onto the bureau.

"Here. How about this one?" Chipper returned with several ties clutched in her small hand. She held out a bright red foulard.

He frowned. "Too loud."

"Well, what about this?" She offered him a dark red in a regimental stripe.

"That might not be bad." He took it from her and she climbed back on the bed.

"Is Julia going to be dressed real plain, too?"

"I don't imagine so. The ladies at a wedding generally do the dressing up."

"Especially the bride," Chipper said.

"Yes, that's right."

"How come I don't get to go to it?"

He flipped one end of the tie over, making a knot. "Because it's a small wedding, and it's at home. Mrs. Bauer, Gretchen's mom, doesn't get around well, and they wanted to have it right there. But it isn't a very big house, that's all, so there won't be many guests."

"I don't take up much room," Chipper muttered.

"Anyway, aren't you doing something nice with Fiona and Bill?"

She nodded. "We're going to the drive-in movie. To see *Beauty and the Beast.*"

"That sounds pretty good to me."

"Mmm. But only if it doesn't rain. If it rains we're going to stay home and play poker, and Uncle Bill's going to make popcorn." She watched as he finished the knot and straightened it.

"Well, what do you think?"

She nodded. "That's a much better fashion statement," she said gravely.

He tried to hide a smile. Where had she picked *that* one up? "Thanks for your help, ma'am," he said in a cowboy drawl.

She surveyed him once more, then jumped down again and ran to hug him. "You don't look dorky, Daddy. You look handsome."

He leaned over to return the hug, his heart suddenly full, the way it often became with her. Unexpectedly, as if somebody had just handed him a gift.

"Okay, you'd better wash up and get ready. Those jeans have something on them—what is it?"

"Yellow paint, from a picture I was making. It had daffodils in it."

"Better put on a clean pair. I'll be ready in a few minutes. I have to make a phone call."

Chipper hurried off, still holding several neckties, then whirled around at the door and brought them back. He replaced them in the closet, then picked up the bedside phone and punched in a number. While he waited he glanced at his watch. There was still plenty of time to pick up Julia and drive to the Bauers'.

It took several rings before an answer came. "Hello?" It was slightly breathless, but he recognized his younger brother's voice at once.

"Hi, Randy, how's it going?"

"Oh, hi. Okay, I guess."

"I thought you might be out at baseball practice. Just get in?"

"Well, yeah, I just got in, but I wasn't at practice."

"Didn't you go out for baseball this year?"

"No."

Tommy tried to keep his tone upbeat, but the going was difficult. Seventeen-year-old Randy sounded bored, indifferent. "How come? You were doing great last season."

"Yeah, well, this year I got a job."

Tommy felt a moment's anxiety. "But you're still in school, aren't you?"

"Oh, sure. Louise has a fit if I talk about dropping out."

He decided not to lecture on that subject for the moment, trusting his sister to hold firm. "What's the job?"

"McCarthy's Shell station."

"Oh? Aren't those places pretty much self-service now?"

"Yeah, but some of the old ladies like full service, so I do that. Mostly I fix up cars. I've been taking a course in auto mechanics at school."

"Are you that good?" It surprised him somehow.

"Well . . ." Tommy could picture his brother's thin shoulders lifting in a shrug.

"Guess you're the one I should be talking to about one of my heavy-duty trucks, then. It's started to clank and lose power when it's loaded up."

"Probably should run a compression check on all the cylinders. Is it an old piece of equipment?"

"Pretty old, yes. Bill Vernon used it first."

"Well, might not even pay to fix it, then."

Tommy could hear a note of interest, but it quickly faded into silence. "How come you're home in the middle of the afternoon?"

"Just gonna have something to eat, then I have to go back. Saturday nights I close the place up late."

A wisp of worry blew across Tommy's mind. A young kid like that working alone on a Saturday night? How wise was that? "What made you decide to get a job?"

"I need the money."

"For something special?"

There was a moment's hesitation. "Yeah. I'm gonna buy a car. A guy I know's gonna sell me his."

A job was a good thing, wasn't it? Tommy's thoughts were scattering about rapidly. Working and saving for something he wanted, that couldn't hurt Randy, could it?

"Well. Sounds great. Everything else all right? How are Louise and Stan?"

"They're okay."

"Good. I'll get back there and see you soon."

"Okay." The indifferent voice on the line indicated Randy doubted this. After he'd hung up, Tommy stared at the telephone for a while, wondering if the call had accomplished anything.

It had started to rain softly when he left Chipper at the Vernons' house. Fiona pressed an oversize umbrella to his body. She looked disapprovingly at the pickup. "Take my car, why don't you?" she urged, and when he shook his head she scolded, "Then buy yourself one."

"This'll do fine." He grinned. "And thanks for letting Chipper stay over tonight."

Fiona waved her hand. "That's no chore. It's when she doesn't come that Bill and I start snapping at each other. We miss her."

He blew her a kiss and, getting in the truck, he placed the umbrella on the seat beside him.

The rain was coming down harder by the time he got to the farmhouse on Firebush Road. Julia came to the door wearing a raincoat over her dress and carrying her new shoes in her hand. On her feet were a pair of barn boots. She was laughing.

"I've been thinking all week how impressed you were going to be at the way I looked today."

"I'm impressed, anyway." He smiled down at her and gave her a quick kiss. Then she tucked her free hand under his arm and leaned close to him under the big umbrella. Feeling her body pressed to his, he realized, as he had all week, how much resolution it had taken for him to walk away from her that night after the dance. He wasn't sure he'd be able to do it again. But there were questions that kept coming up in his mind—disturbing questions. Had she made up her mind to take the job in New York? He'd be damned if he'd ask. He'd promised not to push her, and he wouldn't.

"At least we can be pretty sure of not running into Don Owen at this affair," she said as she climbed into the pickup.

"No danger of that." He grinned and went around to his own side and climbed in. "The less I see of him, the better."

"I have the feeling there's more to your dislike of Don than the rest of us know."

"Uh-uh." He turned the key in the ignition. "I guess I'm carrying a few old grudges. And I don't like his attitude toward you."

He saw her look quickly in his direction. Then she asked, "What kind of old grudges?"

The wipers cut half-moons through the rain that was gathering on the windshield as he turned the truck around and headed toward the county road. "Mostly unprovable stuff. Ever since he's been running things, I've had qualms about the contracts the town's awarded for municipal jobs—that kind of thing. I sure didn't get any of 'em, although I kept submitting good bids. But that fact makes it pretty hard for me to pose as a neutral party. I'd look as if I was just griping. Only I know some of the companies he's hired, and Bill Vernon's told me about others. One or two have been in trouble in other towns."

"Is Don taking kickbacks, you think?"

"Try to prove *that*."

"How'd he ever get elected?"

"Well, you know Don—the original glad-hand kid. He knows everyone around here by their first name. And the Owen family's lived here forever. Old loyalties count pretty heavily in small towns."

He changed the subject. "Chipper was sore because she wasn't invited to the wedding. She picked out my tie for me."

She laughed and moved a little closer to him on the seat. His heart started to hammer in his chest.

"I think the house is going to be pretty full as it is," she said. "There'll be both families and a few of Van's friends from the college, as well as Gretchen's staff at the library. Oh, and get this. Fred Bauer invited Gina Blakely."

"No! You swear you didn't set that up?"

"Absolutely not. But it's kind of nice, isn't it?"

He smiled down at her. Driving through town in the pouring rain, feeling her warmth beside him, listening to her voice, he felt happiness welling up in him, surrounding him like sunshine.

Only Van, Gretchen and Mrs. Bauer were there when they arrived. Gretchen greeted them at the door, radiant and bubbling in her yellow dress. As Tommy and Julia stamped off water on the front porch, Gretchen said mock-seriously, "Oh, is it raining? I hadn't noticed."

Julia leaned on Tommy as she put on her shoes. The simple intimacy excited him. *Careful,* he reminded himself. *It doesn't mean she's made some momentous decision. It could be just wedding-day happiness.*

Van, his ponytail skinned back neatly, looked like a stranger in his dark suit. He was smiling, but it was obvious he was a little nervous. Mrs. Bauer was out of her wheelchair today, looking elegant in a deep rose dress that complemented her white hair. "I'm certainly not going to sit in that thing to see my daughter married," she said crisply.

Julia slipped out of her raincoat in the front hall and said, "What can we do to help before the others get here?"

Tommy's breath caught in a small gasp as he saw her standing there in the spring-flowered dress, the fluffy white collar framing her face and rippling across her breasts. "Wow," he whispered, and was rewarded by her answering smile.

"I think everything's ready," Gretchen said. "Not that I'd know if it wasn't. I'm not quite tuned in to reality today. But the flowers are here and every-thing's ready in the dining room. We just have to pop the hors d'oeuvres in the microwave. Van's already taken care of chilling the champagne.''

Tommy glanced around the flower-filled house. Through the doorway he saw tall white candles ready to be lit. His eyes followed Julia as she moved through the house with Gretchen, her dress floating softly around her legs. Her hair was brushed loosely and fell to her shoulders.

"Here," Van said, interrupting his thoughts, which were escalating rapidly in sensuality. He handed Tommy a ring. "This is your job, friend."

The guests began arriving moments later. Fred Bauer and Gina were the first, followed by Van's parents, who had traveled from Ohio for the occasion. Several of Gretchen's library staff appeared and then some of Van's college associates, along with the two students who'd helped paint Julia's farmhouse. Um-brellas were parked on the porch and raincoats were shaken out. Then the minister, Reverend Simmons, arrived. With the house full to overflowing, Julia took the bride's bouquet out of its box and handed it to Gretchen. She and Tommy followed the bride and groom into the living room, where the minister helped them into the correct positions in front of the flower-bedecked mantel. Windy rain was gusting around the house.

"Dearly beloved..." Reverend Simmons began, and all the lights promptly went out. There was a murmur of dismay from the guests. Tommy moved quickly into the dining room and brought back the four tall tapers he'd seen on the table. He placed them on the mantel and lit them, and there was an audible sound of pleasure through the room as the whole scene was suddenly bathed in a soft trembling glow.

The minister smiled approvingly and began again. "Dearly beloved..."

Throughout the ceremony, Tommy's eyes kept returning to Julia, now holding the bridal bouquet for Gretchen. He produced the ring when it was called for, but again his eyes went to her, knowing she was listening to the solemn words just as he was. "With this ring I thee wed..."

He saw her violet-blue eyes turn to him as Van slipped the ring on Gretchen's finger, and something in the look seemed to speak more plainly than words. He wasn't mistaken, he told himself. He couldn't be. Not this time.

The minister pronounced the couple husband and wife, and as Van bent to kiss the bride, the lights came back on, causing a ripple of laughter and then spontaneous applause.

She hadn't thought the ceremony would affect her that way, Julia told herself as she moved among the guests moments later. She knew it would be an emotional experience—what wedding wasn't? But she hadn't been quite prepared for the jolt she felt at the sound of the familiar old words, and at the knowledge that Tommy was standing only a few feet away from her listening to every word. When their eyes met, she knew her feelings had been open to him. There wouldn't be any more sparring, at least not on her part. No more equivocating, no more stalling for time.

She'd made her decision, and she wasn't going to let her chance at happiness slip away again.

The knowledge produced a curiously calming effect. She felt contentment drop quietly around her shoulders like a soft warm coat. Everything would be all right. She and Tommy had found each other again.

She and Gina and Van's mother began warming hors d'oeuvres in the microwave, while Tommy and Van's father dealt with the champagne. There was laughter over the possibility that another power outage might blitz the microwave, but there was no sense of panic.

"We'll eat 'em cold," Mrs. Lightner said, and Julia liked her at once, just as she'd liked Van the first time she met him. Trays were passed and glasses filled. Van and Gretchen saw to it that Mrs. Bauer was comfortably settled on the couch. Then Tommy was tapping his glass for silence.

"I believe it's customary for the best man to propose the first toast," he said. All the talking stopped and everyone turned his way. Julia put down the tray she was carrying and picked up her glass. Her eyes were fixed on him.

"A toast to Gretchen and Van, the new Mr. and Mrs. Lightner, or Dr. and Dr. Lightner, if you want to split hairs. But I think Mr. and Mrs. is what they'd prefer today. It goes without saying that we wish them every good thing life has to offer, and we're all here today to present those wishes in person. And even if the wedding had been held in the Wiltonburg Municipal Auditorium, there wouldn't have been room enough for all the people who love them. Long life and happiness, Gretchen and Van."

His eyes went at once to Julia. She smiled at him and took a sip of wine before putting her glass down and starting around again with the tray.

"That was beautiful," she whispered when she reached him.

"Pretty ordinary, I'm afraid." He took an hors d'oeuvre, but his gaze stayed on her. "I dragged out every book in the house looking for a good quotation to use, but none of them seemed right. 'Marriage and hanging go by destiny,' for instance. I forget who said that."

Both of them laughed, and she said, "But don't forget, 'Marriages are made in heaven.' I think that's Tennyson. Anyway, it was a beautiful wedding. And you did a fine job as best man, running for the candles like you did. It made the whole thing nicer."

"Not the best honeymoon weather," he said, with a nod at the streaming windows.

"They won't care."

"No, I'm sure they won't."

Their eyes locked, caressing without touch.

"I'd better circulate," Julia said at last, motioning toward her tray.

After Van and Gretchen had lingered long enough to greet everyone and accept all the good wishes and kisses, they changed into more sensible clothes— slacks, boots and raincoats. They paused in the hall- way before leaving only long enough for Gretchen to toss her bridal bouquet, which was caught in a tall stretch by Gina Blakely. Julia and Tommy, standing next to each other, exchanged startled looks and then smiled.

"For a relationship no one expected to go anywhere, that one seems to be right on track," she whispered. He grinned back at her, nodding.

After another hour or so the guests began to straggle out. Julia and Tommy helped tidy up the house, and Fred and Gina stayed behind with Mrs. Bauer, keeping her company and making sure she was comfortable. Julia could see some signs of pain in the older woman's features, but her eyes were radiant with happiness.

"Wasn't it beautiful?" she kept saying. "You know, I'm glad those lights went out."

When at last Tommy and Julia got ready to leave, Fred was prescribing bed and a cup of tea for his mother, while Gina was fetching her medication. Tommy looked at Julia. "Are you as hungry as I am?" he asked as they headed out the door, once more bundled in raincoats.

"Starved. Champagne and munchies seemed to just work up an appetite."

"How about the De-lite Diner?"

"Perfect."

The wind was gusting harder as they parked in front of the diner, and Tommy opened Fiona's big umbrella and came around to help Julia out. But as she stepped toward the curb, holding his arm, her foot slipped and went into the streaming gutter. She let out a little cry of dismay, while at the same moment the wind yanked the umbrella inside out.

"Forget this," he muttered, lifting her almost bodily back into the pickup. "We'll go to my house. At least you can warm your feet by the fire. How's that sound?"

"Heavenly. But you said you were hungry."

"I can cook, remember?"

She was suddenly chilled to the bone and shivering. Water was running down her neck and her hair was plastered flat. She remembered the big living room and the crackle of the fire the night they'd all had dinner there.

"Sounds wonderful," she said. It sounded more than wonderful. It sounded exciting and tempting and slightly dangerous, but today she didn't care.

He parked as close as he could to the front door, and they made a run for it, holding hands. Even so, they were drenched before they got inside. He looked her over. "I'm not sure just sitting close to the fire's going to do it," he said doubtfully, regarding her sodden shoes, soaked-through raincoat and dripping hair. "Why don't you give me a minute to put on something dry? Then while I start dinner, you can take a hot shower. I'll give you something dry to put on."

She nodded, removing her coat and shoes and following him in her stocking feet as he went to light the fire already laid in the fireplace.

"Be back in a second," he promised, taking the stairs two at a time.

Julia stood close to the fire, watching it catch and curl around the logs, yearning toward its warmth. In moments Tommy was back at the head of the stairs, calling down to her.

"Come on up. I'll show you where things are." He was in a pair of fresh jeans and a sweatshirt, and his hair was mussed as if from toweling. She went up the stairs and followed him down the hall to his room.

"There's the bathroom through there. Just help yourself to everything. I put a fresh towel out. My clothes would be pretty big for you, but there's a robe on the back of the door that'll probably go around you two or three times. It'll be good and warm."

"Okay. Thanks." Her teeth were still chattering, but now she was not sure whether it was from the cold or from being in his room where everything seemed so intimately his. "I won't be long," she said.

The flowered dress was hanging limply. After he'd gone downstairs Julia went into the bathroom and took it off, wet panty hose following. Then, in bra and panties, she stood for a moment looking around at the bathroom. It was so thoroughly masculine—dark blue mat and towels, off-white tile, a handsome pedestal sink with his shaving things above it on a shelf. Julia ran her finger over the razor's handle. Then she finished undressing and stepped into the roomy stall shower, letting the hot needles of water refresh and warm her.

The towel he'd laid out for her was an enormous navy blue one, big enough to wrap herself in completely. She rubbed her hair, too, getting it almost dry, then slipped into the dark red terry-cloth robe she found hanging on the back of the door. It hung to her ankles and did indeed go around her almost twice, but it was soft and warm and smelled faintly of Tommy. She held up one lapel and buried her nose in it.

She had nothing to put on her feet, so she tiptoed out into the hall and called down, "May I borrow a pair of socks?"

"Oh, sure. Sorry I didn't think of it." He looked up at her from the open kitchen where he was making something to eat. "They're in the bureau drawer—the upper right one. Take anything you want." His eyes lingered on her. "Everything okay?"

"Yes. The shower felt wonderful. I'll be right down."

She went to his room and opened the upper right drawer carefully. The socks were neatly arranged. She longed to look in the other drawers to see if they were similarly tidy, but she refrained, not wanting to pry. The top of the bureau was clean and bare except for a picture of Chipper when she must have been two or so. Julia took a pair of heavy dark blue cotton socks and closed the drawer.

When she came back downstairs, feeling slightly foolish, she saw him grin.

"Fetching," he said. "Absolutely fetching. As Chipper would say, now *that's* a fashion statement."

She grinned. "Anything for me to do?"

"Not a thing. Besides, you'd be apt to trip over your socks. Are you thawed out enough for some chilled white wine, or would hot coffee suit you better?"

"Wine would be lovely."

She moved to sit in front of the fire and he brought her a glass. "Dinner'll be ready in a couple of minutes."

"I don't feel very useful."

"Highly decorative, though. Actually, it's going to be pretty simple. Just an omelet and salad." He went back to the kitchen and began beating eggs with a whisk. Julia sipped the wine, watching the fire dreamily. Finally, warmed through at last, she removed the socks and stretched her bare toes toward the heat.

"It was a great wedding, wasn't it?" she said. "A little unorthodox, but all the better for it."

Something sizzled in a pan. "I thought so. You wouldn't expect those two to do anything in an ordinary way, anyhow. Do you know where they've gone?"

"To the Poconos, I think. But just for the weekend. Fred's leaving tomorrow, and Van and Gretchen will be back the next day." Julia was beginning to feel a warmth that had nothing to do with the firelight or the wine. Her heart was behaving in an erratic way. "I bet they wouldn't have gone on a honeymoon at all if Mrs. Bauer hadn't talked them into it."

She stole a look at him where he stood behind the tall counter, concentrating on the business of cooking. His hands were out of sight, but she could guess what he was doing by the sounds. Silver clinking against a bowl—he must be tossing the salad. And the unmistakable crunch of a French loaf being sliced. She pictured his hands doing those things, saw in her mind the long square-tipped fingers. In a moment he appeared, setting up a low table by the fire. The larger table where they'd sat the last time had been moved to its proper place in the now-finished dining room.

"What happened to the socks?" he demanded at the sight of her bare feet.

"My feet have thawed out."

"Well, I hate to tell you, but taking them off detracts considerably from the outfit's sexiness."

"Does that mean I'm safe, after all?"

"Oh, I might not go that far," he said, and Julia felt her pulse start racing again. Something was making them easy with each other tonight, letting them tease in a way they hadn't been able to manage before. Yet behind the teasing was a thin thread of seriousness, a consciousness she knew both of them were aware of.

"Okay, here it comes," he said, and went back to the kitchen. When he returned, he was carrying a tray with two filled plates, the salad bowl and a basket of bread. He poured more wine for both of them.

"This looks wonderful," she said. The omelet was golden brown, smelling faintly of mushrooms and green onions. "I can't believe you're such a good cook."

"Just one of my many accomplishments."

They ate hungrily, talked again about the wedding and laughed together over everything and nothing. Outside, the rain continued, lashing against the windows in a way that doubled the comfort and intimacy of the inside. When they'd cleaned up the last crumbs, Julia insisted on helping, carrying dishes back to the kitchen while Tommy made coffee. Then they sat together by the fire, which had burned lower now. They held their steaming mugs and leaned close to each other.

"That was absolutely delicious," she said dreamily. "Everything about today was delicious."

"Including stepping in that gutter on Main Street?"

"If I hadn't stepped in it, you wouldn't have invited me here."

"I might have. I'd have had to work a little harder to find an excuse, that's all."

She put her mug down on the table and met his gaze. "You wouldn't have needed an excuse."

She saw the muscle in his cheek flex.

"I wouldn't?" He put his mug beside hers.

Suddenly her breath deserted her. She whispered, "I'm not going back to New York, Tommy."

He studied her face in disbelief. He seemed unsure of what she was saying. "You mean you've made up your mind?"

She nodded slowly. "I've already called Bud Winter and turned down the job. My landlord will ship my things and rent my apartment." She paused, looking up at him. "I can't bear to think about leaving you again."

She saw the sudden joy flood his features. He took her face in both hands and bent to kiss her, brushing her lips with his tongue until she opened her mouth to his kiss.

When they pulled apart, she murmured, "And I want to hear all those things you've been trying to tell me. Everything I was too stubborn to listen to before." She paused and let her glance move lightly past him, up to the balcony where his room was. "Only not tonight."

THEY WERE TEN YEARS older, their bodies tense with the stored longing of those years. Nothing that had happened since the days of their first love had filled the special places left empty by their separation. Julia could feel it in herself; she could sense it in him.

"How could we have stayed away from each other all this time?" he murmured as he pushed aside the robe and kissed her shoulder. The robe fell to the floor. He turned on a night-light and pulled her into the bed beside him. And suddenly all the empty places, all the dry beds of wanting began to fill up as they discovered each other again. His eyes feasted on her body and his fingers cupped her breasts.

"There was never anyone but you, Julia," he said hoarsely.

"For me, either. Only you, Tommy." Her breath came in gasps as she kissed him wildly, then held his head against her breasts, rediscovering the lost magic of their youth, now doubly precious because it had been so unexpectedly regained.

CHAPTER TWELVE

SHE AWOKE to the sound of rain still lashing the windows, but it was a slow waking, full of luxurious warmth that made her snuggle deeper under the covers. Then her eyes flew open as memory struck and happiness flooded over her. This was the way it was going to be, she thought, suddenly aware of a future she hadn't dared contemplate before. This was what all her mornings would be like—waking up in this bed with the impression of his head on the pillow beside her. Why had she agonized for so long over such a simple decision?

She looked at his side of the big bed—empty now, but she could hear him moving around somewhere in the house. Moments later he pushed open the door. He was wearing the dark red robe, and there was a mug of fragrant coffee in each hand.

"I borrowed it back," he apologized, glancing down at the robe. "I admit it did look better on you. Actually, I think I like you this way best of all." He sat down on the bed beside her and his eyes swept over her as she struggled to sit up, yanking the covers over herself inadequately. He handed her one of the mugs and she took a sip.

"Delicious," she murmured.

"My sentiments exactly." His eyes were still on her.

"You know what I was just thinking?" She smiled at him.

"Same as me, I hope."

"Probably. But I was also thinking how we complicate simple things. Why did it take us so long?"

"Us?" He gave her a lopsided grin.

"Well, all right, me."

"Doesn't matter, does it?" He put his mug on the bedside table. She put hers beside it and reached up to him with both arms. "This is how it all turned out. Good enough for me."

She giggled as he slid under the covers beside her.

Later she dozed again, and when she awoke he was standing by the window looking out.

"What is it?"

He turned to smile at her, and she thought how that special smile would be for her from now on. But she sensed his concern, too.

"Are you worried about it? The rain?"

"Not worried exactly. Not yet. I'm starting to give it some thought, though."

"I should dress and go home. Chipper'll be coming back. Mind if I use the shower again?"

"Help yourself."

Once, over the sound of the shower, she thought she heard the telephone ring. And sure enough, when she came out he was talking to someone. She'd put on her clothes from the day before, dry now but somewhat wrinkled, and was about to make a funny comment about her appearance when she saw his face. It was creased in a worried frown.

"All night?" he was saying into the receiver. "Have you talked to him?" He paused. Julia could hear the voice, but not the words on the other end. "What about a lawyer?" Another pause. "No, I'm glad you called me first. And, anyway, it's Sunday, you might not..." He glanced toward Julia. Anxiety darkened his brown eyes. "All right. Just sit tight and try not to worry, Lou. I'll be there as soon as I can. Are the roads okay down your way? We're having a hell of a storm... No, don't worry, I'll be all right."

He hung up and turned to Julia. "It's my kid brother, Randy," he said without preamble.

"What's happened?"

"That was my sister, Louise. She lives in Goldmont—it's southeast of Morgantown. Randy moved in with her when Mom died three years ago. He's been working in a gas station there. Last night he stole money from the register. There doesn't seem to be much doubt about it—they found it on him. So, they held him in jail overnight."

"Oh, no," Julia breathed.

"I have to go there."

"Yes, of course." She glanced nervously at the window, streaming with rain. He caught the look.

"I know. It's not the best day for travel. But my truck's a four-wheel drive. It'll go through just about anything."

"Call me if you can."

"I will." He returned to the telephone and made a call. "Fiona? I need a little more help, I'm afraid. Can Chipper stay with you a while longer?... What?... Oh yes, it was great. Everything was wonderful." His eyes sought Julia's and his hand reached for hers. "But I have to drive to Louise's. There's been some trouble with Randy. I'll tell you all about it when I get back. Is Bill there? He's probably been listening to the road reports... No? Where did he... Oh, Lord, I hope he doesn't start heaving sandbags around and throw his back out. All right, tell Chipper I'll give her a full report on the wedding when I get back."

"Bill's gone down to the embankment in town with some of the other men," he said to Julia when he hung up. "He never did think it was built right."

"You get ready," she said quickly. "I'll make you some breakfast." Even in this crisis she was comforted by the warmth of their being together, the decision they'd made last night without words. He pulled her against him and held her tightly for a moment, then released her and headed for the shower.

"Just toast," he called through the open door. "I'd better get going. Turn on the radio, will you? Maybe they're giving weather and road reports."

She longed to cling to him for a few precious minutes when he took her home, but not for the world would she have delayed him when she knew he had so much on his mind. So she gave him a quick kiss and hopped out of the pickup into the rain, stopping on the porch to turn and wave. She gave no last warnings about driving carefully, no reminders of how much she would worry about him, no urging him to hurry back. There was no need. The last twelve hours had made all these things understood.

She hurried upstairs to change into jeans and her warm red sweater, for the gentle spring weather had been transformed by the storm into bone-chilling damp. She flipped the thermostat up a notch and then went into the kitchen to brew fresh coffee and confront the last two cartons from the attic. Today was definitely the day to dispose of them. All the bitterness of the past held no power to touch her now. She'd just lifted the first one onto the table when the phone rang. She hurried out to the front hall to answer it.

"Dan Westfall, Julia." The real-estate agent sounded cheerful despite the day. "I know this is the worst time you could imagine for showing the house, but I happen to have a Mr. and Mrs. Sutton here, who've been traveling through this part of the state looking at country property. They're held up in Wiltonburg because of the storm. I told them about your house, and they're interested in seeing it. Would that be possible?"

Nothing was impossible today, Julia knew with soaring heart. "Sure, why not?" she said cheerfully. "They'll be seeing it under pretty terrible conditions, but maybe that's the best way, after all."

After she'd hung up she hurried through the house turning on lamps and patting pillows. She felt a sense of pride at what she and Van and the others had done to transform the dingy old place and bring it to life. Mrs. Bauer's red-and-white quilt was a splash of color in the bedroom, and the yellow of the kitchen walls was as sunny as a June morning.

On a more practical note, she'd be able to point out how well situated the house was on a gentle slope, and how its lower reaches were well drained, thanks to Tommy's engineering skill. Her thoughts darted to him as she felt a moment's anxiety, wondering where he was right now and what lay ahead of him when he reached his family. Then Dan Westfall's sensible Dodge with his company logo on the door was splashing up the lane, and she stepped onto the front porch to welcome the newcomers.

The Suttons—Ralph and Carol, as they insisted on being introduced—were a lively couple in their thirties. Both were lawyers in Pittsburgh and wanted a vacation home in the area. He was tall, lanky and balding. She was small and dark-haired and full of energy. Julia sensed at once that they liked the house. The fact that all the furniture would come with it seemed to please Carol.

"We could move right in," she said enthusiastically.

Julia felt the need to explain that there was still a short wait before the property could be legally sold, but Dan Westfall said his brother, Howard, had assured him it wouldn't be too much longer before the will cleared probate.

When Carol admired the red-and-white quilt, Julia had to tell her that it was a personal possession and as such wouldn't be included in the sale. Carol's face fell, but at once she rallied and said she'd have fun going to country auctions in search of another one.

Ralph poked about, looking at the furnace and inspecting the attic, then inquired about what sort of farm it had been and what, if anything, it still produced.

"Sheep," Julia said.

Carol's face grew soft. "Oh, how sweet," she murmured, and Julia could tell she was picturing frisky lambs and a green hillside dotted with grazing animals. No knowledge, of course, of ticks and internal parasites to be treated. No vision of the breech birth of a lamb on a cold March night.

"The sheep don't come with the farm," Julia said suddenly, and then as the three of them looked at her in surprise, she explained, "I've made other arrangements for them." Why had she said that? What made her sure in that moment that the sheep would stay with her?

"Oh, well, we are just looking for a vacation home, and sheep are no doubt more than we'd want to take on, anyway," Ralph said, and Carol nodded sadly.

Julia gave them all coffee as they discussed price and such practical matters as heating and the state of the plumbing, none of which seemed daunting to the enthusiastic Suttons. They agreed to keep in touch, and Julia said they were welcome to come back any time for another look.

She watched from the front porch as Dan's car left, its tires throwing off angry spurts of water. Then she went back inside, leaving the lights on throughout the house to counteract the gloom of the day. She returned to the kitchen and at last plunged into the contents of the last two boxes from the attic. The familiar musty odor greeted her, but this time it had no power to send her into a tailspin of bleak memories. She even found herself humming softly as she lifted out brittle envelopes and scraps of paper—household notations and reminders, even scriptural references in Gideon's handwriting. "See Second Corinthians for Paul's gratification in penitence and the cleansing of flesh and spirit..."

She was surprised to see several envelopes addressed to Elizabeth Holtz in Julia's own handwriting. They'd been sent during her time spent with the woman she'd called Aunt Delia. She opened some of them and scanned them briefly. Dutiful short letters without warmth or any real affection. She was almost surprised Elizabeth had saved them.

Then came a letter from Delia. "I daresay your plan is sensible, to send the girl away for her education. If she proves to be as clever as you think her, perhaps she will make something of herself. I do caution you, Elizabeth, not to let your foolish fondness for the girl get the better of your good judgment..."

Julia paused in her reading. *Foolish fondness?* She pulled out another letter. "There is no need to put yourself out about the money, sister. I have enough for my needs, and I know how closefisted Gideon is with a dollar. Anyway, I would have to pay a housekeeper if the girl weren't here, and she seems to know what she's about, I will admit."

There were a few more similar messages from Delia, then one that jumped out at her. "I believe you were wise to insist that the young man give her up. As long as he is willing to do so, it will be far better for her. Of course I do agree that it would be entirely wrong for them to see each other again at this point— all kinds of mischief might result. Let her stay with me over the summer holidays. I will need someone,

anyway, as my condition requires constant attendance..."

Julia felt herself starting to tremble. Suddenly she
was seventeen again, lonely and afraid, in a house that
was more substantial than this one, but musty with the
smells of liniment and wintergreen throat lozenges.
Silent except for the querulous voice that summoned
her at all hours of the day and night. Weeks marched
by, then months, all punctuated by those daily trips to
the mailbox where there was never a letter. Then she
was eighteen—although the birthday went unnoticed
by anyone but her. No, there had been a small prim
card from Elizabeth Holtz with a dollar bill folded inside. She remembered it, because she'd never received
another one. For that year she scandalized them all by
marrying Bryce Farnsworth, and contact between her
and her adoptive family was severed for good.

It all rushed back now, even the sad regretful
months of that brief marriage, along with the admis-
sion that she had done something foolishly impulsive
and that it had affected someone else's life, as well.
Bryce's chief reaction seemed to be astonishment that
someone found him less than irresistible. After that
had come the divorce and then lean times, when she
had to scrape money together to pay rent and eat, and
finish her education. Rick had helped, and she'd made
it by waitressing, working in the campus bookstore,
even baby-sitting.

She sank down into a chair at the kitchen table, still
holding Delia's letter in her hand. So this, at long last,
was the reason for it all. This was what Tommy had
wanted to explain to her. Elizabeth Holtz must have

gone to him and made him promise to give her up. And more than that, he had undoubtedly agreed not to write or otherwise communicate with her. That had been crucial if a real wedge was to have been forced between them, of course, she reflected coldly. She pictured her stiff unbending adoptive mother, speaking authoritatively as she convinced Tommy of the wisdom of this course.

And perhaps by that time, Tommy, looking forward to his senior year in college, had probably taken very little convincing. No doubt he'd been only too glad to give up a relationship that had been, after all, only a summer romance and that showed signs of becoming uncomfortably entangling. Julia remembered that last night by the lake, with moonlight silvering the water. She heard their voices making promises as they responded to the demands of their young bodies....

Something began boiling up inside her. For a moment she sat quite still, trying to control her anger, trying to tell herself that all this happened a long time ago and that it had no connection with today or with last night. She and Tommy were not those impulsive kids anymore. They were two different people, grown and matured and presumably wiser—certainly more responsible. Yet the ferment inside her kept rising, bubbling toward the surface until she had to recognize it. It was the same old story. The same pattern reemerging as it had done since her earliest memories.

Someone else had taken charge. Someone else had made the decisions about what was right for her—for *her* life. She'd been shoved into the orphanage, then into foster homes. She'd been sent to the Holtzes, adopted by them without ever being consulted about her wishes. And when she'd at last found the one thing she wanted, the one person she'd thought was truly hers, he had been cruelly snatched away from her as once again others made the decisions for her. Only this time the final decision had been his.

She realized the telephone was ringing. She put down the letter and went into the front hall to answer it.

"Julia? Are you okay up there?" A woman's voice. Julia couldn't place it at once. "Julia? It's me, Suzanne."

"Suzanne! Oh, gosh, I am sorry. Sure, I'm okay. A bit damp, that's all."

She heard the small flurry of the telephone changing hands.

"Jule?" The voice was Rick's. "We've been sitting here with the Sunday papers, and they're full of stories about flooding in western Pennsylvania. Sure everything's all right?"

"Goodness yes. Tell Suzanne I apologize for not recognizing her voice."

She heard him relaying the message. "She's considering it," Rick said, a grin in his voice.

She had a moment's image of Rick and Suzanne sharing the warm intimacy of a Sunday morning with newspapers scattered around them, taking time out to comment and read passages aloud to each other. Immediately she scolded herself for envying someone else's happiness, especially these two who meant so much to her.

"We were worried about you," Rick was saying.

"Worried?" Julia tried to focus on what her brother was saying.

"The flooding. What's it like there? What about the new drainage in the pasture?"

"Oh, it's fine. No problems there . . ."

"Jule? What is it? You sound funny."

Julia's mouth felt dry. Could Rick have known what happened ten years ago? Again, disloyalty gnawed at her.

"I've been going over the last of those cartons from the attic."

"More receipts from those rummage sales?" She could still picture his smile, but suddenly he seemed to sense her mood. "Jule, what's wrong? What did you find?"

The letter was still in her hand. "Listen to this. It's a letter from Aunt Delia to Mother Holtz." She read it to him, then paused. For a moment the empty line hummed between them. At last Rick spoke.

"Oh, my God. Is that what—"

"You didn't know about it?"

"I'm afraid I didn't know about anything that was going on back then. I was so anxious to get away and so pleased with myself for managing it. I wanted to forget about life in Wiltonburg. When I heard you were going to Aunt Delia's, I suppose I talked myself into thinking you felt the same way."

"Oh, Rick. Of course you didn't know anything about it. I know that. It's just that I have an awful feeling that I may have made the same mistake again."

"What are you talking about?"

She was talking about last night. She was talking about loving Tommy all over again, about feeling his arms around her in the night, about feeling safe.

"I told Tommy I wasn't going back to New York. But I don't see how I can trust him now. He's hidden the truth from me for ten years." But he *had* tried to tell her, hadn't he? "Am I being completely unreasonable, Rick?"

He hesitated. "Honest opinion, Jule? Yes, you are. You're ten years older and so is he. Are you the same person you were ten years ago?"

She remembered Gina's sensible voice asking her the same question.

"But why would he do it if he cared for me?"

"Maybe that's why. I don't know what Mother Holtz's arguments were. Only Tommy knows that. I think you should talk to him."

"You're probably right, Rick. But I've got to sort out my own feelings first."

"That's fine, Jule. But I saw the way he looked at you the weekend I was there. He's a man in love if I ever saw one."

"Well, you should certainly know that," she said, forcing cheerfulness into her voice. "I didn't mean to lay all this on you. Apologize to Suzanne for me and I'll call you soon."

When she hung up, the little house that had seemed so cheerful when she showed it to the Suttons suddenly began to close in on her. All its brightness disappeared, replaced by the cold ugliness of ten years ago. Drab linoleum, bleak gray kitchen, cold parlor and colder bedroom. She grabbed her raincoat from its hook near the door, shoved her feet into her high rubber boots and ran out of the house.

The lane was muddy, and rain pelted her face as she splashed toward the barn. Lizzie, dry and lazy at the corner of the front porch, roused herself long enough to peer after her before making the sensible decision to stay put.

At the barn, under a generous overhang, the sheep were huddled, protected from the worst of the storm. It was near this spot that Tommy had stood that morning. She'd been holding a lamb and had looked up suddenly to see his unexpected silhouette against the sunlight. She'd known in that moment that she'd never stopped loving him. Yet he'd been able to turn his back on her and forget her at the urging of a woman whose motives were undoubtedly self-serving, a woman who'd never shown her any scrap of affection. Were men and women so different, then? She wouldn't have thought so once, Julia reflected bitterly, but she could never have turned away from *him* that way.

She slipped into the barn for a moment to escape the cold and rain. But almost at once memory came rushing at her. This was where Chipper had fallen from the ladder. Her screams had brought that stricken look to Tommy's face, and his long strides had covered the distance to the barn in seconds. She recalled his quiet grim concern as they sped to the hospital emergency room. Then his arms had been around her as they'd stood there in the corridor and the young doctor had called her Mrs. Black, assuring her that her little girl would be fine.

Julia drew a deep breath and stepped out into the storm again, headed back toward the house. And it was at that moment, with the rain pelting her face and her boots squelching through the mud, that a fresh thought came to her. Self-absorbed as she'd been all morning with her own concerns, she'd been too blind to look around her and see what was really happening. This was no ordinary spring rain, the kind that brought flowers and vegetable gardens into flourishing growth. This was a relentless storm, an enormous force of nature, one that made tons of melting snow roar down from the higher elevations. In only two days it had men like Bill Vernon down at the embankment anxiously watching the rising water. Who could tell what problems it was posing for Tommy headed straight for the mountainous parts of West Virginia?

Time to take stock, she told herself sensibly. What needed to be attended to first?

Lizzie's anxious face peering through the porch railing gave her the first clue. Supplies. She should get a twenty-five-pound bag of dog food, cans of tuna and boxes of macaroni, as well as dried milk and canned juices—things that could be stored in case power was lost. The house was on high ground. Neighbors or townspeople might need to be taken in. The big new supermarket on the way into town would be open all day. She dashed into the house for her handbag and then ran to the car.

Like most nineteenth-century towns located near waterways, Wiltonburg's old section had been built close to the river, its lifeline and source of commerce. Farther back, however, the newer houses and businesses fanned outward and up the gentle slopes that framed the old business section in a kind of bowl. The main danger would be down below. But the Bauers' house was there, among many others. Julia was glad that Fred Bauer was staying to see that his mother was safe.

The supermarket was just at the crest of the sloping street headed down into the business section. Although its huge parking lot was streaming with water, it was obviously well-drained and would offer safety to anyone coming to replenish supplies. Already a few forward-looking customers were on hand, but they were nothing, Julia guessed, compared to the crowds who'd be converging on the place later in the day. And by that time, she thought ominously, it might be the only dry spot in town.

She parked and dashed, head down, into the store. Grabbing a cart, she headed recklessly up one aisle and down the other. Bottled water might be important, she thought, seizing several gallon jugs of it, then headed for the canned goods, where she picked up soups, corned-beef hash and vegetables. Then she wheeled to the pet-food aisle for Lizzie's kibble. She was just making for the dried milk when she almost crashed head-on into another cart propelled by a tall lanky blond man.

"Fred!" She stopped in surprise. "We must have had the same idea. Is everything all right at your mother's?"

Fred Bauer smiled, but Julia could read concern there. "All right so far," he said. "Although I don't like the look of that water. It's running in the streets now. But the worst of it is, they've been calling me from King's Crossing. There's no other doctor there, and of course you know Mom. She says I have to get back to my post, that she'll be fine and all the rest of it. Well, Gina and I have talked it over."

In spite of his grave expression, Julia saw the faint blush in his cheeks at the mention of Gina's name. "Gina says she'll stay right on top of things and will see that Mom gets out of there at the first sign of danger. I know I can trust her to do it."

"Fred, you can count on me, too," Julia said. "I'll be in touch with Gina, and if any rescue's in order, Mrs. Bauer can come to my house. I'm on high ground. It wouldn't surprise me if a few others wound up there, too. Actually, that's why I'm doing all this shopping right now."

She could almost see the anxiety draining out of him with the great sigh he exhaled. "Gosh, Julia, that would be terrific of you. Takes a load off my mind. And, of course, all this may not even be necessary. This old river's scared us more than once. It may be doing it again."

"Of course," Julia agreed. "That's entirely possible." But in her heart, she knew it wasn't just another scare. This was the real thing. As bad as the storm was, it was getting worse. She'd read real anxiety in Tommy's face earlier. Bill Vernon, who knew the town and the river better than anyone, was pacing and worrying down at the embankment.

Julia felt a knot of anxiety curling inside her.

She phoned Gina the minute she arrived home, giving her the same reassurances she'd given Fred. She told her she'd be standing by and that Gina was to call at once if matters worsened. Under no circumstances was she to hesitate until things reached a pass where there might be danger to Mrs. Bauer. Both women seemed to realize that the old lady would want to stay in her house if at all possible, but if the need arose they wouldn't hesitate to carry her out bodily. There was some discussion of whether Van and Gretchen would be able to make it back as planned, and both agreed not to count on it.

When she hung up, Julia set about putting away all the groceries. A bedraggled Lizzie was invited into the kitchen, and Julia made one more trip to the barn to make sure there was plenty of feed for the lambs and their mothers.

Realizing she hadn't eaten since breakfast, she made herself a sandwich, then started a routine of pacing, in and out of rooms, up and down the stairs. She would put Mrs. Bauer in the downstairs bedroom if she came here. Right now she herself had no longing for bed or sleep. Instead, she stayed in her sweatshirt and jeans and stretched out on the stiff living-room couch, yanking the old Amish quilt over her for protection from the chill. Lizzie crept in from the kitchen and lay beside her on the floor, and from time to time Julia reached down and buried a hand in the dog's thick fur for reassurance. Eventually she fell into a restless sleep.

CHAPTER THIRTEEN

"I'M TAKING HIM back with me." Tommy gripped the wheel and leaned forward, peering through the streaming windshield that was hardly affected by the wipers.

"Tommy, that's not necessary," Louise protested. "I mean, this is the first time there's been anything..."

He took one hand off the wheel to reach for hers. "Never mind. You and Stan have your own three kids to raise. Just sending money doesn't take care of Randy. He should be with me."

Tommy glanced at the two of them seated beside him on the front seat of the pickup. Louise, thin and work-worn, looked older than thirty-five. Beside her, an arm protectively around her, sat Stan Bronsky, her husband, a muscular man with powerful hands—once a miner, now a factory worker. Salt of the earth, both of them, Tommy thought, wishing he could come up with a description that wasn't a cliché.

"Tommy, it hasn't been easy for you, either. You've had Chipper to raise all by yourself."

"I've had plenty of help from the Vernons. And that's another reason I should be responsible for Randy. When I needed help they were there for me.

It's my turn to pass it along. You shouldn't have to do it all.''

Stan made a rumbling noise in his throat and said that wasn't an issue. They'd always treated Randy like one of their own. If they'd just known what was in the kid's head they might have headed off this business of the theft. ''But it looks like the station owner isn't going to press charges, from what the sheriff said—as long as he gets his money back.''

''The kid's luckier than he deserves,'' Tommy muttered. In the back of his mind he couldn't help wondering what all this would do to the plans he and Julia had made—without words—on Saturday night. An unruly seventeen-year-old being shoved into their lives at the very moment they'd rediscovered each other wasn't the most promising augury for the future. But it had to be done. At one time he himself had been as irritating, sullen and resentful as Randy, he supposed. And someone had cared enough to grab hold of him and not let go. Now it was his turn. And if he knew anything at all about Julia, she'd understand. She had to. If there was one thing he couldn't face in this life, it was losing her a second time.

The Goldmont sheriff's office was like those in any small town. There was a plain wooden counter, a coffeemaker with paper cups, a bulletin board bearing notices and pictures tacked up with one pin. The sheriff, a sturdy fellow with a brushcut, greeted them civilly and repeated what Stan had said. The gas station owner was willing to forego prosecution as long as his money was returned. Tommy suspected that Stan's reputation weighed heavily in the decision.

"The boy had it all on him," the sheriff said. "All but fifty bucks, which I guess he'd been throwing around acting like a big shot."

Tommy produced his wallet and handed over the fifty. The sheriff then dealt with the paperwork for discharging the prisoner. After he'd finished, Randy was brought out. Tommy held on to his temper, sorely tempted to grab the boy and shake him until his teeth rattled. Instead, he gave him a curt nod and said to the sheriff, "He won't bother you again. I'm taking him back to Pennsylvania with me. From now on I'll be responsible."

He saw the flash of surprise in Randy's face. He was a thin rangy teenager, with dark hair falling forward and eyes that were deep and restless. A look of sullen resentment was written plainly across his features.

"What's all that about?" Randy demanded.

"We'll discuss it later." Tommy and the Bronskys thanked the sheriff and made their way through the rain back to the pickup.

"I mean it," Randy persisted. "How come you're taking me back there? What if I'd rather stay here?"

Louise and Stan slid into the small jump seats, leaving Randy to sit up front with his brother.

"Stan and Louise have three kids of their own to raise. They don't need a..." He hesitated just short of saying "a damned teenage troublemaker." Instead he said, "...another kid to worry about. And my sending money for your keep and telephoning now and then just isn't enough. You're coming back to Wiltonburg with me."

"Like hell I am," Randy muttered.

Tommy started the truck, teeth clenched. "It's already been decided. You haven't any say in the matter. Look, kid, I want you with me." Surprisingly, despite the anger he was feeling, Tommy found that this was true. "I've even got a job for you. I hear you're a good mechanic, and I've got plenty of heavy equipment that needs work all the time."

"Big deal."

"Big deal or not, that's how it's going to be."

"I've gotta crash some place."

"You'll live with me. There's plenty of room. Okay now, that's enough talk. It's settled. So we'll drive back and pick up your stuff and be on our way."

But once back at the Bronskys' Tommy found there was no easy way to escape his sister's hospitality.

"It's late, you're worn-out, and the driving's going to be awful," Louise insisted. I don't care if you get up and start at four in the morning, but you're both going to need a good meal and a few hours' sleep. Now no excuses."

So once Randy's possessions were loaded in the truck, all of them, including the three children, who stared goggle-eyed at their seldom-seen uncle, sat down and ate fried chicken, mashed potatoes, cole slaw and apple pie. Even Tommy, chafing to be on his way, had to admit he felt considerably restored and found his eyelids beginning to droop with fatigue. He took his shoes off and stretched out on the living-room couch, warning Randy that they'd be starting out soon.

His sleep was restless, and he found himself cocking an ear at every small noise, realizing that he was half worried Randy might attempt to sneak past him and run off into the night. By three in the morning he was wide awake and ready to go. Louise heard him moving around and came downstairs, a pink chenille robe wrapped around her thin frame.

"He's up," she whispered. "Tommy, are you sure you're doing the right thing? I'd hate for Randy to cause trouble for you back in Wiltonburg."

"There won't be any trouble, Lou," he answered with more assurance than he felt. "Now quit worrying and get on with your own life and your own family. There's nothing here that can't be handled." He gave her a quick hug and looked past her to where Randy was coming slowly down the stairs. The boy's expression looked as sullen and uncommunicative as it had in the sheriff's office.

Something inside Tommy plummeted when he thought of what lay ahead of him. But with an act of will he summoned up Julia's face, forced himself to remember that no matter what else he had to confront, she would be there with him. Together they would see it through.

"Okay," he said brusquely. "Let's go."

Stan came hurrying down the stairs, doing up his jeans. He'd been listening to the police band on the radio. The roads were in pretty bad shape, and it looked as if Wiltonburg, King's Crossing and some of the other small towns in western Pennsylvania were going to get the worst of the flooding. West Virginia roads would probably be passable, but Tommy might run into trouble farther along.

Tommy felt a moment's fear, but then reminded himself that Chipper was safe on high ground with the Vernons, and that Julia's farm was equally well situated. They'd be all right. Bill and Fiona were solid as rock and wouldn't let anything happen to either of them.

"My pickup can make it," he told Stan, "but we'd better go before the flooding gets worse. Okay, pal," he said to Randy, "let's get moving."

The first fifty miles out of Goldmont was through teeming rain, but their progress was good. Neither of them spoke, and only the swipe of the windshield wipers broke the silence in the truck's cab. Then the first ominous sign appeared—flashing blue lights ahead of them and a barricade across the road.

THE SHRILL SOUND of the telephone cut through Julia's sleep, and she instinctively looked at her watch. Nine-thirty. She'd been dozing for two hours. She rushed to the phone and heard Gina's voice.

"Julia? I think it's time we got cracking. I've called Mrs. Bauer and told her to pack her toothbrush. Of course you can imagine how that went over. She said to give it another couple of hours to see if it looks any better and she promises to go without a whimper. I think that'll be okay. But there's another problem."

"What?"

"I have five brand-new IBM word processors all set up here at the office. They just arrived Friday, and of course I couldn't wait to see them installed and operational. Now the water's lapping a couple of feet from them, and if it gets much closer there's my first major investment shot."

"What's it going to take to move them?"

"I figured the two of us could do it, if you're willing—"

"Hang on. I'll be there as fast as I can."

"Better not try to bring the car here, though."

"I'll go to the supermarket lot up the hill and walk down."

When Julia got to the lot, water was pouring off the wide expanse of asphalt, but it was still a safe place. She parked as close to the sidewalk as she could, then went pelting down the street in hooded slicker and boots toward the newspaper office.

She found Gina on her hands and knees, disconnecting cables, taking apart connections and swearing profusely. Julia ripped off her rain gear and dived in to help.

"Do you know anything about these things?" Gina asked frantically, her forehead wet with sweat.

"I used to work on one at the publisher's. We'll manage. Where's that screwdriver thing we need?"

"Here. I found two of them. But we can't disconnect anything without labeling it. I brought masking tape. We'll have to put it on every plug and wire or I'll never get 'em back together right."

"Where will we put them when we've gotten them apart?"

"We'll have to carry them upstairs—it's high and dry and there's plenty of storage space."

"Right. So let's get moving."

They were both sweating and exhausted by the time the feat was accomplished, but at last the five units were lined up in the dusty loft out of harm's way.

"Now I'll call Mrs. Bauer and tell her we're on our way," Gina said. "Why don't you make a pot of coffee to tide us over?"

They took five minutes out to gulp scalding coffee, and Gina said, "I'm not even going to try to thank you for this, Julia. All I can say is, if you're by any chance thinking of staying on in Wiltonburg, I could sure use you on the paper. In whatever capacity."

"It's funny," Julia said. "Until just a few hours ago that's exactly what I'd decided to do—stay on."

"And what happened?" Gina pushed her hair back, leaving a black smudge on her forehead.

"Oh, it's about what happened ten years ago—I told you a lot of it. Earlier today I found a letter among Elizabeth Holtz's things." Briefly she described it.

"Oh, hell, Julia. That was ten years ago. What's it matter why he did it? It's all in the past now."

"Except that he betrayed me. And he did it on the say-so of someone who was a virtual stranger to him. Not once, in ten years, did he ever try to get in touch with me, to explain things to me...or to tell me he still loved me." Julia shook her head slightly and looked at Gina. "I spent ten years wondering what I'd done wrong. I just can't forgive him. He's not the person I thought he was. I can't love a man who could betray me that way. I can't let that happen again."

"It seems to me he might have done it because he *did* love you," Gina said.

"He certainly managed to find compensation pretty fast."

"Compensation my foot. From what I hear, his life fell apart right after that. Ask anybody. And besides, he tried to explain it to you, but you refused to listen."

"Will explaining bring back the years we've lost?"

"Of course not. But neither will running away from him."

"I'm not running away, Gina. And for once I'd like to make a decision about my own life. I was wrong to get involved with him again, and the sooner I do something about it, the better off I'll be."

THE WATER WAS RISING, though, to emergency levels. Mrs. Bauer had her television on when Julia and Gretchen arrived, watching the mayor, Don Owen, with some of his aides, assure the populace that the new embankments were holding firm and that there was no cause for alarm.

"And if you believe that," Gina said sourly, "what's that song—I've got a nice piece of ocean-front property in Arizona for you?"

They packed Mrs. Bauer's wheelchair and her small overnight bag, and between them managed to carry her, wrapped in a raincoat, out to the car. Julia saw her take a last look inside the house before the door closed. For a moment the old woman's face worked oddly, but then Julia heard her say quietly as if schooling herself, "They're only *things*. Things don't count. People count."

After that there was some anxious discussion about Gretchen and Van, and it was agreed the couple might have to delay their return if the roads were blocked and flooded. Julia scribbled a hasty note to let them know Mrs. Bauer's whereabouts and tacked it on the door. And Fred—what kind of trouble would he be running into at King's Crossing?

Fussing gently, but cooperating without objection, Mrs. Bauer allowed herself to be transported to Firebush Road and installed in the downstairs bedroom.

"And now I've really got to start acting like a newspaperwoman," Gina said.

"Covering the story, you mean?"

"Absolutely. I'm going down to the embankment. Most of the men are there already, I think, and a lot of the women, too. Sandbagging, probably. But I want to see for myself."

"I'll stay here with Mrs. Bauer," Julia said.

"Julia, I can never thank you enough for tonight," Gina said earnestly. "Not just rescuing the equipment, but taking in Mrs. Bauer, too."

Julia smiled. It hadn't escaped her notice that Gina's concerns about the Bauer family had assumed an extremely personal nature.

"Imploded," the officer said. His caped orange slicker was streaming, and water was dripping off the plastic cover of his hat.

"Imploded?" Tommy had jumped out from the pickup at the sign of the barrier and blue revolving lights. But he knew what the term meant. Sometimes it seemed there wasn't a square inch of West Virginia that hadn't been mined, burrowed into, dug under. Sinkholes appeared in roads with distressing frequency, where the surface simply caved in to the hollow space beneath. "Then there's no getting beyond it this way."

"Not a chance. Where you trying to get to?"

"Wiltonburg."

"Oh, boy. Pennsylvania's worse off than we are."

Randy, who'd followed Tommy out of the truck, stood hunched in an inadequate leather jacket. "Great," he muttered, eyes rolling upward. Tommy ignored him.

"Is there a detour you could recommend?" Tommy asked.

The officer's face screwed into a frown. "The only way I can think of would be to go along old Estlebury road. You'd have to go back a couple of miles and take a right. It's pretty twisty, and it goes through foothills. I've got no idea what you'll find there."

"You know it?" Tommy asked Randy sharply.

"Yeah, I know it. Middle of nowhere."

"Your truck might make it through." The officer sounded doubtful.

"Well, we've got to try. Have you heard much from Wiltonburg? Are the embankments holding?"

"Don't know. It didn't sound good last report we got."

Something that felt like a hawser knot tightened around Tommy's heart. "I've got to get back there. Thanks, officer."

Back in the truck he executed the turn around and started back, peering anxiously through the rain-splattered windshield so as not to miss the cutoff.

"What's the big sweat to get back there?" Randy asked. "Your kid's all right, isn't she?"

"Yes, of course. She's with the Vernons. But I've got a lot of other responsibilities. All the company equipment, the house..." And Julia, he thought desperately. More than all the rest, Julia.

"Why'd I have to come back with you, anyway?" Randy growled.

Tommy's jaw clenched. He didn't answer until he'd swung onto the narrow Estlebury Road, a secondary county highway, high-crowned, but still open. He gave the truck as much gas as he dared. "All right, you want the truth?" Randy grunted. "It's because Stan and Louise have enough to do raising three kids and keeping food on the table. They don't need to take on an ungrateful troublemaking kid, too. Why'd you steal that money, anyway?"

"What do you care? You never asked me about stuff before."

"I care because you're my brother, and because stealing isn't the way to get what you want in life."

"You sure never paid any attention to me till I got in trouble."

"I'm not perfect, either," Tommy snapped. "I was probably too worried about my own life to pay attention to yours."

"I suppose you never did anything wrong," Randy said with a sneer.

"Sure I did. I made plenty of mistakes. But at least I got an education and a job. And that's what you're going to do."

Randy gave a snort and turned away to look out through the streaming window of the truck. "Hey, what's that?" he said suddenly.

Tommy came down carefully on the brakes to avoid skidding. Sideways across the narrow road ahead of them was another pickup, slightly smaller. It had obviously gone into a slide and now its rear wheels were firmly embedded in the muddy right shoulder. While they watched, the driver climbed out of the cab and came over to them. He was a young, anxious-looking man with deep lines in his face.

"Hey, you guys, any chance you got a chain in there somewhere?"

Tommy took a breath so deep it was almost painful. Then he let it out slowly. "Sure thing, man. Turn that thing off and we'll see what we can do."

Whether the challenge to his mechanical skill did the trick or whether he simply reacted on impulse, Randy was out of the pickup at the same time as Tommy, surveying the problem.

"You got a hitch on the back, right?"

"Yep," Tommy replied. "And I've got a heavy chain."

"Then you'll have to turn around to haul him out. There's not much room to navigate."

"I can do it," Tommy said grimly. "Pulling heavy stuff is what I do all the time. But he's got no hitch. Where can you fasten it?"

Randy was already slogging through the mud and reaching down to feel for the rear bumper of the stranded truck. "I can fasten it under here. You start turning around."

The truck was turned, the chain was attached, then stretched to fasten under the bumper of the other truck. Slowly Tommy pulled it back on the roadway, and the young man ran over to them.

"Hey, you guys, I sure appreciate that," he said earnestly. His denim jacket was soaked through. "I'd be glad to pay you—"

Tommy, who suspected the man had no more than twenty dollars in his pocket for groceries for his family, said quickly, "Forget it. Get on home and into some dry clothes."

"Sure will. I bet my wife's calling the cops looking for me."

"Will we hook up with the main road north somewhere along here?" Tommy asked him.

"About twenty miles along you'll see the intersection. There's a gas station on one side and a burger joint across the street."

He climbed back into his truck, and Tommy and Randy watched him proceed cautiously ahead of them, turning off on a small road about five miles farther on.

A gas station, Tommy thought. They'd need gas soon. And maybe there might be a telephone. He had to call Julia. He had to hear her voice. He was too far out of range for his mobile phone, but surely at a gas station... He glanced at his watch. The delay had cost them three-quarters of an hour. It was dawn, but the steadily pounding rain obscured any sign of daylight.

JULIA HAD LOST all track of time. Even the kitchen clock failed to register with her. She looked in on Mrs. Bauer, who was resting peacefully under the red-and-white quilt, which Julia had brought downstairs for her. Julia felt so restless she could do no more than pace from room to room, feeling she should be doing something more. Then it occurred to her she might not be the only one pacing and fearful. She decided to call Fiona Vernon, who very likely would be wide awake, too. But just as she made her way to the front hall, the telephone shrilled.

"Julia? Oh, thank heavens you're there."

"Fiona? I was just going to call you. Anything wrong?" Julia heard a hysterical note in the woman's voice that was completely unlike her.

"Everything's wrong, Julia. Everything. I did something stupid and now I'm scared to death. I can't get hold of Bill—he's down there at the river with the others."

"Now wait, Fiona. Take it slow. Tell me what's wrong."

"Oh, Lord, it's Chipper." A cold stone dropped somewhere inside Julia. "I told her she could go home with her little friend Melissa Brown after Sunday school and stay overnight. But Melissa lives down there in the old part of town, and everybody there's in danger. I went dashing out to my car to go get her, but there's mud clear up past the hubcaps. I can't budge it. Julia, what am I going to do? It's the most foolish thing I've ever done in my life, letting her go there. If anything happens to that child I don't know what Tommy and Bill will do. I've just got to get to her somehow, and you're the only one I can get hold of. The police aren't even answering anymore."

"All right, hang on." Julia rubbed her hand across her forehead, trying to think. "Won't the Browns be thinking the same things we are? Surely they'll get the children to safety."

"But there isn't any Mr. Brown. I mean, it's just Melissa and her mother, Patty. And Patty isn't—she's not very good in a crisis. Oh, Lord, why'd I ever do such a stupid thing? I never realized it was going to get this bad. Not that that's any excuse. I haven't the sense God gave a goose."

"Sit tight, Fiona. I'll go get her. Just give me the address. My car's working fine. And stay by the phone. I'm sure I can manage. There'll be plenty of people down there to help." She was less than certain of that, but she had to stem Fiona's panic.

When she'd hung up she returned to Mrs. Bauer and told her about Chipper. "I have to go find her, but I'll leave Fiona Vernon's number right here." She scribbled it on a scrap of paper. Neither woman would be able to help the other, she realized, but sometimes a voice in the night was the biggest comfort of all.

"Don't give it a thought, dear," Mrs. Bauer said, sitting up in bed. "Just go after those children. I'm snug as can be."

As Julia drove toward town, she made up her mind to take the car right into the downtown area. If it stalled in water and mud, she'd leave it, but maybe she'd be lucky enough to get Chipper and the others out and onto high ground first.

The moment she topped the crest of the supermarket lot, she knew that plan would never work. The water was deep in the streets now, lapping up over storefronts and porches. This was major flooding. In all likelihood the embankments had been breached by the destructive power of the river. Silently she damned Don Owen and his greed, which had been responsible for the shoddy work. There was no point in driving farther.

She abandoned the car and started running down the sloping street, directly into deep water. She knew where the Browns lived—it wasn't far from Mrs. Bauer's place. But now the water was no longer ankle-deep but almost up to her waist. Hampered by her slicker, she pulled it off and let it float away in the swirling waters.

For the first time she felt the cold creeping edge of doubt. Could she do it? Had she the strength? She'd slept only an hour or two out of the past twenty-four, and weariness sat on her shoulders like a twenty-pound sandbag. She saw men in boats, poling about in the gloom. She tried to hail them, but they only waved back and said they'd get to her as fast as they could.

"What about Gedney Street?" she shouted.

"Not good," a man shouted back. "We'll be over that way as quick as we can."

Julia slogged on, pushing every step of the way. She found the Browns' small frame house, but her heart plummeted as she saw the water lapping up over the first floor. Fiona'd said Melissa's mother wasn't good in a crisis, but wouldn't she at least get the children up close to the roof? Desperately, her heart pounding so hard it seemed her chest would burst, Julia pushed on.

Then, from an upstairs window, a small familiar voice reached her. "Julia! We're up here! Help us!"

Julia looked up and saw the frightened face, the big eyes—but no tears, she thought. Spunky and hanging on gamely.

"I'm coming, Chipper!" she shouted. Inch by inch, hanging onto fences, shrubs, small trees, she moved through the waist-deep water and up onto the flooded front porch. The place was an almost exact copy of the Bauer house, so she found the stairs easily. The first floor was already under water and all the lights were out. At the top of the stairs Chipper stood calling to her. When Julia reached her, the small arms clasped around her waist tightly.

"I *knew* somebody'd come for us," she said. "I just didn't know it'd be you. I thought it might be Uncle Bill."

Behind her in a small bedroom, Melissa was whimpering fearfully and sticking close to her mother, a thin frightened-looking woman who was, at the moment, blowing with all her strength into a plastic raft, trying to inflate it. Two helpless kids and a woman who seemed barely able to function, Julia saw with a sinking heart. She pressed all the courage she could summon into her voice.

"I'm Julia Marshall, and I guess you're Patty Brown. I'm sure we'll be fine. It's not too bad out there yet, and there are plenty of men in boats out rescuing people. If that raft has a line attached to it we may be able to use it. Do you have a flashlight? While we try to do something with the raft, the kids can keep signaling."

"I do, yes, I thought to bring one," the woman told her, handing Chipper the flashlight. Julia thought she heard a note of pride in her voice. *At least I did one thing right,* the woman seemed to be saying.

"Keep flashing that light, kids," Julia called. "Watch for any boat that comes by and yell at them. And don't drop it out the window, for heaven's sake."

"We wouldn't do that," Chipper said with a touch of wounded dignity.

Julia succeeded in helping Patty Brown inflate the raft. It looked a poor fragile thing against the raging floodwaters, but they couldn't discount any possibility. Then the prayed-for sound came, a feeble put-put below the window.

"Here's a boat!" Chipper shouted.

"How many in there?" came a voice Julia recognized. She flew to the window. "Fergus? Is that you?"

Fergus Halley was in a tiny boat that looked about the same vintage as his truck. He peered upward. "Julia? What in the name of Sam Hill are you doing way down here?"

"Tell you later. Fergus, there's two children and two adults here. Can you help us?"

"I sure can take the kids. My boat won't hold two adults, too, though, but I'll take the kids and I'll get another boat to come back for you."

"Good enough. I'll get them down to you." Julia turned to the little girls. "All right, you're going first. We'll come in the next boat."

"Mommy!" Melissa wailed.

"No, darling, do what Julia says. We'll follow right after you," Patty assured her.

"Okay, let's not waste time." Julia was busy securing a line to the small raft. "When we get down to the water, one of you stretch out this thing—you've got to hold on tight. Chipper, you can do that, can't you?" The little girl nodded. "And Melissa, you hang on to me, piggyback. Mr. Halley will bring his boat in as close as he can."

The waters seemed darker, the current more powerful than only moments before as they reached the first floor and the flooded porch. Fergus's small but sturdy-looking boat bobbed twenty yards away.

"Can't come any closer," he shouted. "Afraid of running into something that'll put a hole in 'er. Can you get 'em out here to me?"

Melissa's arms were clutched around Julia's neck as she gripped the raft by its rope and pushed it ahead. She was using every ounce of her strength. Would it be enough?

CHAPTER FOURTEEN

THE YOUNG TRUCK DRIVER'S information proved accurate, and after a harrowing twenty miles on the narrow roadway, Tommy could finally make out ahead of them an intersection with a gas station. Best of all, the wide interstate highway that led straight to Wiltonburg lay in front of them now. Tommy refused to consider any obstacles. The interstate *had* to be passable.

He drove into the service station and leapt out of the truck. "You take care of filling the tank," he ordered Randy. "I have to make a phone call."

In the outside phone booth he dug frantically in his pocket for change and dialed Julia's number. The voice that answered after several rings had a frail faraway sound.

"Julia? Who is this? Is this Julia Marshall's number?"

"Yes. Yes, it is. It's Geraldine Bauer. Is that you, Tommy?"

"Mrs. Bauer! What's happened? Is Julia there?"

"No, Tommy, she's not back, yet. She and Gina brought me here when the water got high, but then she went back downtown."

"Back where it's flooded? What for?"

"Oh, dear, it's Chipper, you see."

"Chipper!" A cold fist closed around his heart. "Isn't Chipper with Fiona?"

"She was staying overnight with her friend Melissa Brown, and when Fiona realized there might be danger she started out after her, but her car got stuck in the mud, so she called Julia. And now Julia's gone to get Chipper."

"But the Browns' place is near the river!"

"Yes, I know. Not so far from my house. Tommy, try not to worry. I know Julia has her by now. And men will be out with boats—we can count on that."

"I'm about an hour away. I'll be there as fast as I can." He slammed the phone down, dashed into the station and paid for the gas, then sprinted back to the truck.

Randy was gone.

"Ran-dee!" It was more than a summons. It was a roar of sheer fury. If the stupid kid had taken advantage of his brother's back being turned for a matter of minutes to run off, then that was that. Nothing was going to keep Tommy from pushing on as fast as he could to Wiltonburg. The very image of Chipper and Julia floundering through the dark waters drove every other thought from his mind. Saving Randy had seemed a high priority only hours ago. Now all that mattered was getting home.

He jumped into the driver's seat and turned the key in the ignition. Then suddenly from across the road he saw Randy running through the rain, his jacket streaming, his jeans soaked. He was carrying a bag.

"I figured we might need some food," the boy panted. "I got burgers and coffee. Did you get your call through?"

Tommy let out his breath slowly. "Yeah. Things are bad there. I'm really worried. We've got to try to make up some time." He hesitated. "And you were right, Randy. Food's just what we need." He couldn't say more right now. Instead, he slammed the truck into gear and pulled out onto the interstate.

Randy unwrapped one of the hamburgers and handed it to him. "But she's all right, isn't she? Chipper, I mean?"

"I sure hope so. She's at a friend's house down where the worst of the flooding is, but Julia's gone after her. I'm sure she'll handle it. I mean, she just has to." Yes. His whole life was riding on it—on the safety of his little girl and the woman he'd lost once and now knew he could never live without.

Randy studied him curiously. "Who's Julia?"

Tommy eased the pressure on the gas pedal as the thickening traffic created a temporary delay, but then the traffic thinned, and he sped up again.

"She's the woman I'm going to marry," he said simply.

"No kidding." Randy considered this as he bit into his hamburger. "Guess I really messed things up bad for you."

"Well . . ."

"You didn't have to come for me, you know," Randy said, showing a flare of his old resentment.

"I know I didn't."

"Why did you, then?"

"I already told you. Because we're brothers. Family. Only right now I've got other things to think about. We'll sort all that out later."

Randy studied him for a moment. "They'll be all right."

Tommy's jaw clenched. He didn't answer.

When they reached the exit for Wiltonburg, state troopers were turning cars back.

"We can't let anybody in, Mac. If anybody wants to leave, it's okay, but things are too dangerous."

"But I have to get in there. My family, my little girl's there. I just have to see to their safety." Tommy's voice had taken on a desperate pitch. "Look, I'm going in no matter what you say. You can arrest me later. But they must need extra hands to rescue people..."

The trooper seemed to weigh his orders against the rock-solid determination he could hear in Tommy's voice. Finally he waved him along. "Okay, but you'll have to ditch the truck before long. As soon as you hit the flats you'll lose it, anyway."

From the other side of the road they could see a long line of cars leaving by the exit ramp. Tommy pressed forward cautiously, but it was obvious the officer had told the truth. There was no way they could continue except on foot. He pulled over to the side and parked the truck where it would still, for the moment, be safe. Then he and Randy jumped out and began wading forward toward the surging floodwaters.

"Good God! I didn't imagine anything like this." Small sheds and trailers were sweeping by them, along with trees and timbers of all sizes—boards, planks, scrap lumber that might have been someone's garage. Panic began to close in on Tommy as he thought of Julia and Chipper. He swallowed and concentrated on breathing deeply to stay in control.

"Which way?" Randy asked.

"Straight ahead. Watch for men with boats. They can tell us where they need help. Maybe Chipper and Julia are out of danger already."

And if they weren't? The thought clamped down around his chest like a band of steel.

JULIA, CLINGING to the porch supports along with Patty Brown, watched Fergus's small boat bear the two children away. When they were out of sight she strained to hear what Fergus was shouting over the noise of the rushing water.

"They're okay! Stay there, Julia. We'll send a bigger boat...you hang on tight...gotta find a searchlight..."

The dawn was so murky that searchlights were necessary to find people leaning out upper-floor windows or standing on porch roofs. The boat that came for Julia and Patty was fitted with a searchlight so powerful it was blinding. Although the two women couldn't see the craft, the sound of its motor told them it was relatively large.

"All right, this is it, Patty," said Julia, gripping the small inflatable raft. "Hang on to me and we'll be safe in a jiffy."

It proved an unworkable way to proceed. Patty was trying her best, but she was an unbearable drag on Julia in her fatigued state. "Wait. Let's try it differently. You go ahead of me and I'll push from behind."

Patty allowed herself to be shoved ahead. The water was moving more swiftly now, and even worse, Julia felt the last of her strength ebbing away. Hands reached out to pull Patty up into the boat, Julia was sure of that much. Then she was aware only of the blinding light shining in her face. There must have been people behind that searchlight, but suddenly it no longer mattered. She'd never be able to summon up the strength to get into the boat. She'd never—

"Grab my hand, Julia!"

She could have sworn she heard Tommy's voice. But Tommy was in West Virginia, wasn't he?

Another voice shouted, "Watch out!"

She felt a sharp pain in her head as something struck her and she was swept away into darkness. Her panic began to disappear as she drifted with the powerful current. She was almost comfortable in this dark world where there were no hard choices to make. What had her life been but a series of bleak adjustments to circumstance? And Tommy, the one thing she thought she had found, had never been hers, anyway....

She heard men shouting somewhere in the distance, and wanted to tell them not to worry about her. She'd be all right; she was safe and comfortable, and the river would take care of her.

"We need a rope here! Fergus, you got a rope?"

"I can't wait for a rope. I can barely see her."

"Wait, Tommy. You go in there without a rope, we'll never get either one of you back."

Tommy? Julia tried to open her eyes, but the pain in her head stabbed like a lightning bolt and she slipped under the water.

Suddenly she was jerked to the surface. Coughing and sputtering, her head throbbing, she managed to get her eyes open. Where was she? And who was it holding her from behind?

"I've got her! Shine the light over here."

"Tommy?" she cried weakly. "How did you... where..."

Strong arms held her above the current. What had seemed so benign and comforting a moment ago was now a raging menace. Debris was sweeping past them. She heard children crying somewhere. Behind them, water was nearly to the second floor of the houses on Gedney Street.

She realized that Tommy had one arm around her and the other holding fast to a utility pole.

"Over here, Bill!"

She saw the boat coming closer and suddenly she started to shake violently.

"Chipper's all right, Tommy," she said through chattering teeth.

"I know, darling. Just hang on another minute."

She could hang on another minute. She could hang on for an eternity as long as his arms were around her. What was it that had been bothering her only hours ago? She didn't remember.

"You're freezing, aren't you?" he said. "There are blankets on shore. We'll get you warm in no time."

"Tommy, don't leave me."

"I'm never going to leave you again." They were the last words she heard before blackness closed over her once more.

"WHAT ABOUT THE SHEEP?" The voice sounded like Chipper's. Julia thought it was Bill Vernon who answered.

"There are twenty-five of them up there filling sandbags, but we're going to need more boats."

The sheep were filling sandbags? Julia couldn't make any sense of it.

Another voice said, "I think it's crested. The worst may be over for us."

Someone answered, "It's hitting King's Crossing now."

The voice she was sure was Chipper's said, "I'm worried about the sheep. They're going to get wet, and some of them are babies."

Julia was aware that a rough blanket had been wrapped tightly around her, but her teeth were still chattering and the pain in her head was a dull constant throb. She longed to reassure Chipper that the sheep were safe, but she still couldn't speak.

"I think she's coming around. We can move her now."

"I'll take her." Tommy's voice.

His arms were around her again, lifting her, holding her close. She managed to whisper, "Tell Chipper... the lambs are all right."

His voice was hoarse against her ear. "I just want to hear that *you're* all right."

"Tommy, I thought it was over. "

"It almost was."

"No. I mean you and me. I thought it was over—again."

"You and me? You and me will never be over, Julia. I told you that the other night."

"I know that, too, now. Nothing in that letter matters."

"Letter? What letter?"

Bill Vernon's voice interrupted. "All right, you two. You can talk later. Let's get her in out of the weather and into some dry clothes." He put his rough hand on her forehead and said, "You're very brave, Julia Marshall. We can't thank you enough for what you did, saving Chipper."

Julia smiled weakly.

"Randy's brought the truck as close as he dared. We can carry her that far," Bill said. "All right, Chipper, hold my hand good and tight."

"What about Melissa and her mama?" Chipper asked.

"Fergus is taking them to Melissa's grandma. They'll be fine."

Tommy handed Bill the keys. "You drive, Bill."

"I figured you'd want me to."

With Chipper and Randy in the jump seats, Julia was wedged between Tommy and Bill. She drifted in and out of consciousness, aware of Tommy's arm securely around her. She heard scraps of conversation from behind.

"Are you my real uncle?"

"I guess so, squirt."

"I'm not squirt. I'm Charlotte Black, but you can call me Chipper. That's what most people call me. Where do you live?"

"No place special." There was something familiar about his voice....

She heard Tommy say, "Randy's going to be living with us, Chipper."

Living with us. Julia heard this through a fog. What did it mean? She would think about it when the pain in her head went away. For the moment she was content to rest in the shelter of his arms.

The Vernons' kitchen was lit by barn lanterns. Soup was bubbling on the old-fashioned gas stove. Lack of electricity obviously hadn't proved an obstacle to Fiona. She bustled around supplying dry clothes to everyone, and Julia found herself wearing a pair of Fiona's purple stretch pants along with a bright green sweatshirt. She wore a pair of socks she was sure belonged to Bill. Her hair was stiff with mud, and she noted the cuts on her hands. Tommy had gone to his own house to change and to get Chipper into dry clothes. Julia saw no sign of Randy and guessed that he'd gone with Tommy. The steaming mug of tea Fiona had made for her was helping to bring her back to reality.

"Fiona, I should call Mrs. Bauer. Are the phones working?"

"You stay right where you are, dear. I'll call her."

She bustled to the phone and dialed. "Geraldine, are you all right?... No, we're all fine. Chipper's back and so's everybody else. Any problems at Julia's house?... Oh, my goodness, they must have been frantic. And what about Fred? . . . All right, I'll tell everybody.''

"Tell her she's to stay right there and make herself at home," Julia said.

"Did you hear that, Geraldine? . . .''

After a moment Fiona hung up and turned around. "Gretchen and Van were pretty frantic when they couldn't get hold of her on the phone. The roads are in bad shape—they couldn't make it back. Then they thought to call Fred, and he explained where she was. Once they reached her and found she was safe, they decided to pitch in and help right where they were—sandbagging and so on. Fred says King's Crossing is getting hit pretty bad, but his clinic is on high ground. He's coming for his mother tomorrow to take her back to live with him until the flood stops and they get the mud out of her house.''

It amazed Julia that Fiona had been able to find out so much in a three-minute phone call. She sank back in her chair at the kitchen table, and when Fiona put a bowl of soup in front of her, she began eating it ravenously. She'd had no idea she was so hungry.

The door opened and Tommy came in holding Chipper by the hand, with Randy following. Tommy's eyes went at once to Julia and he slid into the chair beside her. "Love your outfit." He grinned.

Chipper insinuated herself between them and climbed into Julia's lap.

"How about letting Julia eat her soup, Chipper," Tommy said.

"No, it's all right," said Julia. "This is better than soup.''

"Maybe I could share a little of that," Chipper suggested.

"I'll get you your own bowl," Fiona said.

Chipper addressed the room at large. "Julia saved us, you know. Us and Melissa's mama, too. Melissa cried, but I didn't. I held the flashlight and I didn't drop it, either."

Fiona placed a bowl in front of her and Tommy slid her onto his lap. He leaned over and whispered to Julia, "Are things starting to look a little more normal?"

"Things have never looked better."

Between mouthfuls, Chipper went on talking. "Uncle Randy steered the boat when Daddy jumped in to save Julia from drowning. I was on shore, but I saw the whole thing. Uncle Randy's going to live with us now."

"You two haven't been formally introduced, have you?" Tommy said.

Julia's eyes moved to the slender youth, and at once she thought, *It takes one to know one.* That lonely look of not belonging anywhere, of not being wanted by anyone. She'd felt it often enough to recognize it in someone else.

"You didn't get a very good welcome to Wiltonburg, did you, Randy?" She smiled. "But we're going to make up for that. Where'd you learn to drive a boat in West Virginia, anyway?"

Randy looked down at the floor. "Mostly anything that's got an engine in it, I can handle." He raised his eyes to look straight into Julia's, and a ghost of a smile appeared at the corners of his mouth.

There was a knock from outside, and Gina Blakely stuck her head into the kitchen. "Can I come in if I bring good news?"

Fiona reached for another soup bowl. "Even if it isn't good, come on in and start drying out. Bill says the river's crested by now."

"Seems to be the case. But my news is something else entirely, and I just witnessed it with my own two eyes. Mayor Don Owen's red Corvette is totally submerged in the city hall parking lot."

A cheer went up, after which Fiona said hastily, "Dear me, that isn't very kind of us, is it? Still..."

"Hizzoner convened an impromptu press conference and explained that a task force would be assembled to assess responsibility for the shoddy workmanship that resulted in the embankments being breached. However, among the sandbaggers and others who were listening in, there seemed to be a groundswell of opinion that the mayor should have no part of such a task force."

"Like putting the fox in charge of the henhouse," Bill Vernon said gruffly.

"Exactly." Gina sat down at the table and started eating soup hungrily. "Mr. Vernon, your name was the one I heard mentioned most. Don't be surprised if a delegation shows up on your doorstep this time tomorrow."

"What are you saying?"

"Sounds like they're picking the best man for the job, that's all," Tommy said to Bill with a grin.

"Well, anybody who takes on that job is going to need plenty of help. I assume I can count on you and Van?"

"I know the mayor will love your choices," Tommy said.

Bill grunted. "Nobody's asked me, yet. Let's not jump the gun."

"Don't underestimate the power of the press." Gina smiled knowingly.

"My uncle Randy steered the boat when Daddy jumped in to save Julia from drowning," Chipper announced again.

"So I hear," Gina said. "I was covering the wrong story, I'm afraid. Mrs. Vernon, many thanks for the soup, but now I have to get over to Julia's house and see how Mrs. Bauer's doing."

"I just got off the phone with her," Fiona said. "She's doing fine, but take a jar of that soup with you. Tell her if she wants to come here with us she's more than welcome."

"Thanks, but maybe I'll just stay there with her. Is that okay with you, Julia?"

"Of course it is. Make yourself at home and eat whatever you find."

"If you want to know more about anything you missed, I can tell you," Chipper volunteered. "I might be a reporter myself when I'm bigger."

"That's a deal," Gina said, pointing a finger at the little girl.

When she'd left, Fiona said, "Nice girl, that Gina. She's a lot like her grandpa. You remember him, don't you, Julia?"

"Best friend I ever had in this town."

"Only now you've got us," Chipper declared. "And there's a lot of us."

Julia heard her chattering, but fatigue was overtaking her. Her eyelids were growing heavy and the muddy smell of her hair was in her nostrils. She put a hand gingerly on her head and felt a swelling the size of a golf ball. Tommy, watching her, said, "You're exhausted. I'll take you home."

She nodded wearily, her head pounding.

But sitting in the car in the dwindling rain, she said, "I don't want to go home, Tommy. Mrs. Bauer's fine and Gina's on her way to take over, anyway. And besides..."

"Besides?"

"I don't want you to leave me. I want to stay with you."

His eyes moved over her face. "Come on. We'll go to my house."

CHAPTER FIFTEEN

JULIA SHAMPOOED her hair twice and stood under the pounding shower trying to get her muscles to loosen up. But when she finally stepped out she still felt stiff and sore all over. She wrapped her hair in a towel and went over to the big white tub hoping there was still enough hot water for a good soak. Once it was filled she sank into it gratefully, and at last began to feel some of the tension easing out of her.

She tried to remember the sequence of events from the time Chipper had called to her from that upstairs window and she'd arrived at the Vernons'. But all she could remember was how important it was to save the little girl because . . . because why? Was it because she thought of Chipper as her family now? What made a family, anyway? Certainly she'd never felt like part of a family with Gideon and Elizabeth Holtz. She'd seen that familiar look on Randy's face. *I don't belong here.* But that would work out. The problem with Randy had a solution. Tommy would see to that. And so would she.

Her thoughts began to lose focus and drift. Gingerly she touched the swelling on her head and winced. She looked at her hands. Where had all the scrapes and cuts come from?

There was a soft tapping on the door. "You all right in there?"

"Uh-huh. Be right out."

She dried herself with one of the big fluffy towels and then wrapped the dark red terry-cloth robe around her. She took the towel off her head, and her hair fell in a damp tangle. Then she opened the bathroom door and gaped in amazed surprise. Tommy stood there holding a Donald Duck hair dryer.

"It's Chipper's," he explained. "I thought maybe you'd need it."

"It's a wonderful idea, but I don't think I could hold it." She turned her hands palms up. "I seem to have scraped myself here and there."

"Back into the bathroom, young lady," Tommy ordered. He put the dryer down and rummaged in the medicine cabinet for a tube of antibiotic ointment, which he rubbed gently into her palms.

"Okay, that's step one. Now let's see what we can do about this hair. I've only ever worked on Chipper, so I may not do it exactly right."

Julia closed her eyes as he brushed and dried her hair. The distance between bathroom and bed began to look like a long corridor she couldn't possibly summon up the strength to travel. But she needn't have worried. Once her hair was dry he scooped her gently up into his strong arms, carried her down the hall to his room and tucked her between clean white sheets. In his sweatshirt and jeans, he lay on top of the covers with his arms around her.

"Julia, I never wanted to leave you ten years ago." His voice was almost a whisper in her ear.

"I know what happened, Tommy. I found a letter. I know Elizabeth Holtz talked you into it. It doesn't matter anymore. I thought it did, but now I know it doesn't."

"It wasn't a question of talking me into it."

She blinked and murmured, "What do you mean?"

"You meant so much to her."

"To Elizabeth? I did?"

"She was so afraid you'd end up like her—a prisoner in this town."

"She never cared about me."

"Maybe Gideon didn't. But Elizabeth loved you dearly."

Julia couldn't believe she was hearing right.

"After you left for New York State," Tommy continued, "Elizabeth came to see me. She begged me not to get in touch with you so that you could have a chance at life. She knew Gideon would never let you get a college education under any other circumstances. She saw you as being lost like her."

Julia could hear the hesitation in his voice. After all this time it was still hard for him to speak of it.

"She loved Rick, too," he went on. "But once he joined the air force, she knew he'd escaped. He'd be all right. You were the one she was worried about."

Dimly Julia remembered the photo she'd found, the one where Elizabeth Holtz had been sitting beside her on a bench, leaning toward her with a yearning look.

"But did you have to... Did you have to promise her?"

"I never was much good at saying no to a woman who's crying."

"Is that what she . . . You mean she . . ."

"All I promised was that I wouldn't get in touch with you for a year. But by the end of the year I heard you were married."

"I married Bryce. I was so hurt and bewildered and . . . lonely. It was a disaster and unfair to him, too."

If only she wasn't so tired, Julia thought, she could make sense of all this. When he'd heard she was married, was that when all his wild weekends had started, all those other women? Chipper's mother?

"At the time a year didn't seem so long. I figured we'd get through it and then we'd be together again. But then I realized it was the worst decision I'd ever made. And when, after ten years, I saw you again, I knew I'd never gotten over you—and never would. I was afraid I could never make you understand."

Julia snuggled closer to Tommy. She remembered thinking, when he'd told her to hang on as they waited to be pulled from the swollen waters, that she could hang on for an eternity as long as his arms were around her. Now, floating to sleep in his arms, she knew she could never let him go. The ten years melted together, ran into one stream and lost its identity. This was now and they were together. They must stay that way. That was all that was important. She longed to explain this to him, but the words kept sliding away from her.

Hours later when she finally began to wake up, he was still there with her, sprawled on top of the covers, sleeping heavily. She watched him for a moment—the mussed dark hair, the hand thrown across his forehead—and experienced some of the same feelings she'd had the other morning. From now on every awakening moment would have him in it. As if feeling her gaze on him, his eyes flew open.

"Julia," he said. "Julia darling."

WILTONBURG WASTED no time starting the cleanup that would bring it back to normal. Its citizens had suffered the ravages of the river before and were out with brooms and shovels the moment it was humanly possible.

Julia had slept the rest of that afternoon and straight through to the next morning. Then Tommy bundled her up and drove her home. Van and Gretchen had already picked up Mrs. Bauer. Gretchen had left a letter thanking Julia and explaining that they were taking her mother to Fred's place in King's Crossing. "We'll see you when we get back and start the cleanup on Mom's house," it read. "Your brother called several times. I assured him you were fine and the house was fine, but I think he wants to hear it from you. We fed the dog and I think the sheep are okay. You'd better look at them...."

"Sounds as if everything's in pretty good shape here," Tommy said. "I'd better pick up Randy and get the heavy equipment moving. We can do a lot of the cleanup with that."

"Yes, go ahead. They need you, and I'll be fine here."

His dark eyes twinkled at her. "Hey, wait a minute, we have some things to settle first."

"I thought we already settled everything."

"Well, then, when's the wedding going to be?"

"I guess as soon as we get the barn built." Julia grinned.

"Barn? What barn?"

"The one we're going to need for the sheep."

"Of course. Why didn't I think of that? But it's warm weather. The sheep'll be fine without a barn, won't they? We're not going to hold up the wedding for that, are we?"

"I was only teasing. We can get married any time you want."

"Whew. That's more like it," he said, kissing her.

After he left, she put on boots and walked up to the barn to check on the sheep. Lizzie, overjoyed to see her, ran ahead of her yipping and bounding. Then Julia headed for the lower pasture where Tommy had diverted the stream; it had already drained and was in good shape. As she walked back to the house, she saw Dan Westfall's car pull in. He got out, looked around and said, "Everything looks great here. The new owners'll be happy."

"Dan! You mean the Suttons want to buy?"

"They're pretty eager. Howard says another few days and the will should clear probate, so you can go ahead and sell. I think you'll be happy with their offer."

"Well, if all that rain didn't scare them off, they'll probably love it here."

"I'll talk it over with Howard and get back to you in a couple of days."

"Okay, Dan. I'll go call Rick and tell him the good news."

She hurried inside and dialed Rick's number. There was no answer at his apartment, so she called the base.

"Major Marshall here."

"Rick! Guess what? It looks as if the house is sold."

"Never mind that. I've been trying to reach you for two days. Are you all right?"

"Couldn't be better."

"Suzanne and I were worried. What happened to all of you up there?"

"Oh, it's a long story. I'll tell you about it at the wedding."

"But that's not until June."

"I mean *my* wedding—mine and Tommy's."

She heard her brother's gasp of pleasure. "Well, I'll say this for you. Once you make up your mind you don't waste any time. This is wonderful. I couldn't be happier for you. When's the big day?"

"We have to wait until some of this mud's cleaned up, but maybe by the end of next week."

"Suzanne and I will be there as soon as we can make it. Maybe we can lend you a hand with some of that mud."

When she'd hung up, Julia phoned the newspaper office. Gina answered, sounding out of breath. "Oh. Julia. How are you feeling now?"

"Absolutely slept out and raring to go. Let's bring those computers back down and hook them up."

"I've got most of the mud out of the place now, and they've told me the power will be on by this afternoon."

"I'll be there in a jiffy."

Someone had located her car and brought it back to the house. She suspected it had been Fergus. Many of the streets were ankle-deep in mud, but much of the worst hit areas had been cleared. Store owners were out with brooms and shovels, and some had spread merchandise out to dry in the sun. The attractive store where she and Gretchen had shopped for their dresses had a movable rack on the sidewalk, clothing billowing in the breeze. The shoe store up the street was advertising slightly damp sneakers, greatly reduced.

She found Gina doing what so many of the others were doing, shoveling mud away from the entrance of the newspaper office. Her face was smudged and her hair hung limply.

"Hey, you look as if you could use some help."

Gina sighed. "I just had a call from the printer in King's Crossing who puts out our newspaper. They're underwater and won't be able to print the paper this week. That means I have to drive an hour and a half to Larson's Ferry if we want to publish this week."

"Oh, come on, Gina. Buck up. It's only temporary."

Gina sighed again. "The floors are a mess—they'll probably have to be refinished. It's already starting to smell like mildew. All the computers have to be hooked up again. And Ed Persky's truck was washed away in the flood—he's the one who made my deliveries for me. So it looks like I'll be delivering the paper, too."

"But you've got friends. I'll help you deliver the papers. I'll help you hook up the computers, too. We took them apart. We can get them back together again."

Gina still looked discouraged. "Let's face it, Julia. This was a shoestring operation to begin with. It'll take a ton of money to get things going again. You know what flood insurance costs in this town. I couldn't even afford that."

Julia took the shovel out of Gina's hands and leaned it against the building. "What if you had a partner? I've decided not to go back to New York, you know."

"You know how much I'd love to have you working with me, but it's going to take more than that."

"Well, then, how about this. The house is as good as sold, and this is something I've been wanting to talk to you about, anyway. I'd like to invest in the *Courier* as a working partner. Not only will I have my share of the money from the house, I'll have a small legacy, too." She paused and then added slowly, "From my mother."

Gina sat down in the mud and began to cry.

"No time for that, partner. Let's go haul those computers downstairs."

FOR THREE DAYS Tommy and Randy worked steadily on the heavy equipment of the Vernon-Black company, shoving mud and debris out of the way, removing washed-up trees, making way for the city's normal commerce. The schools were open again, and Fiona and the women of her church were supplying lunches for anyone who needed them, children and adults alike. Gretchen and Van had dug their way into the

Bauer house and were airing out the place and hanging rugs on the front-porch railings to dry.

Rick and Suzanne arrived to find Julia, bandanna around her head, hard at work in the office of the *Wiltonburg Courier,* tapping out a story about the new planning commission headed by Bill Vernon. Suzanne had put together a collection of clothing, mostly for children, and was soon coordinating her efforts with Fiona's church, so that sizes were matched appropriately.

"But I have something special for you," the tiny blonde told Julia. "As soon as you get your nose out of that story you're writing."

Intrigued, Julia said, "For me?"

"Mmm. A wedding dress."

"Suzanne! You didn't."

"Well, yes and no. A couple whose wedding I helped with ordered it, but then they broke their engagement. You don't think that's bad luck, do you?" Suzanne gave her an anxious look.

Julia laughed. "Good heavens, no. It was sweet of you to think of it. But is it my size? Will it fit me?"

"I think it's going to be close. Anyway, I brought my needle and thread."

"When can I see it?"

"I told you. As soon as you finish being a newspaperwoman."

"I'll just put the ending on this story. Be with you in five minutes."

The dress proved to be almost a perfect fit, needing only a tuck here and there. It was off-white cotton damask, tea length, with a dropped waist and softly pleated skirt.

"Suzanne, it's beautiful. It's just what I would have chosen. Now, will you help me pick something for Chipper? She's going to be my maid of honor."

"Oh, Julia, how lovely. Of course I'll help you. I'd make it myself if I thought we had time."

"Please, Suzanne, you've done so much already. I saw something cute in the Rose Boutique. Let's go take a look."

The dress they picked was white eyelet over yellow, high-waisted and ankle-length, with yellow ribbons streaming down from the neckline. Chipper, when she tried it on at home, was delighted—with the dress and her role in the wedding.

"What does a maid of honor have to do?"

"You get to walk up the aisle and then stand there and hold my bouquet during the ceremony."

"That's it?" Chipper sounded disappointed. "Does Uncle Randy do more? He's the best man."

"He hands the ring to your daddy."

"Well, I guess it's all right if he's got more to do. Aunt Fiona said he needs a purpose in life, and we all have to do our best to make him feel wanted. We've already cleaned out most of the box room—that's his bedroom now. We're going to keep our junk in the barn after it's built."

Julia glanced out the window and saw Fergus stretching wire fencing where the sheep would be enclosed during the summer. He and his nephew had promised to help Tommy build a barn for the animals.

"Fiona's right, you know, Chipper. But I don't think we need to worry about Randy. He'll be fine. And guess what? We even get to practice before the ceremony."

"How come? It doesn't sound very hard."

Julia smiled. "Well, we just want to make sure everything's perfect."

"Where's the wedding going to be?"

"In the backyard of your house."

Chipper considered it. Then she said a little shyly, "And after the wedding, are you going to be my mom?"

Tears welled up suddenly in Julia's eyes. She was surprised at how the question touched her heart. She hugged the little girl. "Yes, of course. Except that I feel I'm that already."

JULIA HAD LEFT by the time Tommy arrived home muddy and tired. He wanted nothing more than a hot shower and then to hurry over to her place as fast as he could. But as he let himself in the front door he could hear a full-scale argument in progress between Chipper and Randy.

"But you have to be!" Chipper's voice was anguished. "You have to hand the ring to my daddy."

"Anybody can do that. The only reason he asked me was because he thought he had to. I don't want to be a dumb best man, anyway."

"But I want to be the maid of honor. I want to hold the bouquet and wear that pretty dress," Chipper wailed.

"So do it. That's got nothing to do with me. Listen, the rest of you've known each other for a long time. I don't want to be in this stupid wedding."

Chipper spotted Tommy. "Daddy, Randy says he won't be the best man. Can he do that?" She started to cry. "You're mean," she raged at Randy. "I don't even want you for my uncle."

"All right, all right," Tommy said wearily.

"You can't just treat me like one of your kids, you know," Randy said defensively.

"No, of course not. And the wedding won't be ruined, Chipper. I'll be disappointed, but Randy's a grown-up—he can do whatever he wants to."

"You just want to make me part of things here, that's why you asked me. Well, I'm not part of things and I don't want to do it."

"Of course you're not part of things here. You haven't even been here a week. The reason I wanted you to be my best man is because you're my brother."

Randy flushed. "Yeah, but look at us. We're no kind of family."

"Maybe not yet, but we're going to be. A family is having people you depend on, people who support each other. The Vernons weren't my family when I came to Pennsylvania, but they are now."

Chipper sniffled. "Julia's going to be my mom. She said so."

Tommy's look grew tender. "Of course she is. And there's a place for you here, too, Randy. But the first thing you've got to do is get that chip off your shoulder."

"Nobody has to do me any favors." Randy climbed the stairs two at a time and banged the door to his room shut.

Chipper whined, "Daddy—"

"Things will be okay, honey. You'll wear the pretty dress and hold the bouquet."

"What about Uncle Randy?"

"Let's give him a little more time and then let him do whatever he wants. Hey, how about showing me that dress?"

As he followed the little girl up the stairs, he knew this scene with Randy wasn't the last one they'd have. What was he asking Julia to take on?

Later, discussing it with her, he asked, "Are you sure you know what you're getting into? Getting married in my backyard with my daughter and seventeen-year-old brother attending wasn't exactly what you had in mind ten years ago."

They were sitting in the kitchen having coffee. Rick and Suzanne were out for a stroll in the meadow. They said they enjoyed the country air, but Tommy suspected they were using their own kind of tact.

"You know how much I love Chipper. Could it be you're having trouble with Randy?"

He gave her a wry smile. "I guess I wouldn't love you so much if you didn't know me so well."

She reached out and touched his hand. "Don't you remember what it was like to be seventeen?"

"Yeah. I guess that's about the age you say you don't want to be in stupid weddings."

"Is that what he did? And what did you tell him?"

"I told him it was up to him. He's almost an adult. He can do what he wants."

"That was exactly the right thing. But if you really mean it, then you have to treat him that way. He just came from living with Stan and Louise, sharing space with three younger kids. Now he's got a room next to Chipper's. Maybe he needs a place of his own."

"But the whole idea of bringing him here was so I could keep an eye on him."

Julia was silent for a moment, thinking. "What about that new barn that Fergus is going to help us build? Suppose we were to make it a little bigger and Randy were to have his own quarters upstairs. Separate from the main part of the barn, of course. I bet he'd even enjoy helping to build it."

Tommy turned the idea over in his mind. "Julia, you are amazing."

"This is something I've had experience with. Why don't you go and tell him right now?"

His face fell. "But I came over here to see you. I haven't seen you in two days."

"After Saturday you won't be able to get rid of me."

He gave her a long look. "If anybody'd told me that even a month ago I wouldn't have believed it." He got up and came around to lift her out of her chair. Turning her to him, he enfolded her closely in his arms and for a moment simply rocked her back and forth. Then his head bent and his mouth found hers. She responded eagerly, her lips opening warmly to his.

After long moments she whispered close to his cheek, "How many hours have you slept in the last three days?"

"Not enough," he admitted.

"I knew it. Now go on home and have a good long sleep. We have the rest of our lives, darling."

"Is that a promise?"

She put both hands up to cradle his face. "Absolutely. And I don't want you keeling over just at the moment you're supposed to be saying I do." She knew the sleep they'd shared together on his bed the night of Gretchen's wedding had been the last real rest he'd had.

"All right then, maybe I will catch a few winks. But don't go changing your mind or anything while I'm doing it."

"That's a promise, too."

HE LET NUGGET OUT for his run when he got home, then filled the dog's water dish, let him back in and trudged upstairs. He could see a crack of light under Randy's door. When he looked in on Chipper he saw her curled up with the cat beside her, her new dress hanging where she'd see it first thing on waking. He went back to his own room and began pulling off his shirt. There was a soft knock at the door.

"Come on in."

Randy was still in T-shirt and jeans and looking somewhat more subdued than he had earlier.

"I was thinking about that old truck you talked to me about a while ago," he said, standing uneasily inside the door.

"Oh?"

"You know, the one you said loses power when it's loaded up."

"Well, it's a pretty ancient piece of equipment. Guess I just feel a little sentimental about it. It belonged to Bill when I took over the company. You might say I learned on it."

"Okay, well, I was looking it over, and I think I may have figured out what's wrong."

"Rings or valves, you think? Probably cost an arm and a leg to fix."

"I did a compression check and the valves don't look that bad. One of 'em, maybe. But what it looks like to me is the carburetor. Something's causing the fuel-air mix to go out of whack. A new carburetor wouldn't be as expensive as valves or rings, and I could do the work myself."

Tommy studied his brother's serious young face. "That sounds like a fairly sophisticated diagnosis. How'd you figure it out?"

The boy flushed slightly. "Oh, it's not that tricky if you've got a feeling for engines."

"Which you obviously do. Well, go to it. I'll leave it in your hands. Good work, Randy."

"Okay, I'll get right on it." He hesitated, his hand on the doorknob. Then he blurted, "And I'll be your best man, if you still want me."

"Of course I still want you." Tommy walked over to his brother, caught him by the neck in a loose hold and gave him a gentle shake. "Why do you think I asked you?"

He dropped a hand onto Randy's shoulder. "Maybe this could wait for another time, but I'd like to know how you feel about it. You've been cooped up with younger kids for a long time. What would you think about having a place of your own when we put up the barn? Separate outside entrance, maybe a kind of studio apartment. It wouldn't take much to add it to the plans."

Randy looked at Tommy, at first in disbelief, then with joy. A broad smile spread across his features. "You mean it?"

"Certainly. It's not a big deal when new construction's going up, anyway. Just a little additional plumbing and then the finish work."

"Gee, I could help with that."

"Don't tell me carpentry's something else you're good at."

"Well, not really good. But I know one end of a hammer from the other."

"Why do I get the feeling that's an understatement?" Tommy grinned. "Okay, it's a deal. We'll start right after the wedding. Fergus and his nephew have promised to help, and I imagine you'll have to fight Bill off, too."

"I know I've caused a lot of trouble for everybody. And I didn't mean what I said before about not fitting in—you know."

"Believe me, I do know. You wouldn't believe how bad *I* messed things up once. I never thought I'd get a second chance, but I did. And you will, too."

"Thanks, Tommy."

CHAPTER SIXTEEN

THE CLOUDS THEMSELVES looked like fluffy white sheep on Saturday morning, but all Julia could see was the rear end of the fat ewe she was trying to push into Fergus's trailer. Fergus and Tommy had come early to transport the sheep to their new pasture.

"If the lamb goes in first she'll follow," Julia said, panting.

Behind them Lizzie was hopping and yipping. Tommy managed to get hold of the lamb and push it in ahead of the mother. Julia gave a mighty push, and Tommy quickly closed the tailgate. The thirty sheep were milling and bleating.

"When you get there, just head them in the right direction and Lizzie will herd them in," Julia said.

Tommy wiped his forehead on his sleeve. "I bet you're the only bride in America rounding up sheep on her wedding day."

"Never mind. I want them at my wedding."

"Then so do I." He leaned over to kiss her.

Rick, in sweatshirt and jeans, came dashing out of the kitchen door. "Suzanne just kicked me out. She said from here on it's all bride stuff. How about if I come help with the sheep?"

"Sure, come on. We can put you to work. There's a lot to do to get the backyard ready."

Inside, Suzanne, in pink sweats, was making coffee. "What else will you have for breakfast?"

"Just coffee will be fine for me. I have to run down to the newspaper office."

Suzanne's eyes widened. "What on earth do you have to do at the office on your wedding day?"

"A story I was working on."

"Which somebody else can finish. Today is the most important day of your life, and you've already been out herding sheep. That'll be enough of that. From now on you're going to be pampered."

Julia hugged Suzanne and gave in gracefully. "Okay, you're in charge. What's first?"

"A manicure." Suzanne looked with dismay at Julia's hands. "Here. Have some coffee and we'll start those nails soaking. After that, a shampoo, a facial, and then we're going to style your hair."

As Suzanne took over, fussing happily, Julia had to admit it was a pleasant sensation being the object of so much attention. Suzanne buffed and filed her nails, and then applied pale pink polish. She lathered Julia's hair with herbal shampoo, rinsed it and set it on big loose rollers. Then she took an avocado facial mask from a drugstore bag.

"Avocado?" Julia smiled. "Isn't that going to be green?"

"Never mind. Tommy won't see you in it. I'm sure the green will wash out by the time of the wedding."

It was still on her face, however, when the florist's truck pulled up in front of the door. Suzanne flew to answer. "Oh, Julia, how beautiful," she breathed, lifting out from its tissue-papered wrapping a bridal bouquet of yellow roses, stephanotis and baby's breath with a trail of ivy. She handed Julia the card. It read, "First and only love...second chance." Tears sprang to her eyes.

"Stop that crying. Your avocado is running."

"You're crying, too."

"I know, but it doesn't matter with me. Oh, Julia, I'm so happy for you. I'll put this in the refrigerator to keep it fresh until we're ready." She started to replace the tissue in the box and said, "Wait a minute. There's something else in here."

"What is it?"

"Well, see for yourself."

Then Julia noticed a small box tucked into the corner of the larger one. She opened it. A sparkling diamond solitaire winked back at her.

"Oh, my gosh, it's beautiful." Suzanne's voice was hushed.

Julia stared at the ring. "Suzanne, dear, get this green goop off me so I can have a good cry."

THE YARD BEHIND Tommy's house was mowed and trimmed. New leaves were coming out on the trees, and pots of daffodils stood on the steps. The guests were already assembled and were mingling on the lawn between the two big oak trees where the ceremony was to take place. Van and Gretchen were there, along with Mrs. Bauer. Gina held Fred's arm as they chatted with staff members from the paper, including the photographer who'd been at the high school dance. Patty and

Melissa Brown were there, as well as Fergus and his nephew. Bill Vernon moved easily among all of them, playing the host, stopping to speak to Bud Winter.

Bud Winter! All the way from New York. Rick must have arranged it, and Julia's eyes grew misty at his thoughtfulness. In the distant meadow, sheep were already dotting the new green field. Randy and Tommy were standing near the minister. Randy looked totally unlike himself in a blue blazer and gray pants. Julia's heart turned over as she saw Tommy, his head bent to hear what Reverend Simmons was saying. His dark blue suit made him look slim and serious.

Fiona was waiting for her and hustled her quickly into the house.

Suzanne said, "Rick and I will wait right outside for you."

Fiona was holding Chipper's dress ready to slip it over her head. Chipper was hopping from one foot to the other.

"All right, now first go to the bathroom," Fiona ordered. Chipper went scampering up the stairs. Fiona was wearing a bright blue dress that set off her eyes, which right now were misted over.

"Ever since Tommy came to live with us this is what I hoped for," she said. "I know I'm not his mother, but I feel as if I am. I think of Chipper as my granddaughter. I love them both, but our family wasn't complete until now. You were the missing part, Julia."

Julia embraced her, and Fiona dashed away the tears as Chipper came hurrying back downstairs.

"All right, let's get this dress on you, girl, and remember to walk slowly and stand where Reverend Simmons told you."

"Oh, Chipper, you look beautiful!" Julia exclaimed.

"So do you," Chipper replied shyly.

"*That* goes without saying," Fiona said, brushing the little girl's hair back and fastening it with a clip. Then she placed a small crown of spring flowers on her head.

"I get to wear flowers on my head because I have to hold the bride's bouquet," Chipper explained importantly.

"Now," Fiona said, looking around. "That ought to be it. Are you sure you have all the right things? You know—something old, something new . . ."

"Well, I certainly have something new." Julia extended her hand to show Fiona the diamond solitaire. This time Fiona's eyes sparkled with delight; the ring was clearly a surprise she'd been in on from the beginning. "Isn't it wonderful? You wouldn't believe how many he looked at before he found the one that satisfied him."

"And my dress is borrowed, even though I have no intention of returning it. I have something old, too," Julia said a little diffidently. "Here in the pocket." In a slim pocket cut into the dress's side seam she'd slid the picture of Rick and her, with Elizabeth Holtz sitting beside her on the bench.

"Oh, Julia, I'm so glad you thought of that." Fiona's eyes threatened to grow misty again. "Well, then, all that's missing is something blue, and I thought of that. Here's a blue hanky you can slip into that pocket, too. Okay. Now I think we're really ready."

Rick poked his head in the door and smiled. "Everybody's waiting."

"I'm ready," Julia said.

"Wait, we've got to put some music on." Fiona hurried to adjust the CD player. "There, now we'll leave the screen door open." Soft strains of Mozart followed them outside. Bill was there to escort Fiona and Suzanne. Julia took Rick's arm, and Chipper piped up, "Is it my turn now?"

"It sure is, sweetheart. We'll be right behind you." As the little girl started to walk toward the two big oak trees, Julia turned to Rick. "We've been through a lot together, haven't we, Rick?"

"We sure have. But wasn't it all worth it?" He reached out to pat her hand.

Funny, Julia thought, how she'd never seen herself as part of a family. It was always she and Rick alone against the world. But now she had Tommy. They had each other.

She saw the way his dark eyes looked at her, the way his hair threatened to fall over his forehead, and it was like meeting him for the first time all those years ago. But seeing Chipper and Randy standing with him brought the present back to her, and she knew she was walking toward her new family. And what was a family, anyway? she asked herself.

She still wasn't sure she knew the answer to that. But she did know that sometimes life gave you a second chance at happiness.

HARLEQUIN SUPERROMANCE®

WOMEN WHO DARE
They take chances, make changes
and follow their hearts!

Too Many Bosses
by Jan Freed

According to Alec McDonald, Laura Hayes is "impertinent, impulsive, insubordinate and totally lacking in self-discipline"— all negatives in an employee. Mind you, he also has to admit that she has the legs of a Las Vegas showgirl.

According to Laura Hayes, Alec McDonald is "a pompous bigot who considers Kleenex standard issue for his female employees." But while these are negatives in a boss, Laura doesn't intend to remain his employee for long, because it's obvious that Alec needs Laura—in his business and in his life.

Within twenty-four hours of their first meeting, Laura and Alec are partners in a new business. *Equal* partners. Yet two bosses is one too many for any business—especially when the boss is falling in love with the boss!

Watch for *Too Many Bosses* by Jan Freed.
Available in May 1995, wherever Harlequin books are sold.

Bestselling Author

Jasmine Cresswell

**May 1995 brings you face-to-face with her
latest thrilling adventure**

Desires &
Deceptions

Will the real Claire Campbell please stand up?
Missing for over seven years, Claire's family has
only one year left to declare her legally dead and
claim her substantial fortune—that is, until a woman
appears on the scene alleging to be the missing
heiress. Will DNA testing solve the dilemma? Do
old family secrets still have the power to decide
who lives and dies, suffers or prospers, loves or
hates? Only Claire knows for sure.

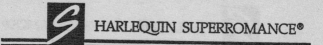

HARLEQUIN SUPERROMANCE®

presents

EVERY MOVE YOU MAKE
By Bobby Hutchinson

This May, meet the first of our FOUR STRONG MEN:

Mountie Joe Marcello. He was hot on the trail of his
man, but what he got was...a woman. Schoolteacher
Carrie Zablonski found herself in the wrong place at the
wrong time, and when Joe learned there was more to the
lady than met the eye—and she was quite an eyeful—he
assigned himself as her personal guardian angel. Trouble
was, Carrie didn't *want* his protection....

Look for *Every Move You Make* in May 1995,
wherever Harlequin books are sold.

4SM-1

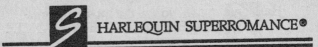

HARLEQUIN SUPERROMANCE®

presents

a new book by

Bestselling Author Janice Kaiser

MONDAY'S CHILD

Kelly Ronan was on vacation; Bart Monday was on the
lam. When the two met in Thailand, more than sparks
began to fly. Chased by a rain of bullets, they swam to
relative safety, dodging snakes and pirates on a small
but dangerous island. It wasn't Kelly's idea of a dream
vacation, but her mother had always told her she needed
a little excitment in her life....

Look for *Monday's Child* in May 1995,
wherever Harlequin books are sold.

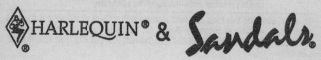

HARLEQUIN®

Don't miss these Harlequin favorites by some of our most
distinguished authors!
And now, you can receive a discount by ordering two or more titles!

HT #25607	PLAIN JANE'S MAN by Kristine Rolofson	$2.99 U.S./$3.50 CAN. ☐
HT #25616	THE BOUNTY HUNTER by Vicki Lewis Thompson	$2.99 U.S./$3.50 CAN. ☐
HP #11674	THE CRUELLEST LIE by Susan Napier	$2.99 U.S./$3.50 CAN. ☐
HP #11699	ISLAND ENCHANTMENT by Robyn Donald	$2.99 U.S./$3.50 CAN. ☐
HR #03268	THE BAD PENNY by Susan Fox	$2.99 ☐
HR #03303	BABY MAKES THREE by Emma Goldrick	$2.99 ☐
HS #70570	REUNITED by Evelyn A. Crowe	$3.50 ☐
HS #70611	ALESSANDRA & THE ARCHANGEL by Judith Arnold	$3.50 U.S./$3.99 CAN. ☐
HI #22291	CRIMSON NIGHTMARE by Patricia Rosemoor	$2.99 U.S./$3.50 CAN. ☐
HAR #16549	THE WEDDING GAMBLE by Muriel Jensen	$3.50 U.S./$3.99 CAN. ☐
HAR #16558	QUINN'S WAY by Rebecca Flanders	$3.50 U.S./$3.99 CAN. ☐
HH #28802	COUNTERFEIT LAIRD by Erin Yorke	$3.99 ☐
HH #28824	A WARRIOR'S WAY by Margaret Moore	$3.99 U.S./$4.50 CAN. ☐

(limited quantities available on certain titles)

	AMOUNT	$
DEDUCT:	**10% DISCOUNT FOR 2+ BOOKS**	$
ADD:	**POSTAGE & HANDLING**	$
	($1.00 for one book, 50¢ for each additional)	
	APPLICABLE TAXES*	$_____
	TOTAL PAYABLE	$_____
	(check or money order—please do not send cash)	

To order, complete this form and send it, along with a check or money order for the
total above, payable to Harlequin Books, to: **In the U.S.:** 3010 Walden Avenue,
P.O. Box 9047, Buffalo, NY 14269-9047; **In Canada:** P.O. Box 613, Fort Erie, Ontario,
L2A 5X3.

Name:_____

Address:_____ City:_____

State/Prov.:_____ Zip/Postal Code:_____

*New York residents remit applicable sales taxes.
 Canadian residents remit applicable GST and provincial taxes.

HBACK-AJ2